INTRIGUE IN ITALICS
A Claire Gulliver Mystery

Also by Gayle Wigglesworth

GAYLE'S LEGACY,
RECIPES, HINTS AND STORIES CULLED FROM A
LIFELONG RELATIONSHIP WITH FOOD

TEA IS FOR TERROR

WASHINGTON WEIRDOS

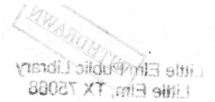

INTRIGUE IN ITALICS

A Claire Gulliver Mystery

by

GAYLE WIGGLESWORTH

To Janice
(Hope you'll enjoy this
visit to Italy

Gayle Wigglesworth

Library of Congress Control Number: 2006935844

ISBN-13: 978-0-9759621-8-3

ISBN-10: 0-9759621-8-3

Koenisha Publications, 3196 – 53rd Street, Hamilton, MI 49419
Telephone or Fax: 269-751-4100
Email: koenisha@macatawa.org
Web site: www.koenisha.com

This book was completed with the help of my husband, David, and my daughter, Janet, who as always were dedicated editors as well as strong supporters. This time a special thanks is due to my son-in-law, Dave, who helped me with the wine "talk", to my neighbor, Clare Perkins, who edited the draft to make sure it stood alone and to my friend, Carol Barraco, who knows Italy, their food, wine and language. She kindly read it in draft form to make sure I didn't embarrass myself with mistakes.

This book is dedicated to my baby sister, Teresa Grill, who has always been an enthusiastic fan of my stories and even more so now that she can read them in print. It is thanks to her efforts that my website is always working and, I hope, pleasantly interesting to those who access it.

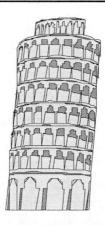

CHAPTER 1

Claire felt wilted as she waited curbside for a break in traffic when the light changed at the next block down. The street in front of her seemed to shimmer in air heavy with exhaust fumes from the profusion of mopeds, bicycles, motorcycles and occasional tiny auto. It was hot. The sun bounced ferociously off the ancient stone buildings. There were no trees, no shade.

She needed to get back to the hotel to nap. Maybe it was only jet lag from her night flight to Milan, then immediate transfer to a flight to Florence. She had arrived in time to lunch with her mother and Ruth, her mother's longtime friend, who had arrived a few days before her. Now she realized her schedule had been too ambitious; now she was paying for it.

Numbly she watched the people passing. Her eyes followed a motorcycle driven by a handsome man with a toddler sitting precariously in front of him while a young woman with an infant strapped to her back sat sideways behind him, clutching him around the middle. None of them seemed concerned about how dangerous their mode of transportation appeared. Tired as she was, Claire almost laughed at the sight of a very prim older woman, dressed in a conservative navy dress, her gray hair tightly twisted into a bun, sitting very straight on her cherry red moped. Her tiny poodle rode in a bag secured between her feet on the floorboard. She chugged along serenely, unruffled by the traffic. Following her closely was a group of younger people, perhaps students, judging by their backpacks and ragtag bikes. Some of them were trying to pass others, some calling out to friends; all of them seemed intent on arriving at their destination as quickly as possible. Behind them came a redheaded woman. Just as she pulled even with Claire, their eyes met. Claire saw her own surprise reflected in the woman's eyes. She felt a smile spread over her face as she started lifting her hand in greeting. Then a shutter seemed to come down in the woman's eyes. She quickly averted her head just as she swept by and the greeting died on Claire's lips. Her head swiveled, her eyes followed the woman, confusion rocking her.

It was Kristen. And she was sure Kristen had recognized her, too; she saw it in her eyes.

But then her own eyes widened as she realized it couldn't be Kristen. Chills ran down Claire's spine causing her to shudder.

* * *

"I just can't believe it."

"Hush, Ruth, you'll wake Claire." Millie's whisper woke Claire instantly.

She lay there a minute remembering where she was, blinking at the afternoon light which was pleasantly dimmed by the louvered shutters. Then she rolled over and said, "Believe what?"

"Oh, now, see what you did." Millie accused Ruth.

Ruth rummaged through a drawer, pulling out a clean shirt while at the same time she struggled to get the one she was wearing over her head.

"Ugh. A pigeon got me. Pigeon? It felt like a pelican. A direct hit; it's disgusting."

Millie, Claire's mother, couldn't keep the shadow of a smile from reaching the corners of her mouth. "Ruth, it could happen to anyone. Some people consider it a sign of luck."

"With all those people on the street I was the one that got it. It was lucky for all those others. Trust me; I could have happily lived my entire life without this experience." Ruth was indignant. She took great pains with her grooming. She would never have worn anything even slightly soiled, and wearing the dirty shirt back to the hotel was odious for her. Even now, well into her sixties, she kept up with current styles, wearing what was fashionable regardless of what was suitable for her age bracket. She bragged she still wore the same size she did in high school, ignoring the fact she now appeared to be poured into her clothes, which only further accentuated the bulges. And of course, no one mentioned the sagging muscles and wrinkles which clearly told her age.

Claire was wide awake now. "Mom's right. It could happen to anyone. Mom, remember my friend, Pat? She was in her bridal gown, getting out of the limo at the church when a seagull got her good."

Ruth looked shocked. "What did she do?"

"She went on with the wedding of course. Her mother cleaned her up at the church. I'm sure it wasn't easy. She had a beautiful gown with lace and beading, but she got it clean. And it wasn't an omen or anything."

"Well, I don't know about that, Claire," her mother said. "As I recall, after about ten years and three kids, she finally got tired of her husband's philandering and divorced him."

"Philandering? Come on, Mom. Sometimes marriages just don't make it. And I'm pretty sure it didn't have anything to do with the seagull."

Millie shrugged, obviously not convinced. "Anyway, dear, are you feeling better now after your little nap?"

"Yeah, I do." She was a little surprised at how revitalized she felt. "I think I'll shower and change my clothes, and then I'm ready to see Florence. What do you two have planned?"

"I'm writing some postcards." Millie sat down at the little desk beneath the generous window, shuttered to keep out the hot afternoon sun.

Ruth sank down on her side of the big bed she shared with Millie. "I'm going to take a nap, and then we'll decide what to do tonight for dinner."

Claire straightened the covers on the bed the hotel had rolled into the generous-sized room so she could share with the two women. Then gathering up her toiletry kit, she headed for the bathroom. The large room was completely tiled, including the ceiling. It took her a moment to realize there was no bathtub, not even a shower stall. She poked her head out and whispered to her mother, "Mom, where's the shower?"

"See the spigot in the middle of the wall?" She nodded in the direction of the shower. "That's it. I've already learned to move the toilet paper out of the way. Put your clothes on the shelves at the far end away from the spray. And be very careful, because the floor is like a skating rink when it gets wet."

After she got over the shock of standing in the middle of the room to shower, Claire found the spray very satisfactory. She let the water flow over her, remembering how pleased she had been to find her mother in such good spirits and obviously enjoying this trip she had been so reluctant to take.

When Millie had announced last year she would retire at the end of the year, her boss at Richman Cadillac had been justifiably alarmed. He and his two brothers had immediately tried to talk her out of the idea, not wanting anything to interrupt the smooth flowing dynamics of their company. The dealership had grown to be one of the biggest in the West and they had always said it wouldn't have been possible without Millie's management of the support functions. If she retired, they believed, everything would change and not for the better.

Rich Richman, the oldest of the brothers, couldn't believe she was intending to start a second career. "That's not retirement, Millie. Retirement is doing something fun. Something you want to do, but don't have time to do while you're working."

"That's it exactly. I love to cook. And I don't have the time or any reason to cook now. That's why I plan to provide meals for a few busy career people and cater some small dinner parties. I think it will be perfect. It won't be work, you see; it will be fun!"

And he did see, so he convinced his brothers her retirement was inevitable. And then, in an effort to show their appreciation of her contribution, they had signed her up at the prestigious Italian Culinary Retreat, which was being held the following year at the posh Villa Tuscany outside Florence, Italy.

Millie had been touched and grateful. But she flatly refused to go. She wasn't adventurous. She didn't travel. She thought the classes she was taking at the California Culinary Academy, just a bus ride away, were all she needed.

Of course she didn't tell the Richman brothers any of that.

Her friend, Ruth, and her daughter, Claire, argued endlessly with her trying to change her mind. They saw this as a chance to help Millie spread her wings a little; to stretch her boundaries as they say in all the magazine articles. They were convinced she was passing up an opportunity of a lifetime.

At last they succeeded by pointing out the cost of the gift, a sizable amount, would be wasted if she didn't use it. That was a very distressing thought for the ever frugal Millie. Finally, Ruth promised to accompany her, even agreeing to take the classes at the Retreat, so Millie, reluctantly, capitulated.

Of course, then Millie tried to talk Claire into going with them. Not to the Culinary Retreat; she knew Claire had little interest in cooking. But why not join them in Florence and Venice, she wheedled.

Claire had lots of reasons to resist. The most important were the two trips she had taken the previous year which had both turned out to include harrowing experiences, which she was still trying to forget. Those trips had cooled her ardor for travel considerably. Of course, her mother didn't know about the near disasters and Claire didn't intend she ever learn of them.

Then there was the universal horror of 9/11 which had occurred shortly after she returned from her second trip. That disaster had stunned the world. Claire's business, Gulliver's Travels Bookshop reeled from the public's sudden aversion to travel. Claire had laid off staff and cut hours in an effort to make it through the slump. And luckily, after the beginning of the year, business had started improving. People once again wanted to hear the travel lectures she had scheduled at the store. And customers started buying books for trips they were planning.

Claire's mother continued to nag her to go to Italy with them and in early February, Marianne Peabody's inspiring lecture at the store kindled Claire's desire to see Italy. That's when her assistant manager and friend, Mrs. B, got on her case.

"Look, Claire, if we want people to travel we need to show them it's safe. It would be great for business for you to go and send back lots of postcards for our bulletin board."

Claire countered with, "Why don't you go? You could use some time off. And you get along well with my mother. It would be perfect."

"I'm too old." Then seeing Claire's skepticism, she shook her head firmly. "It's true. I like reading the books and talking to the customers. But I've done my traveling. I've been there, everywhere. I don't want to schlep my luggage on and off trains and planes. I don't want to sleep in a strange bed every night. I'm too old. Getting up and coming to work every day is enough adventure for me."

Claire didn't even know how old Mrs. B was, but suspected she was in her eighties, even though she looked twenty years younger. But she could see Mrs. B didn't intend to travel again.

"You have the free pass on Vantage, so it would be a pretty cheap trip. What's keeping you from going?" She continued, looking at Claire shrewdly, "You're not scared are you? You're not letting those past two experiences turn you off of traveling, are you?" She shook her head, an expression of disbelief on her face. "Travel is fun. It's enriching. And believe me, it's safe. And don't forget we rely on it for our livelihood. You should go!

"Tuffy-Two, Theroux and I can handle the store."

Claire smiled to herself. It was hard to win an argument with Mrs. B; she always seemed to know the right buttons to push. Tuffy-Two, the West Highland Terrier puppy, was no longer a little ball of fluff that customers mistook for a stuffed toy. And Theroux, the bookshop cat had him well in hand, treating him as if he were her kitten instead of a puppy. The customers of the book store loved them both. Mrs. B was right; the three of them could handle the business in the store, which still had not returned to the level it had been before the terrorist attacks.

Claire turned off the shower and concentrated as she carefully made her way over the slick floor to the thick towel she hung from a hook earlier. She toweled her hair and checked her face in the mirror. She looked okay, the years were being kind. She thought she looked in her thirties a good ten years younger than she was. That was encouraging. It made her feel more energetic. The shower had really perked her up and she was getting a little excited about exploring Florence.

Her mother and Ruth, had arrived in Florence on the previous Thursday, so they had several days to acclimate themselves before Claire joined them today. They were due to start their Culinary Retreat on Wednesday, leaving Claire to explore Florence on her own and then proceed to Venice where they would meet her when "school" was over. And Claire had a whole list of "things to do" and "places to see," some she had taken from Marianne Peabody's lecture, some were suggestions she had collected over the years from travel magazines and newspapers, and some were recommendations from her customers. She knew she wouldn't do everything but she fully intended to make a big dent in the list.

Finally, hair dried, dressed in her underwear, she quietly entered the big room, nodding at her mother. She quickly selected and donned a pair of khaki slacks and a sleeveless knit sweater. She was fastening her sturdy sandals when Ruth's gentle snoring abruptly stopped.

"Okay," Ruth said stretching on the bed, "a little nap was just what I needed. So what shall we do this evening?"

"Well, it's Claire's first night, so I think we should do something special."

Ruth nodded her agreement.

"Remember that area of little shops we saw on the other side of Pont Vecchio?" she asked Ruth. "That lady from Toledo said she ate at a very nice restaurant there. Wait, I marked it in my book." She rummaged around in her bag and came up with the book. "Here it is, Momma Mia's. And we could show Claire the gold shops on the bridge and look in some of the art galleries and shops in that area. What do you think?"

"Fine with me." Claire thought anywhere with food was sounding good about now.

"Let's do it," Ruth agreed, swinging off the bed and looking for her shoes. "But let's take a taxi to Pont Vecchio. I've walked enough today."

It didn't take long for the taxi to drop them at the foot of the ancient stone bridge over the river Arno. The bridge itself was golden, bathed in the rays of the setting sun, and was crammed with shops clinging along both sides selling their gold. Even though it was early evening all the shops were open, their proprietors eager for every sale.

The women slowly made their way through the pedestrians, examining the endless variety of jewelry, comparing prices. Claire couldn't resist an intricate gold chain bracelet, deciding to wear it on the same hand as her watch. She was certain it would look perfect with the beautiful gold and diamond Cartier watch Vantage Airlines had given her last September. Of course, she wasn't wearing it now; she hadn't even brought it. She knew enough to leave her expensive jewelry safely at home, and that watch was the only expensive piece of jewelry she owned. Then just before leaving the bridge she purchased a pair of earrings she thought would make a wonderful birthday gift for her friend, Lucy Springer.

"Well, now you must feel like you're on vacation, Claire. You've spent your first wad." Ruth's droll comment made Claire laugh.

But it was true. She had napped and showered, so she felt good. She had bought herself a trinket. And she was in Florence.

The evening was warm and beautiful. They strolled down a street parallel to the River, glancing in the windows at beautiful paintings, works of art and artful displays of shoes, purses and other leather goods.

"There it is. See, where those people are turning in." They picked up their pace, the thought of food drawing them.

"Wow, our timing was right," Claire exclaimed a few moments after they had been seated at one of the last available tables in the dimly lit restaurant. They noticed the people who had arrived after them were already crowded into the bar, glancing enviously at the diners, hoping some would be finishing soon. But they forgot about the people waiting as they turned their attention to a mellow red wine from the generous carafe placed on their table while they nibbled nuts and olives and considered the menu choices.

"Millie, can I see that phrase book?" Ruth held out her hand, explaining, "I thought I ordered rabbit the other night, but when it came I just couldn't figure out what it was."

Millie laughed. "Maybe it was rabbit tripe. Fortunately my dinner was large enough for us both," she explained to Claire.

Ruth studied the menu carefully consulting the little book of Italian translations that Millie carried.

"This doesn't look like the menus from one of our Italian restaurants, does it?" Claire had been thinking of having Petrale Sole Meuniere with mashed potatoes and wilted greens, one of her favorites served in the many Italian restaurants in San Francisco, but she couldn't find anything like that on the menu.

"No, we're in Tuscany, dear, not San Francisco. I'm sure we can find you something good in the local dishes." Her mother was in her element, but of course, food was her passion. "We found a first course and an entree is plenty, unless you're really hungry. If you're starved you might want to order a pasta course too?"

Claire shook her head. "I'm going to order a salad and fish, because I'm intending to have some luscious pastry for desert."

"Why don't you try the Triglie Alla Livornese? See it?" Ruth suggested helpfully.

"It would probably help if I had a clue as to what it was."

"It's a local fish I had the other night. It was very good," her mother encouraged.

"Sounds perfect, and a salad; do you have a suggestion?"

Her mother nodded and gave the waiter their selections. Then Ruth, with a serious face, ordered Piccioni Sul Crostone.

"Stuffed Pigeons? Ruth, are you sure?" Millie looked up from the book she had retrieved from Ruth.

Claire choked on her swallow of wine. Her mother patted her on the back while she gasped and wheezed, finally getting her breath back after a sip of water.

Ruth's eyes gleamed in anticipation. "Revenge comes in many ways. And I feel obligated to do my part in controlling the numbers of pigeons Italy has to cope with. I'm sure the dish will be superb."

And the meal was wonderful. Claire's fillet of fish was very tasty and served with wilted greens with pine nuts and tiny steamed potatoes. Her mother's heaping plate of pasta was fragrant and she claimed, tasted wonderful. And while the plate set before Ruth holding four tiny birds seemed a little obscene to Claire, Ruth ripped into them with gusto. Finally, finishing their wine they waited for their desert and coffee.

"Oh, look Ruth, there's that couple we met at the hotel." She and Ruth nodded pleasantly when the couple waved to them across the room. "It's really a very small town, isn't it? We keep seeing people we know, and we don't even know anyone in Italy."

That's when Claire remembered.

She looked at her mother. "Mom, the funniest thing happened when I went back to the hotel this afternoon. Well, not funny really, but very odd." It must have been the tone of her voice, because Millie and Ruth both turned and gave her their full attention.

"I was standing on a street waiting to cross and Kristen rode past me on a bicycle."

Her mother's head jerked. "Kristen? Kristen Bonnibelli?"

"I'm sure it was her. And she recognized me. I saw it in her eyes."

"That's not possible, dear." Her mother reached out putting her hand on Claire's arm. "Maybe you were dreaming."

"I know, I know, but I swear it was Kristen. Right here! In Florence! Kristen was on a bicycle riding along the street in the midst of a bunch of other people."

"Claire, that's crazy. It couldn't have been Kristen. You were dreaming or in jet lag or something." Her mother's voice had sharpened with her effort to convince her daughter.

"Wait a minute, Millie. It's not impossible to see someone you know on the other side of the world. People do it all the time. Why couldn't Claire have seen her friend?"

"Because Kristen died, that's why," Millie muttered grimly. "It couldn't have been Kristen." It was as if she could make it not true. "Kristen died in an auto accident last year. Claire went to the funeral. It was very sad. I remember it well."

Ruth's mouth dropped open and it was a moment before she recovered enough to swallow the last of her wine.

"So it was just someone who reminded you of Kristen, Claire. That's all. You didn't speak to her, did you?" Then seeing Claire's head shake, she said vehemently, "There, that's it! You were tired and someone passed who reminded you of Kristen. If you had spoken to her, you would have realized it wasn't her. But because she then vanished, you keep thinking it might have been her." Millie was fully satisfied with her reasoning.

But Claire wasn't convinced.

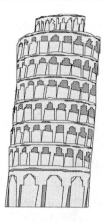

CHAPTER 2

The day was already hot when they rounded the corner, only to stop aghast at the long line snaking down the block.

"Is this the line?"

Ruth asked the lady at the end. "Are you waiting to get in the Accademia?"

She nodded her head vigorously as she replied in some language they didn't recognize any words but "Accademia?"

A woman standing several people ahead of them turned around and assured them in English. "It looks worse than it is. It seems to be moving quickly."

Already there were several people lined up behind them asking the same question.

"You two wait here and I'll go up to the front and check it out," Ruth told them and then marched ahead.

Millie started a conversation with the lady behind her who was from Houston. The woman had been to

Florence before, so she had several suggestions for them to try for dinner.

Claire scanned the street, watching the natives going about their business, seemingly totally disinterested in the large group of tourists hungering for a look at Michelangelo's *David*. The line did move steadily and soon Ruth was back.

"It's a good thing we decided to come this morning because a lady up in the front said she was here Sunday and the line was so long they couldn't get in before closing. So they finally gave up. But because the museum only opened a bit ago, it will take a while for it to get so crowded they will have to stop allowing people to enter until some leave." Ruth was pleased with herself as she was the one who insisted they visit *David* the first thing this morning.

Claire hadn't been eager as she had already seen two copies in various parts of town and she had been here less than one day. But Ruth was adamant. She said they couldn't visit Florence without seeing the real *David* and, of course, the Accademia housed all the other works by Michelangelo as well. And the deciding factor was the Accademia was right around the block behind their hotel. Ruth said it would be easy to come out after breakfast and visit this museum before they did anything else.

Claire watched while her mother introduced Ruth to the new friends she made in the line and then listened to their conversation as they all discussed their decisions to make the trip to Italy.

Claire smiled to herself watching her mother. She was proud of her even though she frequently became impatient with her tendency to be overcautious. She wished she looked more like her mother. They had the same hair color as Millie's blonde hair was now streaked with a pretty gray and Claire had her light brown hair professionally highlighted with blonde. But Millie was several inches shorter than Claire. Her shape was not model thin, but compact, and she looked well in the clothes she wore. And Millie was pretty. The age lines couldn't disguise her beauty and her interest in people showed in her eyes and the animation on her face. No wonder people were drawn to her.

Claire's Great Uncle Bernie always told Claire she took after his mother, but Claire had never been comforted by any similarity to the stern faced woman in the old pictures he showed her. And when in high school she began to grow she thought she would never stop. So she was tall, slender and very strong, which was good as she was always slinging boxes of books about at the store. She always looked older than her friends, and she realized now that had probably impacted her life. She had friends of both sexes, but she had never been into the party scene, nor had she dated much. She seemed more interested in her studies, reading and then her library career than the silly activities her friends enjoyed.

Then in her mid-thirties two things happened which drastically changed her life. First, she noticed her looks had finally come into fashion or maybe she had just grown into her features. Anyway, where as a young girl and woman she had always been aware she was not attractive, now she seemed to be. That gave her increased confidence and a burgeoning interest in style and fashion. Then of course there was the incident where she almost lost her life. She was only doing a favor for Ruth while she was away. She agreed to stop by Ruth's house to take care of her cat. That led to a very scary few weeks, two near-death experiences and the realization that leading a cautious careful life did not guarantee longevity. Eventually that and subsequently inheriting Great Uncle Bernie's book store led to a complete turn-about of her life. She no longer wanted to read her favorite mystery novels, she no longer was content to observe life; she wanted to spread her wings a bit, take some risk and take charge of her life.

She shook herself out of her daydreams as she saw they were nearing the front of the line. The conversation around her was now about other special destinations in Italy. The people behind them had just spent four days on the Cinque Terre.

They were having a great time bragging about walking the high trails between the five little villages perched on the cliffs over the sea. Actually, it did sound nice. Claire remembered Marianne Peabody had waxed ecstatic about the area she called the Italian Riviera as she flashed her incredibly beautiful slides on the screen. But Claire was more interested in seeing the art and history of Florence and Venice, so she hadn't even considered a visit to that area. But now, listening to these fellow tourists rave about their experiences, she wondered if she had made the correct decision. Finally, they came to the front of the line and were able to buy their tickets and enter.

The inside of the museum was a blessed relief of coolness after the long wait in the sun. They followed the crowd into a high rotunda and Claire halted in her tracks, transfixed by the sight of *David* in front of her. She heard her mother's gasp and knew just how she felt. It was incredible. There was no comparison between the copies of this statue and the real thing. Of course the light in the rotunda lit the statue so the gleaming marble became luminescent, highlighting the tiniest details of the sculpture. It was breathtaking.

She was so glad Ruth had been adamant they see it, and she told her so. When she had her fill of looking she pulled her camera out of her backpack and tried to take a picture that would somehow convey this perfection to film. It was a while before they were willing to wander into the other rooms. They marveled at the carvings, the richness and variety housed in this one gallery. And they found amazing the blocks of marble with figures emerging, which had been works in progress, only to be abandoned when Michelangelo died.

When they emerged, they were momentarily dazed by the sunshine. They huddled in a bit of shade and conferred over the maps, finally agreeing on the appropriate direction to take. Next on their itinerary was a visit to the Mercato Centrale, a huge food market serving both retail and wholesale customers. This visit was scheduled so Millie and Ruth could complete a homework assignment for their Culinary Retreat. They had been given a shopping list and instructed to locate each item in a market and then price them for use in their class. However, when they entered the cavernous building and saw how huge the market was, they decided to split up. The meats and fish were upstairs, so Ruth went there. The fruits and vegetables were on the main floor. Claire tagged along with her mother enjoying the conversations half in English and half in Italian with lots of hand gestures. But eventually they were able to locate even the most obscure item on the list and head back to the main entrance to find Ruth already at the little café sipping coffee and reviewing her list.

Claire sat and ordered bottled water while her mother opted for a coffee. The women compared their lists, discussed a few of the items and decided they were done.

"Great, now for the fun shopping." Ruth had a gleam in her eye. "Look, this next market is really big, so we need a plan in case we get separated."

"Can't we just stay together?" Millie was nervous, uncertain about how she could cope if she found herself alone in this strange city.

"We'll stay together, Mom, but Ruth is right. A plan is a good safety tool. I think since we're so close to the hotel, if one of us gets separated we'll just meet back there. Does that sound good?"

Ruth nodded.

"Here, Mom, this is the hotel's card with a little map. See that's where we're going and here's how to get back. But don't worry, if you do get lost just grab a taxi and give them this card; they'll drive you back." Then seeing the fear in her mother's eyes she smiled. "I'm going to stick to you like glue. Remember when I was a kid and you made me hang on to your jacket when we went out in crowds? Today you can hang on to my backpack, okay?"

Millie laughed then nodded. Claire decided to use the facilities before they left. Ruth pointed her in the right direction and made sure she had the proper coinage. "It's a little different than in the States, but this is what foreign travel is about, different customs."

Claire found out what she meant. The toilet had a men's room door and a women's room door, but they both led to the same big room. Each side had an attendant who collected the coin, handed out a piece of toilet paper and ushered the patrons into one of the stalls. And the attendants, a man and a woman were carrying on a loud, seemingly amusing conversation the whole time. While it was perfectly private it seemed very strange to Claire.

"You survived, huh?" Ruth grinned at her when she joined them again.

Claire just shook her head, bemused by her experience before announcing, "I'm ready. Let's see what this great market has for us."

The market was wonderful. Most of the booths had canopies to protect the goods from sun or rain but others were just tables laid out to display the goods. Claire was especially taken with a selection of silk scarves.

"Look Ruth, these look just like the designer ones that cost a couple hundred dollars. Are they knock offs, stolen or what?"

"I don't know, but they look great. Don't pay more than ten dollars each, because I saw some over on the other aisle for that price."

Claire, who had been about to close the deal, put the scarf back on the table to the disappointment of the vendor.

"You not like? Good deal. Only twenty dollar U.S. Silk, real silk." She spread out the one Claire had especially liked, bargaining, "You like? Two for thirty-five dollars."

Claire shook her head with regret.

"How much you pay?"

Millie spoke up, "Ten dollars each, U.S."

The vendor looked shocked, then when she saw the determination in their faces and they started to turn toward the other aisle, she changed her price. "Okay," she whispered, "but only for you. Ten dollar U.S. each. Okay?"

Claire nodded, relieved to be able to buy the ones she had already selected. She ended up getting five, not only were they a great buy but they were small enough to fit in her small suitcase. They would make perfect gifts.

And they couldn't get by the leather goods section until Ruth had bought a purse. Millie purchased belts of fine Italian leather for the three Richman brothers, and Claire bought a beautiful pair of sandals for a fraction of what they would have cost at home. But while the wares were tempting and the prices reasonable, eventually they stopped buying only too aware of their limited luggage space.

They moved without speaking to a shaded table at a sidewalk café and ended up ordering large dishes of gelato (ice cream) instead of lunch. Two things they found were plentiful in Florence, coffee and gelato. There was no reason they shouldn't treat themselves every day they told each other, but agreed they had to be disciplined so as to not do it several times a day.

"Did we miss siesta?" Claire asked checking her watch.

"Well, we may have missed Italy's nap time, but mine is coming up soon. What say we head back for the hotel and a little quiet time before going out later this afternoon?" Ruth suggested. "I thought we might want to visit the Uffizi before we have dinner. It was closed yesterday and I have to see it. My god, it would be like visiting Paris and not going to the Louvre.

"My guidebook says if we call, we can make reservations with only a fifteen minute wait. If it's all right with the two of you?" Ruth paused and then seeing their nods, went on. "There's a restaurant located very close to the museum which those people behind us this morning said was very good. Perhaps we could try it?"

Claire nodded. "I'm anxious to see the Uffizi. I've heard so much about the art there. But we need to decide what we're going to see, because my brain goes numb when I'm in a museum more than an hour. I can't even remember what I've seen after a while."

Ruth nodded. "You're right. I think my book recommends several of the rooms. When we get back to the hotel I'll check it out.

"Is that Rick Steves' book?"

Ruth nodded smiling. "Of course, my travel bookstore recommended it."

"Okay, nap, reservations, plan on what to see and then dinner as a reward. That sounds good!" Millie checked each off on her fingers as they moved quickly toward their hotel, anxious for that rest.

* * *

"Well, I think we got it all." Ruth looked again in the large armoire, checking the drawers along one side.

"Are you sure you don't want to move into a smaller room? We could help you pack up."

Claire shook her head at her mother's suggestion. This was about the tenth time she had suggested it. She forced her tone to be calm, trying to eliminate any hint of her impatience at her mother's repeated concern over keeping this big room. "Really, Mom, I'll be fine here. I'm going to use that big bed you and

Ruth shared and sleep right in the middle. It's such a nice room. So big and airy, it somehow reminds me of the room in that Merchant and Ivory movie, *A Room with a View*. It's perfect, really. And since you and Ruth have been paying for the room, I think I can afford to splurge on my last few days here."

Her mother shook her head, obviously not convinced it was a wise decision. But she seemed to realize Claire wasn't going to change her mind. "Now, you'll be careful. Don't talk to strangers. Watch out for those Italian men; they like to pinch."

Claire and Ruth laughed as they said in unison, "Millie!"

"Mom!"

"Give it up Millie, Claire is all grown up. She can handle a few days on her own. And you see how safe it is. What kind of trouble could she get into?" Ruth was impatient with Millie's insistent worries.

"What kind of trouble? You say that? And you know she was almost killed just doing you a favor. Have you forgotten that? The world if full of crazies and for some reason Claire just seems to attract them."

Ruth was stricken by that reminder. Even after all this time she felt terribly guilty about the mess Claire had gotten into when she had gone to Ruth's house in San Francisco to care for her cat while Ruth had been away.

"Come on, Mom. Look, now you've upset Ruth. That's all in the past." Claire took a deep breath and pasted a cheery smile on her face. "Come on the two of you, let's go have a nice breakfast and forget all of that history."

Millie nodded, and Ruth brightened at the thought of coffee. They left their bags by the door for the boy to bring down and headed for breakfast.

By the time they had traversed the large room to the little table available near the window, Claire felt that her mother had stopped to speak to everyone in the room.

"Mom, you've only been here five days. How do you know all these people?"

Millie waved brightly at a couple just coming through the door. "Well dear, we see them here for breakfast, in the elevators and even out on the streets. Everyone has been so kind about sharing their experiences at the different restaurants and museums."

"And you know how your mother is, Claire. She's never met a stranger, but she'll worry herself to death thinking you might talk to one."

Claire smiled. It was true; her mother was very social and made friends everywhere, even though she worried constantly about Claire doing the same thing. For some reason she thought she was such a good judge of character it was all right for her to be friendly. She spent most of her life in the same neighborhood, working at the same job and going to the same church, which had created a safe environment for her and her daughter. But here she was in Italy, acting just like she was in her own neighborhood. Claire looked at Ruth, her eyes reflecting her concern.

"Don't worry, Claire. I'm watching out for her. So far, we haven't run into the big bad wolf, even if we do get a pinch or two occasionally."

"Oh, for goodness sake, Claire, you're always fussing about me worrying too much and here you are worrying about me. I'm sixty-three years old; I think I know how to take care of myself. You're the one who is always getting into trouble."

Fortunately the waiter interrupted them to take their breakfast order. While they had been warned that breakfast in Italy was usually a roll and strong coffee, this hotel catered to the English tourists and provided huge breakfasts to keep their clients happy. It was one more advantage to choosing this hotel besides the large airy rooms and its central location.

It wasn't until they had finished eating and Ruth had gone to the desk to settle their account that Millie grabbed Claire's hand, leaning over the table to whisper. "Claire, I want you to promise me that you'll leave that Kristen thing alone."

Claire jerked, startled and suddenly feeling guilty, because she realized she hadn't really forgotten about Kristen.

"Really, Claire, it couldn't have been her. And it's just like you to get all involved in something that could cause problems."

"Mom, I have a whole list of places to go and things to do while I'm here. I'll be plenty busy. Don't worry about me. And besides, how could I get in trouble about Kristen? She's dead. As you said, it couldn't have been her I saw."

Her mother didn't look quite satisfied.

"Mom, you just go learn to cook Italian goodies so I can look forward to you practicing them for me when we get home. Okay?"

Millie wasn't sure it was okay, but what else could she do? Just then she saw Ruth wave at her from the doorway. "Oh, oh, I guess our ride is here." They hurried to the front and followed the driver and their bags out the door.

There was a little confused flurry and then Claire was waving enthusiastically to them both, promising to call and laughing at her mother's worried expression. She knew they were going to have a marvelous time.

She stood there until the van was out of sight and then with a feeling of excitement at her total independence, she turned back to her room to gather up her things. She was anxious to get out and about. Florence was hers and she wanted to explore.

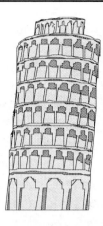

CHAPTER 3

Claire was transfixed by the Etruscan art in the Archeological Museum. She had seen some of these pieces before on slides shown in her Art History course at the university. Here were the bronzes, the decorated pottery and tomb sculptures which were the inspiration for many of the Renaissance works of art. It was hard to believe the Etruscans were so sophisticated, so advanced that they could produce these wonderful pieces and yet, disappear off the face of the earth. Who were they? What happened to them? It reminded her of the riddle of Stonehenge she encountered on her trip to England last year. That visit inspired her to delve into ancient English history. Now she knew she would have to expand her studies to the Continent.

She studied the map of the Etruscan digs and saw how close to Florence many of them were. Now she wished she had allocated some time to visit Orvieto which seemed to have produced the majority of the

Etruscan findings. She would have loved to see where these pieces were actually found.

Reluctantly she decided she had absorbed as much as she could in one visit, so she left the museum to head for the next stop on her agenda.

The Duomo Cathedral in Florence was truly magnificent. A cathedral of pink, white and green marble set in a piazza in the busiest part of the city. She, of course, had already seen it. Actually several times, as she passed it whenever she went from her hotel toward the river Arno. Even so she had yet to visit its museum. And that is where the famous Ghiberti doors were housed. In San Francisco, Grace Cathedral sitting on top of Nob Hill had copies of those door made from casts of the originals. She had seen and admired them many times and now she was going to see the real thing. She wondered idly if she would see as big a difference between the copies and the originals of the doors as she noticed in Michelangelo's *David*. She felt a small shiver of excitement. She hoped so.

As an American she still had trouble under-standing "old." "Old," such as the California Missions, was synonymous with simple or primitive. In the Americas "old" meant hundreds of years. Yet, here in Europe, they lived surrounded with art objects and buildings which were thousands of years old.

She remembered her awe when she saw the York Minster in England the previous year. It was unbelievable to her how people had the skills to build it more than a thousand years ago. And it was so grand. And it was still standing.

* * *

Millie and Ruth followed the young man carrying their luggage, heads swiveling, trying to see everything and still keep up with him.

His heavily accented English was quite understandable. "Check the Agenda in your package. Lunch will be served in there," he nodded at a room off the entry, "at one o'clock. You have time to get settled before then." He led them up the stairs and down a hall before he opened the door to a spacious room with windows overlooking the hills and a tiny balcony barely holding the two chairs. "Welcome to Villa Tuscany, Signoras. Please enjoy your stay with us."

Villa Tuscany was even more beautiful than the brochure indicated. Perched on the top of one of the rolling hills, partially shaded by ancient, gnarled trees, it was built of stone that almost blended into the hillside except for the touches of red paint on the windows and doors. Everywhere there were urns and pots of flowers. Inside, the thick walls kept the heat out and the terra cotta tiles looked as cool as they felt. The furnishings were old but comfortable. Big overstuffed chairs and couches invited guests to sit and relax. Windows everywhere were open to the views of the countryside allowing the smell of grasses and the flowers to drift in as well as the occasional bee. The gardens and outdoor patios were invitingly furnished with chaises and benches, shaded with vine laden trellises and trees.

Ruth and Millie looked around their room and smiled widely. Millie went to the balcony and breathed the fresh warm air deeply. "Look, Ruth, there are still red poppies in the meadows on the hills. And look at the vineyards. Everything is still so green, not like our California hills which have already turned brown.

"Come on, let's unpack and explore the grounds a bit before lunch. I know they have a pool, a vineyard and an herb garden, let's check it all out."

Ruth nodded, quickly thumbing through the package of materials they were given on checking in.

* * *

5th Annual
Italian Culinary Retreat
2002

Villa Tuscany
Jean Claude Martin, Head Chef
May 8, 2002 – May 15, 2002

Agenda

Day 1 Wednesday, May 8th
- 9:30 Transport from Florence to Villa Tuscany
- Settling in at Villa Tuscany
- 1:00 Lunch, Introductions and Orientation
- 3:00 Tour of facilities, equipment lecture, review of pre-work
- 5-7:30 Free Time
- 7:30 Cocktails in main salon
- 8:30 Dinner

Day 2 Thursday, May 9th
- 7:00 Breakfast
- 8:00 Lecture and demonstration
- 9:30 Break
- 10:00 Hands on kitchen work
- 1:00 Lunch and free time
- 4:00 Break-out groups
- 7:30 Cocktails in main salon
- 8:30 Dinner

Day 3 Friday, May 10th
- 7:00 Breakfast
- 8:00 Winery Tour Bus leaves from main lobby
- 5:00 Free time
- 7:30 Cocktails in main salon
- 8:30 Dinner

Day 4 Saturday, May 11th
- 7:00 Breakfast
- 8:00
  - Group A Leaves for market from Lobby
  - Group B Kitchen work/Lecture
  - Group C Lecture and demonstration
- 1:00 Lunch and free time
- 3:00
  - Group A Lecture/Demo
  - Group B Tour/lecture in wine cellar
  - Group C Kitchen work
- 5:00
  - Group A Kitchen work
  - Group B Free Time
  - Group C Free Time

- 7:30 Cocktails in main salon
- 8:30 Dinner
- 10:00 Jazz and after-dinner drinks in the main salon

Day 5 Sunday, May 12th
- 7:00 Breakfast
- 8:00 Transportation to local churches
- 10:00 Lecture and demo of pasta
- 1:00 Lunch
- 2:00 Kitchen hands-on: Pasta workshop
- 5:30 Free Time
- 7:00 Cocktails in main salon
- 7:30 Dinner

Day 6 Monday, May 13th
- 7:00 Breakfast
- 8:00
  - Group A Lecture and demonstration
  - Group B Leaves for market from lobby
  - Group C Kitchen work/Lecture
- 1:00 Lunch and free time
- 3:00
  - Group A Kitchen work
  - Group B Lecture/Demo
  - Group C Tour/lecture in Wine Cellar
- 5:00
  - Group A Free Time
  - Group B Kitchen work
  - Group C Free Time
- 7:30 Cocktails in main salon
- 8:30 Dinner

Day 7 Tuesday, May 14th
- 7:00 Breakfast
- 8:00
  - Group A Kitchen work/Lecture
  - Group B Lecture and demonstration
  - Group C Leaves for market from lobby
- 1:00 Lunch and free time
- 3:00
  - Group A Tour/lecture in Wine Cellar
  - Group B Kitchen work
  - Group C Lecture/Demo
- 5:00
  - Group A Free Time
  - Group B Free Time
  - Group C Kitchen work
- 7:30 Cocktails in main salon
- 8:30 Dinner, Awards Ceremony/Graduation
- 10:00 Graduation Party in main salon

Day 8 Wednesday, May 15th
- 7–9:30 Breakfast
- 8–12 Transportation leaves from main lobby

* * *

The Villa was full of surprises; everywhere they found nooks and crannies inviting their inspection. The garden was especially intriguing with its vegetables and herbs mixed attractively with flowers and shrubs. But time had been passing and suddenly they realized they were going to be late for lunch. And when they arrived in the private dining room, they found they were the last. All the seats were taken except two at opposite ends of the table. They split up, hurrying to claim the seats.

"Is this seat taken," Millie asked politely. The man on her left stood up, bowing stiffly from the waist, pulled out the chair for her. The man on her right just smiled at her as she sat down.

"Ladies and Gentlemen, welcome to the 5th Annual Italian Culinary Retreat. Our host, Geno Giambono," the speaker graciously gestured to the man sitting on his right, "is the owner of this five star facility and has graciously agreed to host us this year."

Everyone clapped enthusiastically. Everyone had heard of the Villa Tuscany. In the food circles it was up there near the top for innovation, presentation and continuous quality and, of course, the hotel was well known also.

"My name is Rafael Angelino and I represent the Italian Culinary Association. Our group proudly organizes this retreat. We are pleased to be able to present our fifth retreat here in Tuscany. It is our pleasure to lure world-renowned chefs to some fabulous setting to inspire, to mentor and to reveal to a few lucky souls their secrets for producing wonderful Italian cuisine. This year we have coaxed Chef Jean Claude Martin from his famous New York restaurant, Jean Claude's, to our little bit of heaven here in Tuscany."

The applause was loud. The speaker paused. "Chef Martin, not content to own and run an award winning restaurant has spread his talents to the entertainment arena. Many of you may have seen his cooking show on PBS Television, which I believe has been shown here in Italy as well as in many other European countries. And of course he has been published." He looked at Chef Martin. "What is it now, Chef Martin, number five?...or six? Well, if any of you have his cookbooks, now is a good time to get them autographed. If you don't have yours with you, I believe the Villa Tuscany has stocked a few in the gift shop for this occasion. Right, Geno?"

Geno nodded enthusiastically.

Rafael looked sad. "I am sorry that prior business commitments have kept me from joining this group, but I am leaving my able assistant, Marie Verde, here to make sure everything runs smoothly. If any of you have any issues or questions, see Marie. Stand up, Marie, so people will recognize you." He looked around, and said, "Well, with no further ado, I would like to introduce Chef Jean Claude Martin."

The large, dynamic, gray-haired man stood. His electric blue eyes roamed over the group seeming to single out each person. He smiled slowly, the force of his personality already hypnotizing them.

"I know, I know, those of you who have heard about last year's Retreat are ecstatic to be here, as am I. I am honored to be your chef for the next week. We have an exciting agenda and I guarantee you will find this Retreat meets all your expectations. We will work hard, have fun and everyone will learn something, which will make you a little better at what we all love, cooking. Plan to hone your culinary skills in Italian dishes. And most importantly for some, you will all become even more proficient at selecting the appropriate Italian wines to serve with each dish."

Judging by the enthusiastic response everyone was looking forward to the lessons in Italian wines.

Chef Martin continued his introduction. He described how the Retreat was to be organized, how each person would be assigned to one of three groups. All couples would be separated into different groups so everyone would have equal chances to participate. Each group would prepare a portion of the meal on three days. All three groups would work together in some basic instruction, the pasta class and the wine tour. They could each expect to get hands on experience in all aspects of meal preparation over the duration of the Retreat. Each of them would receive an empty binder and, during the week, would accumulate copies of all recipes used, as well as those used by the Villa itself for the meals their kitchen provided.

"Each night at dinner we will enjoy our meal and then we will analyze the dishes served. I expect all of you to participate with enthusiasm. As that is how we all learn, is it not? But remember we want constructive criticism. Not only will you offer kind criticism, but also suggestions to improve the dish or even to alter it. But of course on Friday, Geno's people will be providing our dinner, as that day we will be visiting the local wineries. After a day of sampling their production right in their own cellars, we're not expecting any of you to be in any condition to cook." His smile widened at their enthusiasm at this announcement.

"Now, those of you who do not speak English do not worry, as Sal will interpret for your benefit." He nodded, and a young man stood and began speaking rapidly in Italian.

"Now, let's eat, and enjoy, and get to know each other. Sal will come around the room and make sure everyone has understood all the information and will identify those who will need his services over the next few days." He held up his glass of wine. "Here's to a great dinner, one of many at the Villa. Salute!"

They all lifted their glasses crying, "Salute, Salute."

Then Chef Martin stood up again. "Excuse me, I am so sorry, but I forgot to introduce Wanda, who is my assistant chef, as well as is Sal. You will all become fast friends. Now sit and enjoy."

When the meal resumed everyone introduced themselves to their neighbors. Millie found the man on her left was named George Binns from Wales. He was the owner and chef of a small hotel. Middle-aged, perhaps in his mid-fifties, he was a solid man of average height and ruddy complexion. His hair was dark and thick and his expression pleasant. He looked like a man who was happy with his life.

"Just a small place, you understand, nothing grand such as this." He gestured around to encompass the Villa. "But we serve a steady stream of business travelers during the week and tourists on the weekend. We've noticed how popular our few Italian dishes are becoming, so here I am, learning more." He smiled. "My wife is quite jealous, but then someone needs to tend to business and I am the chef, you see." He laughed. "For once that is an advantage. And someday soon I'm sure she'll be off on a jaunt of her own to discuss inn-keeping, linen folding or some such topic."

The man on her right and the woman on his other side were a Swiss couple called Fredrick and Helga Lowenthal. They spoke German, Italian and very little English but smiled a lot. Since Millie only spoke English she couldn't breach the language problem enough to find out why they were taking this class.

"I am Renee DeBois," the man across the table said. "I have studied at the Cordon Blue and worked at the George V in Paris for five years." Young and proud of his credentials he puffed up in his chair, looking around him for their approval. "Now I finish up here before starting my position as chef on the yacht, Belvedere, out of Naples."

The woman beside him nodded with appreciation. "Ooh, how lucky! That sounds like a great assignment."

He nodded, trying to keep his expression neutral, but not able to stifle the satisfaction gleaming from his eyes. "Yes, this was very lucky. The owners have dined at the George V many times and I have known them. They lease this yacht, fully staffed. So when their chef had family problems and had to resign I was offered the job. His misfortune was fortuitous for me. And after so many years spent learning my art, believe me, I am ready for the excitement of different ports.

"And I only cook for the passengers and the officers. The crew has their own chef; they even have their own kitchen."

"How wonderful! I envy you." The woman beside him introduced herself. "I'm Marybeth Lewis. I have a restaurant in Connecticut. Believe me there is not much freedom to explore different ports when you own your own restaurant." She glanced across the table. "Is there, George? There is always the buying, the preparing, the staff to manage and the clients to please. Always!" Her smile lit up her face.

She was a pleasant looking woman, Millie thought, she was probably Claire's age, early forties. Her light brown hair was loosely tied back at her nape, the curls springy and wayward. She used little or no makeup other then a bit of lipstick, allowing her freckles to show as they wished. Her eyes were hazel and friendly and she appeared to be a capable women. Millie just assumed it was a good restaurant. How could this woman own anything else?

"This is a busman's holiday for me. Every few years I try to get away and take a refresher course to keep up with what's new in the industry, as well as to hone my skills. Of course, I came because of Chef Martin. I have dined at his restaurant and really admire his style. I was especially thrilled when I learned the Villa Tuscany was hosting the Retreat this year as its restaurant is well known for using fresh vegetables, herbs and fruits from their own gardens, which is a specialty of my restaurant. Have any of you seen the gardens yet?" She looked around and seeing some nods continued. "And I've promised myself to only call home once a day. The restaurant will have to get on without me."

Those close enough to hear her comment laughed. They all knew that feeling of being glad they were gone, but worried about what was happening at home.

Millie realized it was her turn. She was slightly dismayed. Not only did everyone seem to have so much more experience than she did, but they were all much younger. "I'm very new at this," she said tentatively. "I've recently retired and I'm hoping to work in the catering field to supplement my retirement. It's something I've always wanted to do." Her voice was stronger now as her enthusiasm radiated from her. "But I've only had a few classes at the California Culinary Academy and, of course, all those years I cooked out of necessity. I hope I can keep up with the rest of you."

"Don't worry; you'll do fine. Everyone here is coming from a different background and with different skill levels. You'll see they are prepared to teach us all something." George nodded encouragingly.

Then Renee started talking to Fredrick and Helga in Italian with George adding a comment now and then. Rather than try to talk through their conversation to Marybeth, who didn't seem to understand them any more than Millie did, she turned her attention to the rest of the people seated at the long table. She counted fifteen, nine men to the six women, here for the class not including the people who sat at the head table with Chef Martin. It turned out that Millie and Ruth were not the oldest. The Asian couple, who sat near Ruth, appeared to hold that honor. They were very small in stature and despite their age, their expressions were bright and alert. Millie was sure she would hear about them later from Ruth. There was one impossibly young man who looked as if he was in his teens and even wore braces on his teeth. Millie's glance lingered on him, wondering if he really was as young as he looked, or if it was another case of her getting older so everyone else looked younger. And if he was so young, how did he get accepted for this class. But seeing his enthusiasm as he helped himself to the food being passed around family style, she realized he loved food. As a matter of fact, that's what they all had in common. They were there because they loved food; fixing it, eating it, looking at it. She smiled to herself as she took a generous serving of the dish of gnocchi George passed to her. This was going to be fun. She was glad she came.

* * *

As Claire approached the busy corner on her way back to her hotel, she realized it was the spot where she thought she had seen Kristen that first day. A glance at her watch told her it was almost the same time of the day as that occasion. It struck her she might see that person again, so she hurried to the curb, anxious to watch a while. But when she looked to her left at the crush of bikes, mopeds and motorcycles sailing down the road, it seemed a hopeless task. Then she swiveled her head to look at the traffic which already passed. Way down the block she saw the back of a bicyclist with a mass of red hair. Could it have been her? She stood on tip-toe, stretching her neck as she looked for identifying details. It was near the end of the long lunch break, which was the custom here, so she assumed many of these people passed at the same time everyday returning to their business for the afternoon.

Then she remembered with a guilty start her mother's admonishment to forget Kristen. She loved her mother dearly and she truly appreciated all that Millie had sacrificed to raise her. But her mother worried all the time. So much so that Claire had a tendency to hide things from her mother to prevent unnecessary worry. And while most of her life, Claire had listened to her mother's warnings and remained cautious, after that incident where she almost lost her life, she had changed. That's when she realized living carefully wouldn't necessarily keep you safe. That's when she decided her cautious life might be stifling her.

Then Uncle Bernie died and left her all his worldly possessions, including his musty out-dated bookstore in Bayside. That's when Claire began to actually change her life. And she had refused to give up her new dream because of her mother's fears. She had been firm. She had cashed in the retirement benefits she had already accrued at the library. She had invested everything she had, dreams, energy and money in Gulliver's Travels Bookshop, and now it was paying her back. And while her mother argued strenuously against her plan, she now was proud of Claire's accomplishment. But she still worried incessantly about her.

Well, Claire could understand why. Millie's father, a career Army man, had died way before his time, one of the casualties of the Korean War. Millie's mother had died while Millie was still in high school leaving her a total orphan. Danny Gulliver saved her. She married him at eighteen and had Claire a year later. They were a happy family until Danny was killed on duty.

Ruth once told Claire her mother always expected Danny to be killed. She knew it was inevitable when she married a police officer. But while he was alive Danny seemed to be able to keep Millie's worries at bay. He took her and Claire on adventures, the beach, Disneyland and even camping in Yosemite. But after his death Millie just dried up, all the fun was drained out of her. She used all her energy raising Claire. Later, when Claire was older, Millie's part time position became a full time job at Richman Cadillac. But all the time she worried as if her mantle of worry could protect those she loved.

Claire wished she could remember more about those times when her dad was alive. She had the pictures she used to look through. It was almost hard to believe the laughing, carefree woman was her mother. But other than the expression on her face she looked the same.

Claire had been surprised when her mother said she was going to retire and start a little catering business. It was a daring thing for her to do. But her mother loved to cook and didn't get enough time to do it.

Her idea was to provide meals several days a week to a few working couples she knew, who didn't have time to cook and were sick of takeout food and commercial frozen entrees. She was appreciative of the Richman brothers' intent when they signed her up for the Italian Culinary Retreat, but alarmed at the thought of attending.

Claire grinned, as she remembered how she and Ruth had managed to wear her down. This was good for her!

Suddenly she realized she had been standing on this corner while several groups of pedestrians had crossed the street. She turned her attention back to the people on the street.

Yes, her mother's last words had been an admonishment to forget about seeing Kristen. But she knew how cautious her mother was and her mother hadn't seen the woman. Claire had! She remembered how the look of recognition had momentarily widened the woman's eyes. She knew, as impossible as it seemed, it was Kristen.

The pedestrians moved off the curb once more, swarming toward the other side. Claire looked down the street as she crossed but the redheaded woman had long disappeared. She decided tomorrow she would come back. She would be here earlier and she would be prepared.

* * *

What looked like a very generous lunch break of two hours on the schedule just seemed to disappear, and by the time they were ready to leave the dining room they had to hurry to use the facilities before reporting to the kitchen. Here they were each issued a voluminous white apron and a chef hat, which looked like a drooping mushroom cap. Soon the kitchen was filled with chefs as they crowded around Chef Martin, Sal and Wanda.

The kitchen was monstrous. The part they occupied was used when large functions such as weddings or conferences were scheduled in addition to the normal restaurant activities. This week it would be used exclusively by the Retreat students. This way they would be part of the kitchen but well out of the way of the regular staff, who still had to prepare and serve the other guests of the hotel as well as the patrons of the restaurant.

"Wow, this makes my place look pretty shabby." Marybeth whispered to Millie as she looked around with awe.

George nodded his agreement, "My kitchen isn't even as big as this little section we're in. But, it's very efficient," he added proudly.

Millie was also intimidated by the size, the equipment and the obvious skill of the kitchen staff going about their business on the far side of the room.

She looked at Ruth, raising her eyebrows as if questioning what they thought they were doing here.

Ruth, her chef's hat sliding over one eye, righted it and moved a little forward, the better to see and hear everything. Millie straightened her spine and followed. After all they paid the price and if they didn't become experts they still expected to learn a lot from the next week. And Millie, at first reluctant to come, now determined she would make the most of this opportunity.

"Chef Martin," Ruth was not shy, "why are our hats different than the people who work here?" She pointed to the tall, stovepipe hats on the heads of the people busy doing prep work.

"Chef's hats, like nurses' caps traditionally follow the mentor. Since you are in my class, you will all wear my traditional hat." He smiled. "And, it clearly identifies us in the kitchen. Believe me, things sometimes get very hectic in here, and I wouldn't want one of you to be Shanghaied and end up preparing vegetables instead of your class assignment. Please make sure you all wear your aprons, hats and name tags while attending classes and working in the kitchen. Also, for the first few days we'd all appreciate it if you wore your name tags to all functions. That will help us all learn everyone's names."

The students followed him from work station to work station as he described the equipment, the supplies and the workings of the kitchen. Everywhere he went, each way he turned they were all right behind him much as a gaggle of goslings follow their mother.

Finally back in their part of the kitchen Chef Martin discussed the pre-work assignment. Millie and

Ruth were very proud they had located and priced everything on the list. Not everyone was as lucky.

Steven, who was from Chicago, complained that as he only arrived in Italy in time for lunch and still hadn't even seen his room, he hadn't been able to find a market. The markets in Chicago didn't even know what some of the items on the list were.

"Well, each of you will be going to the market with me during the week and if any items on your list were not identified we'll try to find them for you then." He looked at Wanda. "Oops, Wanda's telling me we're running out of time, so I think we all have a break until cocktail time." He looked at Steven. "Get yourself settled, have fun all of you and I'll see you at seven-thirty. It's our first night and Geno has asked his staff to prepare a very special meal. See you soon." He waved and left the kitchen.

"Ooh, my feet are killing me," Ruth complained as she limped out the door. "Tomorrow I'm wearing comfy shoes for sure."

Millie followed her, pulling off her hat and fluffing her hair. No one but Ruth had worn heels but as she had insisted they were the only shoes that went with that particular dress, Millie had just shrugged. She wasn't her mother. She had worn slacks, a cotton, short-sleeved sweater and sturdy, rubber soled shoes. She was dressed appropriately for spending a day in the kitchen or roaming the streets of Florence. She had always been a sensible person, but here, amongst these other colleagues she was feeling younger than her years. She admitted that agreeing to take this course was a good decision; it made her break out of her cautious life. She smiled to herself as they headed back to their room, remembering Chef Martin's blue eyes. Maybe she would wear the more casual of the two dresses she brought. It would make it more festive, she told herself, even while she admitted her decision might be influenced by the fact that Chef Martin was much more attractive in person than she expected.

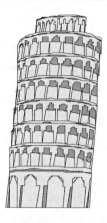

CHAPTER 4

Claire wobbled down the street on the rented bicycle. She was very nervous about the traffic and the uneven streets, but mostly about being on a bike again. She thought once you knew how to ride a bike you always knew how to ride. However, this bicycle had a confusing number of gears and very touchy hand brakes, and somehow pedaling seemed harder than she remembered. When she arrived at the corner she was grateful to stop for a moment. With one foot on the curb holding the bike upright, she felt secure enough to look around. The street was clogged with the usual mid-day traffic all heading one way. She had arrived a full fifteen minutes earlier than yesterday, because she didn't want to take a chance on missing Kristen. As it was, she sat watching the traffic move past, lulled into a trance and almost missed seeing the little old lady with her poodle. Today she was wearing a bright flowered dress and her dog had a big pink ribbon around its neck. Claire watched carefully as a thick cluster of people on bikes passed. Then she caught a glimpse of red hair through the riders and saw Kristen was passing on the far side of the street.

Her heart started thumping with excitement. This was it! Today she would catch up with the red haired woman and solve the mystery. She was certain her mother was right about one thing; when she spoke to the woman it would certainly determine if she was or was not her friend, Kristen. She pushed herself off the curb and into the crush of vehicles.

She was pedaling hard to catch up. Suddenly a bike cut right in front of her, racing to pass the two people ahead of her. She had to apply her brakes to avoid hitting it.

Too hard! The brakes squealed and the back end of her bike lurched to the left hitting another bike as her front wheel stopped dead. Then things happened fast. Claire and her bike flipped over, taking the bike next to her with them. Several bikes close behind were unable to avoid the growing disaster. Claire and her bike ended up near the bottom of a major pile-up.

She lay there a minute gasping, trying to regain the breath knocked from her. Then as people and bikes righted themselves she was able to cautiously test her limbs. Everything seemed to be working. She struggled to her feet, reached out to help another girl up before trying to right her bike. It and she seemed to be functioning except for a torn pant leg and a skinned knee, both hers. She tried to apologize to the other riders, but the language was a problem. They waved her off with looks of disgust. Most were already heading down the street by the time she was back on her bike. She was embarrassed. She had wanted to tell them it wasn't her fault. She pedaled down the street for several blocks but never caught another glimpse of

Kristen, the brown-suited man who had swerved in front of her, or even the old lady with the dog. Finally, she gave up and headed for her hotel. She needed to put something on her knee and change out of her torn pants.

* * *

Everyone was clad in their aprons and hats, their name badges pinned in clear view. They eagerly crowded in front of the work station presided over by Chef Martin.

"...so you see this dish is made from only the freshest ricotta. It must be only one day old, two at the most. If it is not fresh, then use it in some other way.

He looked at them. "Find a source for the cheese. Then you will always have the perfect ingredients. That's essential to creating this delightful dish. And, of course, you will want to make this frequently. It is simple, tasty and oh, so..." He brought his fingertips to his lips and then flung the kiss into the air.

"Here are my raisins. See how plump they are? They have been soaking in a lovely desert wine for several hours. How long, Sal?"

"Since five a.m.," Sal answered, then glancing at the wall clock, "about six hours."

"See what it means to be a chef. Sal was down here at five to soak the raisins while you were all tucked cozy in bed."

They smiled, nodding at Sal, grateful they had been sleeping while he had been doing the prep work. Already they were all in sync with the pace of the class. They moved around to get different views of the demonstrations, making sure everyone could see what was going on and they paused quietly when Sal repeated Chef Martin's comments in Italian for those few who didn't speak English.

"I used Vin Santo but you can use your favorite. Now I will drain the raisins, and while they drain I will prepare my ricotta," Chef Martin explained. And then while Sal translated his words, he placed a sieve over a bowl and using a flat wooden tool he pressed the cheese through the sieve.

"Make sure there are no lumps. Now add the sugar." He dumped the little bowl of granulated white sugar into the cheese and briskly stirred it in. "And gently add the raisins." He stirred the dish carefully. "That's all there is to it." He grabbed a pedestal dish and heaped the cheese and raisins in a mound on it. Then he sprinkled the cinnamon pre-measured in the little dish over the top.

Aahs and oohs rippled from the onlookers. It looked elegant.

"Here it is, ready to be chilled. I usually have this dish or a variation of it on my menu each night. A helping of this with a couple of biscotti is a wonderful way to end a meal.

"Taste, taste," he invited graciously.

They didn't waste any time crowding forward with their spoons and scooping up a taste of the dessert.

As soon as the ricotta hit her tongue Millie tried to discreetly push it back on the spoon. She glanced at Ruth, who hadn't yet put it in her mouth and shook her head slightly. Ruth got the message. Others weren't so lucky. Steven loudly spit it into the hanky he yanked from his back pocket and the Swiss lady, Helga, ran for the sink to spit in. One or two actually swallowed the vile concoction, but couldn't disguise their looks of disgust.

Chef Martin was alarmed at the faces. "What's wrong?" He grabbed a spoon and tried a bite only to spit it into the towel he carried slung over his shoulder. His faced flushed a deep red. "My god, what is this? My ricotta is ruined. Sal, Wanda, taste it. Someone has ruined my masterpiece with salt."

Sal and Wanda tasted a very tiny bit, then with screwed up faces shook their heads in denial.

"Chef Martin, I'm so sorry. I don't know how this could happen. I put the ingredients together myself. Let me check them." Wanda hurried off.

Chef Martin threw down his towel in disgust. "This is disgraceful. Never have I had this happen. I apologize. Please, all of you take a short break while we get this sorted out. Meet back here in twenty minutes." Face still red, he turned and left the kitchen.

Several of the students gathered on one of the piazzas enjoying the coffee from urns kept available for their benefit.

"Wow, he was mad. I wouldn't like to be in Wanda's shoes now."

"I don't blame him; it's his signature dish. How embarrassing..."

"I tried not to make a face, but it was so awful..." Renee had to laugh.

"Wasn't it? Well, even the best chef can make a mistake," Antonio started.

"It wasn't Chef Martin's mistake." Michael Caruthers cut him off. He was a New Yorker who apparently had plenty of time and money. He never said what he did and maybe he didn't do anything. He looked to be in his fifties and was handsome, if you thought his faded blond, slightly dissipated look was attractive. He was very social; he enjoyed participating in the group discussions and he professed to be Chef Martin's biggest fan. He boasted he had dinner at Chef Martin's exclusive restaurant, Jean Claude's, several times a week. That was a clear indication of his standing in New York society, which didn't come cheap. When he heard Chef Martin had agreed to lead this Retreat he told them at breakfast, he just decided he had to come. He didn't really cook, like Ruth, he was mostly a fan of good food.

"He's the best, and this dish is one of his best. I've had it many times at his restaurant.

"And he certainly doesn't make stupid mistakes. He's a pro, the best! Do you know where he's going after he finishes the week here?"

He looked around and seeing only questioning faces he continued. "He's going to lead a team in the Culinary Olympics being held in London. They won last time, four years ago, in Tokyo and I'm betting they do it again. This is not the kind of man who would make a simple mistake and ruin his dish." Michael was hot, prepared to defend his hero from all slander.

Steven Greenery was impressed. Millie had learned he wrote restaurant reviews for several Chicago area newspapers and two airline magazines. Additionally, he did freelance work for other newspapers on food related subjects. Strangely enough he didn't look at all like what you would expect a food critic to look like. He was in his forties, his brown hair receding on top and graying on the sides. He was tall, over six feet, and angular. Boney would be a better word to describe him. And he had already demonstrated he could consume large quantities of food and drink with no apparent affect. He was full of nervous energy and had a wry sense of humor which was apparent from the first meeting. And he obviously knew about the Culinary Olympics.

Millie tried to appease Michael. "Relax, Michael. I'm sure he didn't make a mistake. I'm just sorry he was upset. And even if it was his error, it's really no big deal. We've all had disasters." But then unable to contain her giggles any longer, said through them, "But it was horrible."

"And the look on your faces as you tried to be polite," Ruth chimed in, her laugh hearty, not even trying to suppress it now.

"Well, not the Swiss lady," Steven said.

They roared. Everyone but Michael enjoyed the joke, but even he grudging accepted it had been a funny situation.

Their time was up and they moved toward the kitchen once again. Steven said to Michael, "Do you suppose Chef Martin would talk to me about his plans for the upcoming Olympics? I'd sure like to do an article about it." Then his eyes snapped with excitement. "I'd like to go to it. Are you going?"

They moved out of range so Millie didn't hear the rest of that conversation but she realized it was apparently a big event in the culinary world.

"Antonio, have you heard of this Olympics?"

Antonio Inglaises was an Italian from Sorrento who now worked in a restaurant in London. He spoke with a heavy accent and with many hand gestures that were vital to his communication in either language. He was young, probably in his thirties, olive skinned, slender and with those famous Italian good looks. His smile was charming and Millie felt herself melting under it.

"But of course. We have a team going from London. It is, how do you say, prestigious? Some day I will compete. It is my dream!"

Millie nodded, thinking she needed to spend more time watching the food channel. Obviously there was a lot going on in the culinary arena she didn't know about. She followed the rest into the kitchen anxious to resume the interrupted class.

Chef Martin seemed in control once more. "This was a painful lesson for me and one you all should heed. The chef needs to taste his dishes. Just because something is produced time after time doesn't mean it doesn't need to be tasted before it is presented to the patron." He smiled at the class. "I wish I had heeded my own rule before inviting you all to taste."

He indicated the items set out on the table for the next demonstration. "Wanda found the little dish of sugar actually contained salt. Things like that sometimes happen in a busy kitchen. She and Sal have now checked the contents of all the other prepped items, and they all appear to be correct. So we will proceed. And this time I will taste first."

The rest of the morning session passed quickly. Just as they were dispersing for lunch, Wanda called out, "Wait, everyone gets a copy of the Group Assignments. You'll need to know which group you're in before you meet this afternoon. The locations will be posted on the board after lunch."

* * *

Culinary Retreat 2002
Group Assignments

Class	Saturday	Sunday	Monday	Tuesday
Group A	Market/ Main Cse	Pasta	Desserts	Wine/ Antipasto
Group B	Wine/ Antipasto	Pasta	Market/ Main Cse	Desserts
Group C	Desserts	Pasta	Wine/ Antipasto	Market/ Main Cse

Group A
1. Helga Lowenthal
2. Sam Ng
3. Zoe Yuricev
4. Steven Greenery
5. Antonio Inglaises

Group B
1. Ruth Clarkson
2. Michael Caruthers
3. Marybeth Lewis
4. Jacques Ouimette
5. Frederick Lowenthal

Group C
1. Millie Gulliver
2. George Binns
3. LiAnn Ng
4. Renee DeBois
5. Randy Jackson

* * *

It was peaceful on the piazza. Millie had moved the lounge chair into the shade where she sat reading the book she had brought. Every little while she put it down to observe a bird in the trees hanging over the wall, or to watch the tendrils of the brilliant crimson bougainvillea, trailing over the arbor, sway in the breeze.

George, Sam Ng and the teenager, Jacques, headed across the piazza not even noticing her until they were seated at the table on the other side.

"Oh, Millie, we didn't see you there. We're going to play some cards. Would you like to join us?" George invited, Sam and Jacques smiling with agreement.

"What kind of cards?"

"Poker, dealer's choice." Jacques was excited, obviously planning to win.

She laughed. "I don't think so. I don't know how to play and, even if I did, I'm smart enough to hang on to my money. Thanks anyway."

They had only started to play when Steven and Zoe appeared. In the few days since the Retreat had started Steven, Zoe and Michael had become inseparable.

Zoe didn't say much. At least Millie and Ruth hadn't learned much about her. She was Croatian. She spent a great deal of time in Italy and was fluent in Croatian, Italian and English. Sometimes when Sal had trouble translating Chef Martin's meaning, Zoe helped him find the right words. She was a large woman, shapely in the way Sophia Loren was, her clothes only enhanced her femininity. She had creamy skin and dark luscious hair, neither of which looked as if it had been tampered with. She was probably in her thirties and anyone could see why the men sought out her company.

Millie watched the table for a while, worrying if Jacques was going to be relieved of his money. He seemed very young to be playing with that group, even though he seemed confident. Ruth had taken to him that first lunch and had reported he was the precocious only child of a wealthy Parisian family by the name of Ouimette. He had asked for and received this trip for his Christmas present. He loved to work in his family's kitchen and had done some apprentice work in a prestigious Parisian restaurant. He knew he would never be a chef but thought he would build his own restaurant chain some day. He was still growing; still wearing braces to straighten his teeth and, while very mature for his age, there was no doubting he was only sixteen. The rest of the group treated him as if he was the favored little brother and he graciously accepted their good-natured kidding. Remembering all this, Millie decided the others would see he won a few hands.

She turned her attention back to her book; the sounds from the table and the occasional laughter blended with the sounds of the Villa and the birds.

She woke with a start when Ruth trotted in after her swim. "Millie, you should have come, the water was wonderful. It was so refreshing." Then seeing the game in progress she veered across the piazza. "What are you playing?"

Ruth eagerly joined the table. Millie noticed when Ruth joined the game the noise level increased substantially, as did the laughter and the good-natured jeers. Ruth was a fun person, Millie conceded.

She was lucky to have her as a friend all these years. While Ruth had no aspirations to be a professional chef, she was and had always been a good cook and, of course, she appreciated good food. So she claimed she was enjoying the Retreat, which was a relief for Millie. It was costing Ruth plenty to accompany her and Millie knew Ruth did it because she believed Millie should attend. She felt guilty about that, worrying that Ruth was spending all that money for no benefit to herself.

Millie sighed, she was an adult. Sometimes she couldn't understand why she was so reluctant to try new things, to have new experiences?

Then the answer popped into her head. It was because too many scary things happen! Some had happened to her.

She found being careful and staying in a familiar environment made it all the easier to avoid nasty surprises. While San Francisco frequently had a high crime rate, her neighborhood was relatively safe. She knew the people there, they watched out for each other. She shook her head. She wasn't going to sit here and rehash the past, deciding instead to think about the group break out sessions scheduled next on their agenda.

Millie looked more carefully at the people at the poker table. Three of them, Zoe, Steven and Sam were in one group. Ruth and Jacques were in another, and George was in her group. She had been disappointed when she found out she and Ruth would be in different groups. Wanda had explained their reasoning when she gave out the group assignments, pointing out that it would be better for each person to function individually. That way, she said, each person would get the most out of the Retreat.

So along with their group assignments she told them where they would be meeting and what their assignments were. Each group would use the break-out session this afternoon to select the recipes they would serve when they were responsible for the Main Course, the Antipasto, the Wine and the Dessert during the next few days. Each course would be expected to consist of three selections with the exception of the wines. Each day one of the groups would be responsible for selecting all the wines served with the meal. It was imperative for the group choosing the wines to know what the menu items for that day would be.

She smiled as she sighed with pleasure. She loved being here. The beautiful countryside and the Villa were wonderful, but the excitement of meeting all these people involved in the culinary field she loved, was just the best.

* * *

Once more Claire was poised on the street corner ready to complete her mission. But today she was really prepared. She had found the bike to be very handy in navigating through Florence and used it for the rest of yesterday and even this morning while she was out and about. Now she was more confident. Now she was used to the touchy hand brakes. She wouldn't be caught unaware today. She was smiling with anticipation when she saw the couple and their kids pass on the motorcycle. Then the red-haired woman passed her. Claire glanced over her shoulder, spotting a break in traffic; she pushed off from the curb to smoothly join the stream of riders on the street. She didn't race to catch up today. Today she was content to just keep her quarry in view. She had decided it would be best to approach her when they reached her destination.

Claire had already gone a few blocks when she noticed the man who had cut her off yesterday, thereby triggering the pile up. There was no mistaking his brown shiny suit that flashed olive green when the light struck it. No, she didn't need to see his face, the fancy suit and his gleaming designer loafers made him hard to miss. Today he didn't seem to be in as much of a hurry as he had been yesterday. He pedaled leisurely along in the stream of traffic between her and Kristen. Despite his fancy clothes and his relaxed manner, his bike appeared to have been ridden hard. It was dented and battered from use and on the rack over the back wheel a large padlocked box had been attached to secure the rider's belongings.

So they all moved down the street and, as long as Claire could see Kristen up front, she was content to just be a part of the flow. On her bike, on the street with the other commuters, she felt just like one of the locals.

Then Kristen was gone. Just like that. She had glanced away for a moment and when she looked back she had disappeared. She pedaled faster but then, relieved, she saw the brown suited man turn into a small alley. Deciding it was the only place Kristen could have turned off she headed that way too. When she got there she saw it stretched only a half a block between two buildings ending at a stone wall. She didn't see Kristen's bike, but there were doors leading into the buildings on either side and somehow she was sure Kristen had gone through one of them. The man in the brown suit had just finished attaching his bike to some pipes extending from the wall on one side of the alley. He hurried past her with a scowl on his face, never even glancing at her as she got off her bike and wheeled it into the little space. The pipes were anchoring several bikes in spite of the universal sign of a bike in a circle with a line through it posted on the wall. She boldly attached her bike to the pipes as well.

Now what? She stood in the alley and looked at both doors but there wasn't any indication as to where they led. She walked back out to the street and decided to turn to the right first. There between the alley and the corner she found a store and judging from the display in the windows, it was an art supply store. One of the clerks was just unlocking the door after the lunch break, so Claire wandered in with the other customers. She examined the impressive array of supplies as she headed back to the service desk. She got there just as Kristen came out of the door from the back room. They stood frozen, eyes locking for a moment. Kristen shook her head, held up a finger indicating a "one moment" signal and retreated back through the door.

Claire heard a rapid spate of Italian, then Kristen reappeared. This time she was slipping into a backpack and with a jerk of her head she signaled Claire should follow as she headed toward a side entrance and out on the street around the corner from where Claire had entered.

"So it really was you," Kristen said as they walked down the street away from the store. "I thought I must be mistaken." Then she smiled wryly. "I hoped you would just go away.

"But I know how you are. And you are tenacious, aren't you?"

Claire had a million questions, but they never even got to her lips.

"We're just going down the street for a coffee. I'll answer your questions then, okay?" Kristen told her firmly.

Claire was still stunned, so just murmured, "Okay!" as she meekly walked beside her friend.

At the end of the next block there was a cluster of inviting sidewalk cafes. Kristen selected a table some distance from the occupied ones. The waiter took their order and disappeared. Kristen shrugged out of her backpack, setting it on the ground between her feet.

"Never, never ever put your belongings in a chair or beside you. Believe me they'd be gone in a minute. I love Italy, especially Florence, but the tourists swarm all over the place and, of course, they attract the thieves, pickpockets and muggers. You have to be alert to stay intact."

Claire watched her, noting the changes in the Kristen she had known. She was now in her mid-twenties. Wearing her casual, artsy clothes she looked even younger until you saw her eyes. The eyes looked old. They projected a weariness of the world. Claire didn't know what had happened to Kristen to make such a change. The Kristen she had known was intelligent, hard working and had such a marvelous good humor she was fun to be around.

The waiter returned with their coffees and a pastry for Kristen. She stirred a couple teaspoons of sugar into her espresso before she sat back and looked at Claire. "All right, you can see I didn't die." She shook her head. "Who would have believed I would run into someone I knew? Here? And it would be someone who wouldn't be convinced they were mistaken and therefore, would persevere to track me down."

"But why, Kristen? Why pretend to die? Your parents, your friends, everyone was so upset. And I talked to your brother. He couldn't have known! He was crying for god's sake."

Kristen had the grace to squirm. "I know. I'm really sorry.... But, I had no choice. And my brother knows now. And my parents know. But no one else does. You see, I got involved in a little situation." She stared morosely at Claire then sighing, she proceeded with her story.

"If you remember, I was trying to get my Master's at State while still working at the library part-time. It was really a hectic schedule, but I was almost done. I didn't have much of a life except for working and studying. But once in a while I would go out with friends to the clubs South of Market.

"We liked to dance. That's all, just dance like crazy and laugh. We didn't even drink, only soft drinks. And we made a pact to watch out for each other. You know, make sure our drinks were safe, that no one slipped something in them? And we agreed to make sure we each got home safely? We promised each other we wouldn't let any of us go home with anyone but one of us." She looked at Claire to see if she was following the story.

Claire nodded. She had heard stories of what was happening in some of the clubs. It was a sad situation, but it could be very dangerous for girls who only wanted to have a little fun.

"Anyway, it worked for us and we enjoyed ourselves. We had a favorite, the Gemini Club, in a little alley off of Harrison."

Claire recognized the name of the club. She had heard it was the "in" place.

"Their band was hot. And it had a big dance floor. So usually that's where we went, or if we went somewhere else we would end up at the Gemini before going home. Anyway, I met this guy there. His name was Sonny. He was a dream. Danced like a professional, looked like a movie star and wasn't afraid to show he had manners drilled into him. I probably saw him five or six times over a couple months. He wanted to take me out, but I was stalling."

"Why? He sounds almost perfect."

Kristen nodded, thinking a moment she tried to explain. "I thought he was perfect. But I was very busy then, and I didn't have the time for romance. And to tell you the truth I was leery of one of the guys he hung out with. He made me nervous. I used to feel goose bumps when he looked at me. And that made me worry about Sonny. Like, why did he hang around with him? Was he the same, but just in a nicer package?" She glanced at her watch a moment before finishing her pasty.

"How's our time? Will you get in trouble with your boss if you're gone too long?" Claire asked.

She shook her head. "It doesn't matter. When we're through I just need to go back to get my bike. I'm quitting today."

"Quitting? But..., why?" Claire was shocked.

She gave a half smile. "Because you found me. And if you did, someone else may, so it isn't safe anymore."

Claire sat back dismayed; it had never occurred to her she would be disrupting Kristen's life.

"Don't worry, Claire. I'm just glad it was you who found me." She reached out and clasped Claire's hand briefly. "And I'm really glad to see you. You were always so nice to all of us students. You were always so calm, so patient when we made stupid mistakes. You know we all said we were going to grow up to be a 'Claire'.

"And you know I really felt rotten about letting everyone think I was dead."

The silence stretched out before Kristen picked up her story again. "Anyway, one night at the club I went up to the ladies'. The club is in an old warehouse and the facilities are upstairs down a long corridor to the back. It was a warm night and the windows along the hall were all opened. I was looking out as I walked along, and I saw Sonny and his two buddies down on the street on that side of the building. I almost called out to him, but there was another guy with them and I could tell they were arguing. I couldn't actually hear what they were saying, but it didn't look nice. Then they pushed this other guy into a big dark SUV and they all got in and took off.

"What got me was when they opened the door the interior light fell on the guy's face. His look of absolute terror made my blood run cold."

"Oh my god, what did you do?"

"I went on to the ladies' room. And I told myself I was over-dramatizing the whole thing. Anyway, every time I thought about it I managed to convince myself it was a non-event, and I finally did forget about it."

Now she had a stricken look on her face and Claire leaned forward. "And? What happened? Come on, I know there is more to this story."

Kristen nodded, blinking back tears. "Later that week I was in the lunch room at the library taking a break and I glanced at the Chronicle someone had left on the table. There he was. The guy I saw getting into the SUV with Sonny on Saturday night. They found his body in Golden Gate Park on Tuesday. They said he had been beaten to death. Tortured, they said." The last few words came out in a rush. She looked at Claire, her misery obvious.

"So I hadn't been over-dramatizing things. I might have saved him. But I didn't. I just ignored it all. And he died because I didn't help him."

Claire sat back stunned at this story. She felt so sorry for Kristen. She hadn't done anything. Her sin was omission instead of commission.

"I was really upset. And I was scared, because it was clear Sonny had a part in this. Sonny, the guy I thought was perfect, the guy I was thinking about dating, was a murderer. And worse! They tortured the guy to death.

"I had to call the police.

"It turns out Sonny is the youngest and only son of a major mafia don on the East Coast. He's been coddled and spoiled by his six sisters and his parents. He is apparently amoral. He has been suspected in a number of brutal crimes, but the authorities could never get any evidence. The Feds had been keeping an eye on him for over a year, trying to get him on something that would put him away for awhile. He is destined to take over after his father and while his father is tough, the Feds say they don't want to face what Sonny will do with the power of the crime syndicate behind him.

"With the information I gave them they zeroed in on Sonny. They decided to keep my involvement quiet after they were able to turn one of his buddies, who agreed to testify to avoid the death penalty. It wasn't the creepy one, the other one. Anyway, it didn't save him. He was mysteriously murdered while still in police custody. So then I became the only weapon they had to convict Sonny. They said the only way to protect me and their case was for me to go into hiding. I didn't want to, but they scared me. And apparently there was good reason to be scared.

"It's been one delay after another. Sonny's father's attorneys are apparently very good. But they were never able to get Sonny released on bail, so at least I know he's not going to turn up. Now I understand the trial is scheduled for September. Finally Sonny will get his day in court. That's when they plan to convict him of murder on my testimony.

"And, when it's over, I will go into the Witness Protection Program and start a new life somewhere."

"Kristen, I don't know what to say." Claire shook her head sadly. "Now I'm really sorry I didn't listen to my mother and just assume it was someone who looked like you."

"No, believe me, I've learned it's best not to ignore...."

The plate glass window shattered behind them just as the noise reached their ears; their table rocked violently throwing the dishes to the concrete. Claire grabbed the table, preventing it from toppling over and at the same time steadied herself. Being from San Francisco, naturally she first thought "earthquake," but the loud noise sounded more like an explosion—a very big blast—and it was close.

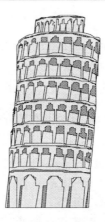

CHAPTER 5

The car park looked over undulating hills softened by the remnants of the night's fog. They milled around the bus talking excitedly while waiting their turn to board. The festive mood was contagious, like a group of school children getting ready for a field trip. And that was what it was, a field trip. They would spend the entire day in local wineries, sipping, eating and enjoying the ambiance.

Sal talked quietly to Helga and Frederick in Italian while Wanda, the other assistant chef conferred with Chef Martin while checking off a list as people boarded the bus.

"Okay people, let's not spend the day in the parking lot. There's wine to be tasted." Chef Martin's voice carried over the noise.

That got a laugh and the pace of boarding speeded up. Millie followed Ruth down the aisle. Ruth was dressed to party in a short cotton sun dress with bare legs and the high-heeled sandals she obviously loved.

She did bring a sweater, a concession to Millie's warning about how cool the cellars were liable to be.

Millie was dressed much more sensibly in lightweight slacks, a sleeveless shirt and a sweater over her shoulders, its sleeves tied around her neck. She had been to visit wineries in California and knew that in spite of the hot dry countryside the cellars used for storing the wines would be cold. And she wore her comfortable rubber-soled walking shoes for walking in the fields, on cobblestones and exploring cellars.

They took the first two seats still available which were behind LiAnn and Sam Ng. The Ng's were an interesting couple. Millie thought they were in their late seventies, but they could be in their eighties. Both were small, maybe wizened was a better word. Sam had become stooped by the weight of his years, but LiAnn, tiny as she was, held herself erect as if there was a ramrod down her back. She was almost regal in her manner. Last night while talking to them at the cocktail party Millie had learned LiAnn was the matriarch of the large Ng family. Their seven children, thirty-five grandchildren and fifteen great-grand-children all apparently catered to LiAnn, as did Sam.

The entire Ng family seemed to be involved in the restaurant business. Many years ago, in anticipation of Hong Kong reverting to the Chinese, the family had diversified. Now they had children and grandchildren running restaurants in Hong Kong, Vancouver, Honolulu and San Francisco. LiAnn and Sam, pioneers in fusion cooking, still played an active role in all their businesses. They mixed Chinese, Vietnamese, Japanese and Italian dishes creating a new craze. They said they came to the Retreat to learn from Chef Martin. Judging by the intense gleam in LiAnn's eyes,

Millie assumed she was another of his fans. And they were here, Sam had added, because they loved Italy.

Now Millie said in LiAnn's ear as she settled into the aisle seat, "Don't forget we need to get some ideas for the wine on Monday."

LiAnn nodded, and then turned to speak rapidly to Sam in what appeared to be some Chinese dialect.

Millie explained to Ruth, "Our group is doing the wine on Monday. LiAnn and I are both admittedly pretty green in our knowledge of wine. We're a little worried about our ability to contribute to the selection of the right wines. Anything we learn today will be a help." Then she leaned across the aisle to answer a question from Michael, who was sitting with Randy Jackson.

Randy was from California, not far from where Millie lived in San Francisco. He told her he had worked long and hard to help build a company which supported some of the newest innovations in the computer field. Now, having sold the company, he was at a crossroads. So he decided to give himself a break and pursue his favorite hobby by attending the Culinary Retreat. After he got back he was going to finish remodeling the kitchen in the little house he bought in Menlo Park before deciding what he was going to do next. His computer expertise was lost on this group. None of them even understood the importance of the device his company developed. But he loved to cook, so in that aspect he fit in here.

Randy was young, probably in his twenties, medium build. In fact he looked like the stereotypical computer nerd. He was quiet but pleasant company and while he didn't belong to the clique with Steven,

Zoe and Michael, he sometimes hung around with them.

Helga and Frederick Lowenthal were last on the bus and therefore had to take a seat in the back while Sal dropped into the seat in front with Wanda. Helga smiled at Millie as she passed. She seemed very nice, but then how would Millie know, not being able to communicate with her. Sal had told her the Lowenthals owned an inn on Lake Garda in Italy. It catered to Swiss, Italian and German tourists. They, as many of the others, were here to refresh their skills in Italian cuisine. Millie hoped before the retreat was over to get the address of their inn. She thought Claire might like it to pass on to some of her customers.

"All right, we're all here. Hang on, we're away," Chef Martin called out as the bus door closed with a whoosh and the bus headed out.

The chatter in the bus was deafening. After only two days together friendships had been formed and alliances made.

The first winery was perfect and Millie assumed that's why they started with it. *Una Cantina Delle Sette Cantine*, Millie let it roll off her tongue, repeating it after Chef Martin. It sounded as lovely as it was. The hills were covered with rows of green vines while the stone buildings of the winery nestled in a little valley. The Seven Cellars Winery seemed an appropriate name as they moved through cellar after cellar cut deep into the stone hills.

"Wow, look at this." They looked around the huge manmade cavern filled with stainless steel vats and rows and rows of racked bottles.

"Smell it. I think I could get high just from breathing the fumes."

"Not me, I'm waiting for the real thing," George retorted, "and I'm starting to feel thirsty."

Their guide heard George's comment and assured them. "Soon, I promise you. Only two more cellars to visit and then we come to the VIP tasting room." He led them into the next cellar, this one containing row after row of beautifully carved, huge white oak aging casks.

"Here are the casks that give our wine that oaky taste we're known for. These barrels were made in the 17th century and have survived the ravages of time, war and natural disasters. They are very valuable to us as white oak is extremely hard to obtain now. And then, of course, the carvers were artists. It would be impossible to duplicate this quality." He was willing to pause long enough for them to examine the barrels closely. The carvings done in deep relief were magnificent, every bit as detailed and beautiful as ones Ruth and Millie had admired in the museums in Florence.

But finally they entered the VIP tasting room, an alcove off the last cellar. This room was dark and filled with racked bottles. In the middle of the room was a bar, bathed in light, where the sommelier was waiting to serve them.

"You understand that all other tours end up in the tasting room where we started. There they are given a taste of a select number of wines and can purchase bottles of wine if they wish. However, for this group, we have a special tasting."

Their guide gestured toward the sommelier wearing his little tasting cup on a chain around his neck. "Henri is here to explain the wines for you. Taste as many as you wish. However, Chef Martin has asked me to remind you there are two more wineries to visit before lunch."

They laughed. It was a gracious way of telling them they couldn't stay forever. They surged toward the small bar where Henri presided, pouring generous amounts in the glasses before him. And while they were being passed around, he described the wine.

"This is a classic red Tuscan wine. It's made from Sangiovese and Cabernet Sauvignon grapes from our own vineyards. Notice the color."

He held his glass up and swirled it. They all followed suit.

"Smell it," he ordered dipping his nose in the glass and inhaling. "Smell the notes of cherries, smoke and vanilla." He looked around as one by one they nodded; either identifying the aromas or saying they did rather than admitting their ignorance.

"Taste it." He took a sip and rolled it around in his mouth, smiling with pleasure when he swallowed it. "Aged twenty-four months in the white oak barrels to get that oaky taste and the body is velvety and smooth; the finish is long and lovely." He took another sip and they followed suit.

"Now tell me, Chef Martin, wouldn't you love to serve this with one of your famous pork dishes?"

Chef Martin's expression conveyed no doubt as to his enjoyment of the wine.

Henri generously poured a bit more in the glasses held out for another taste and then he passed around a little dish of crackers urging them to cleanse their palates before tasting the next.

Finally, several wines later, Henri opened a Moscato d'Asti. "I have been signaled by your leaders you need to be moving on, so I want to give you a taste of this wine. I love this wine. It's equally perfect to start or finish a meal." He poured into the new tray of glasses which had been set down in front of him. "It is fabulously fruity." He swirled again and they all did the same.

Millie was feeling like she was really getting the hang of this swirling business. And she liked the smell of this wine, it was different than the others. She could actually smell the fruity odor. And when she tasted it, she felt the little fizz on her tongue and the slight taste of peach. She would remember this one for sure. But to make sure, she made a little note on the brochure she had picked up at the beginning of the tour.

If the mood had been festive at the start of the morning, it was more so now. The wine had relaxed them and this pleasant visit had only heightened their expectations of what was to come. They were ready for the next winery.

* * *

For a moment everyone seemed frozen, then Kristen was on her feet, her eyes wide with horror as she looked back down the street at the smoke pouring out of the building at end of the next block. Little spots of color identified victims down on the street amidst the rubble.

People were already running to their aid, as was Kristen. Grabbing her backpack, she shouted back at Claire, "Come on. Hurry! It's down near the store..."

The police vehicles, sirens screaming, passed before they even got to the nearest corner, and they could see the police were already cordoning off the street; refusing to let anyone enter.

Kristen paused a moment, then turned to her left running down the street. "This way, we'll go around behind. Maybe we can get closer from the other street."

Claire was noisily panting when Kristen stopped. This street was also cordoned off, but they were better positioned to see what was left of the art store on the corner and the building on the other side of the little alley. There were gaping holes through the rubble that had so recently been solid stone walls. They could see the flames. The firefighters were already on the scene connecting their hoses and forming groups preparing to enter both structures. More police, fire trucks and emergency vehicles were arriving filling the street. Passersby and emergency staff attended to victims lying randomly on the street. It looked like a war zone.

Kristen was in shock. She stood pressed against the barricade with tears running down her cheeks as she recited the names of her co-workers. She started forward; she had to get closer.

Claire pulled on her arm. "Wait, you can't go in there. Can't you see we'd just be in the way?"

"But I have to see if anyone made it out. I have to know."

Claire nodded, understanding Kristen's need. "I know, but everything is chaotic now. They need a little time to sort it all out. Why don't we go back to my hotel and put on the TV. I'm sure they will be reporting on this. Then later you can call the authorities and tell them who was there and find out what happened." She tugged on Kristen until she turned and followed her docilely down the street.

Later Claire stood glumly at the window, watching the still billowing smoke. It was obvious the fire fighters were waging a battle with the flames. Kristen was lying on the bed, a cool wet towel draped across her forehead, a cup of cooling tea forgotten on the table beside her.

Claire had needed a bracing cup of tea and thought Kristen would benefit from one too. Luckily the hotel catered to English guests, so it kept tea kettles and supplies in each of the rooms. They didn't talk. What was there to say? Kristen was still crying. While her sobs had diminished, the tears still oozed from her eyes, trailing down her cheeks. She couldn't seem to stop, but she said the wet cloth helped her head.

Abruptly she sat up. "There, turn it up." She listened intently and repeated in English for Claire. "No survivors from the two buildings. Four people on the street were killed and sixteen more were injured from debris, some seriously."

She turned and looked at Claire. "If you hadn't found me I would have been one more casualty." She looked as horrified as Claire felt. This time Claire cried too until she finally went in the bathroom to get a damp cloth for her own head.

Kristen had attempted to call the authorities on two different occasions but the lines were apparently jammed with calls. Now she stood up and gathered her things announcing she was going home; she would try to call the police again later. It wasn't until she realized she would have to walk, having parked her bike as usual in the storage room at the store that Claire realized her bike was also gone. She groaned. It would take a lot of effort to explain this to the bike rental shop. She suspected she had bought the bike.

Since Kristen was determined to go home, Claire decided to go with her, feeling responsible for her now that she had resurrected her, so to speak. She wanted to make sure she made it home safely. But before she turned off the television Kristen put up her hand to stop her. Her face drained of color as she looked at Claire.

"It was a bomb. They said it was a bomb in that little alley we use between the two buildings. It's like the bombing of the Uffizi a few years back. Someone parked a car full of explosives right next to the museum and detonated it. Luckily, it was at night so no one was around at the time."

Claire felt the blood drain from her face as what Kristen said registered. "But I parked my bike in that alley." She shook her head trying to clear it. "And there wasn't any car there. In fact the alley is so narrow I don't think a car would fit there."

Abruptly she collapsed on the edge of the bed. "There were only some bikes. And there was the bike with the big box on the back. The guy with the brown suit left it there. I saw him."

Stiffly she turned to Kristen, forcing the words out. "I might have seen it. The bomb!" She shook her head hardly able to believe what she was thinking. "It was that guy on the street in front of me. He had a box fastened to the rear of his bike." She closed her eyes a minute. "Wait, wait I don't think I saw the box yesterday. No, he couldn't have had it yesterday; I'm sure I would have noticed."

"Yesterday, what do you mean? You saw the same guy yesterday?" Kristen was staring at her with very wide eyes.

Claire nodded. "It would be hard to miss him. I was waiting for you on my bike. I was going to catch up with you and see whether or not it was really you.

But after I pulled out into the traffic, he cut right in front of me to get behind you. I had to apply my brakes and they're very touchy, so over I went. I didn't see him after that, but I'm sure I would have noticed the box. I certainly recognized him today when I saw him."

"Where was he today?" Her voice had a little catch in it that caught Claire's attention.

"On the street, a few bike lengths behind you." Claire was thinking. "But you don't think...?"

Kristen sat down, taking off her backpack again. "I don't know what to think. Let's talk this through. Tell me everything."

So Claire went through the sequence again. This time she mentioned everyone she had seen more than once on the street before or after Kristen passed.

"What do you think?" she asked Kristen.

"I don't want to think about it. It would just be too horrible if I caused this mayhem."

They sat staring at the television trying to absorb the implications of what they were thinking.

At last Kristen said, "Well, I won't be going home. That would be too big a risk. I'm going to assume I was uncovered and act accordingly."

"What will you do?"

"I'm leaving town. I've got to get out of here right away. That time someone bombed the Uffizi, they closed the city down. None of the buses, trains or even cars could get in or out. I need to get out now before that happens."

"But where will you go? How will you be sure you're safe?"

Kristen shrugged. "I can't be sure, but I have some disguises and I'll try to find somewhere to light until I can connect up with my controller."

Claire nodded, then making up her mind she said, "I'm going with you."

* * *

Kristen moved through the crowded train station with purpose despite the confusion milling around them. Claire glanced longingly at the taxis waiting outside the exit, but Kristen crossed the street without a glance in that direction. Claire wasn't surprised after Kristen's "too easy to be remembered," comment in Florence. They had walked to the train station when the buses along their route never arrived. They assumed the buses were held up in the traffic jam around the bomb site. Fortunately the train station was less than two miles from her hotel.

Now, almost seven p.m., it felt later. Claire was hoping the hotel they picked from her guidebook would have room for them. Kristen inserted some coins in a blue machine, which spit out two pieces of cardboard. These turned out to be passes for the bus which came along shortly after. It wasn't a long ride before Kristen signaled her they were at the stop they wanted. Claire was amazed at how much easier traveling was with someone familiar with the customs and at ease with the language. She didn't say a word as she followed Kristen off the bus. They had decided it would be prudent if Claire didn't give away her American origins, thinking two Italian women on a weekend holiday would be much harder to trace, if, in fact, anyone was trying to trace them.

Now they paused on the curved street running uphill from the edge of Il Campo, Sienna's central piazza.

"I think we should go directly to the hotel and try to book a room, because if they're full, it may take us a while to find an available one. Then we can eat. What do you think?"

Kristen nodded her agreement. "According to this map it's up that way; I think only a couple of blocks."

Kristen still looked pale and her now dark brown, short hair altered her looks substantially. That, plus the dark circles ringing her eyes, made her look older and very tired. Claire imagined she was probably looking even worse. She didn't have Kristen's youth to help combat the ravages of stress.

Despite the stress and the shock, Kristen had calmly gone about making ready to flee Florence after declaring her intention. Claire watched with awe as she pulled a pair of scissors and a package of hair dye from the bottom of her backpack. It didn't take her long to alter her appearance. Then she gathered up the red locks from the bathroom floor, the empty dye packaging and tied it up in a bundle, announcing, "We'll dump it along the way."

And when she couldn't dissuade Claire from coming with her, she then supervised the packing of Claire's backpack. As they left the hotel and turned in the key, Claire told the clerk she would be away for the weekend; shook her head sadly at the clerk's comments on the bombing and then quickly left. Kristen had warned her, if she didn't tell them she was to be gone, they would think the worse when she didn't pick up her key for a couple days. It would be very awkward if the authorities were looking for her and even worse, Claire's mother might become alarmed when she couldn't reach her.

The hotel they had selected had a very nice, albeit small, lobby. Kristen signed them into their last vacant room, handing over their passports and talking to the clerk in rapid Italian. The hotel was housed in an ancient building built into a hill incorporating part of the old wall of the town. Apparently the bottom floors of the building going down the hill were private homes. The first three floors above the lobby were business establishments and the hotel was housed on the upper floors, which had been added more recently. The elevators from the lobby only stopped at the floors the hotel used for rooms, breakfast and lounge. Their room on the eighth floor looked over part of the old wall and down the hill. Claire stood at the large window, but could only see dim lights and an inky sky.

"Don't unpack anything," Kristen cautioned. "From now on we take these packs with us everywhere."

Claire nodded, just then realizing she had not really grasped the seriousness of their situation as Kristen, obviously, had.

"Let's go and have some dinner. When we come back we'll pick up our passports. They should be through with them by then. And I need to call in. They'll find out about the bombing..." Her face fell for a moment. "Christ, I pray it didn't have anything to do with me."

Tears sprang to her eyes and her voice became a whisper as she said, "How could I live with myself if all those people were killed because of me?"

Claire put her arms around her and patted her on the back. "You didn't do anything, Kristen. It wasn't you!"

They stood for a moment, then Claire said, "Maybe you're jumping to conclusions. This is Italy. There could be a million reasons..."

Kristen nodded. Gathering her resolve she stepped away and went into the bathroom to splash water on her face. Drying it she said, "You're right. Let's go. We'll both feel better with something in our stomachs and a good night's sleep."

* * *

They had become slightly rowdy by the time they arrived at Cantina Del Nettare Di Etruscan. This was a very modern winery. All the aging casks and fermenting vats were stainless steel. The bottling apparatus was the most modern they had seen. There were no picturesque cellars here, just big modern warehouses with climate control. They were currently in the bottling shed and the guide was explaining the difference their bottling method had on the finished wine.

Millie stood at the rear of the group. She wasn't used to drinking during the day and, although she had only tasted, the net result was a lot more wine than she was used to consuming. Others in the group had been milling around a bit, some wanting to see the conveyor belt from different angles, some probably just restless as their enthusiastic guide went into excruciating detail about the process. When the guide turned on the conveyor belt, the noise filled the large space. The bottles entered at one end, were filled, then corked and sealed before being labeled and finally packed. The action was mesmerizing.

Millie struggled to keep her eyes open in spite of the noise. She was wondering if she could sneak a few minutes of shut eye on the bus before they reached their final stop for the day. When she rotated her head to stretch her neck she noticed movement behind her. She turned to see what it was.

It was a forklift heading their way. But, she realized with horror, it was moving way too fast. Then she saw there was no driver on board.

Chef Martin stood directly in its path; his back was to the machine as he focused his attention on their guide.

Millie yelled a warning, but it was swallowed in the noise from the machinery. Her heart pounded so violently, she couldn't breathe. She launched herself at him; her fear gave her a surprising burst of speed. She barreled into his back from the side, the impact and surprise staggered him. Off balance, with her weight on his back, he couldn't remain upright. He fell to his knees, then on the floor. Millie ended up on top of him, sandwiching him between her and the hard cement, as the forklift rumbled past with only inches to spare. The noise reached a crescendo when the forklift reached the assembly line, its half raised prongs jamming the conveyor belt. Bottles, machinery parts and shouting spectators converged at the joining of the two machines. A worker raced out of the warehouse section and leaped on the forklift. Somehow he managed to turn it off. Just about that time the guide was able to hit the emergency stop button for the conveyor.

A quiet settled with only little pings from the metal parts settling and the crinkling sound of glass pieces still falling. No one moved; they were shocked into immobility.

Millie glanced down at Chef Martin, who twisted around beneath her to look at her with a confused expression on his face.

"Why, Ms. Gulliver, I swear you just knock me over!" His droll comment was so unexpected Millie couldn't help laughing, breaking the unnatural silence. She flushed as she realized she was still on top of Chef Martin.

"Oh, I'm so sorry, Chef Martin. Did I hurt you?" She struggled to stand without damaging him further. Suddenly people, noticing the two of them on the floor, rushed to help.

"What happened?" Antonio asked while he and Sal lifted Millie to her feet.

"Is anyone hurt?"

"Did it hit you?"

Millie shook her head, holding onto the two of them when she realized how unsteady her legs were. Suddenly she was more than aware of her age.

Antonio and Sal led her to the side where a desk and two chairs were placed and sat her down in one of the chairs.

"Millie, what happened? Are you all right?" Ruth rushed to her side.

Michael and George helped Chef Martin to his feet, but he just shook his head at their questions; it was clear he had no idea what had happened.

"I yelled a warning, but you couldn't hear me. I hope you're not hurt." Millie's voice trembled.

Chef Martin looked at her, then at the forklift caught in the assembly line, then at where he was standing. He got the picture.

He walked over and collapsed in the other chair. His face had a grayish hue as he took his hanky out of his pocket and wiped the beads of moisture from his brow. Then he leaned close to her face. "Ms. Gulliver, you are either very foolish or very brave. Did it occur to you that you might have been crushed with me somewhere in the middle of that mess?"

She nodded, clasping her hands tightly to hide the trembling.

Ruth's expression would have been comical if Millie had felt like laughing. "Millie, what were you thinking? My God, you could have been killed." Then her expression changed to real horror, "Millie..., and I would have had to explain it to Claire!"

Her fear making her sound cross, she scolded, "Millie, you're a sixty-three year old woman. You have no business acting like a superhero."

Now Millie had started to shake. She looked at Chef Martin and then at Ruth. "I didn't even think about that. I just saw the forklift coming and the next thing I knew I was knocking him over."

Three winery employees were now over by the damaged assembly line, shouting aggressively in each other's faces, and more were coming.

Millie turned to Antonio who was still standing next to her. "Do you understand them, Antonio? What are they saying? What happened?"

He shrugged, the way some Italian men do, and explained in heavily accented English, his hands gesturing wildly in accompaniment with his words. "They're arguing. The man who climbed up and turned off the machine says he knows it was turned off and the brake was set when he parked over there before he went out for his cigarette break. That one," he nodded at the man with the beet red face, "says it's impossible. If the motor wasn't idling how could it have slipped into gear to run into the conveyor?" Antonio shook his head.

"The machine operator was at fault." His voice was certain. "He'll most likely be fired and he'll be lucky if he's not held liable for the cost of the damage."

"Oh, dear, how dreadful!" Millie felt sorry for the man, a small mistake and look what happened. She shuddered as she thought about what had almost happened.

* * *

"Millie, Ruth, we have room here." LiAnn gestured graciously to the two seats next to her.

Millie had taken a long nap during their free time after the winery excursion and slept right through cocktails. Ruth, of course, hadn't. But she had more stamina and more practice in holding her spirits, Millie thought.

Antonio smiled at her across the table. "And how are you this evening? No pains from your tumble this afternoon?"

Millie grimaced, and shook her head. She wasn't going to mention the huge bruise she found on her hip when she showered before dinner. It was a small price to pay for saving Chef Martin.

"Tumble? Did you hurt yourself today, Millie?" LiAnn's face was solicitous, but her eyes gleamed with curiosity. Her husband craned forward to look around his wife, his face also interested.

"No, nothing much."

"Nothing much?" Antonio shook his head, waving his arms. "She was the heroine, was she not, George?"

George sitting next to Antonio and across from Ruth turned his attention to their conversation. "What, oh, yes. Millie's quick action probably saved our Retreat, as well as Chef Martin," he added.

"Oh, Millie, tell us what happened. When did this happen? Why didn't we notice? Tell us!"

Her imperial tone worked, so Millie found herself dutifully explaining what happened.

"And I missed it all." LiAnn was obviously disappointed. "I went to use the facilities and when I came out everyone was heading for the bus. I didn't see any of it." She looked at Sam with disapproval. "You didn't tell me any of this."

He shrugged. "I didn't see it. I only saw the problem on the assembly line. It didn't occur to me to tell you about it. It was a management problem. Not our concern."

LiAnn reached over and patted Millie's hand. "You are a brave woman and obviously very capable. Your family must treasure you," she pronounced solemnly.

Millie was uncomfortable with the attention and was glad when the conversation turned back to a discussion of the wineries they had visited.

"A treasure, huh?" Ruth muttered in her ear. "But truthfully, Millie, I can't believe you did that. Didn't you think you might not have succeeded in moving him; that you might have both been run over?"

Millie looked at her as she thought about what Ruth had just said. "You know, I didn't think. I just acted. And it was probably just as well. If I thought about it, I never would have been able to move fast enough to save him." She shuddered. "And Ruth, I think he would have been skewered by the prongs on that forklift."

"Well, I guess I can't complain about you being so timid any more, can I?" And Ruth turned to talk to Jacques, the teenager who sat on the far side of her.

Dinner was over and it was the time Chef Martin usually started the discussion of the items they had eaten. But tonight, after a discussion with Marie, who seemed somewhat agitated, he stood up and held up his hands.

"Please, everyone, can I have your attention? Marie Verde has just brought us some sad news." He nodded. "A bomb exploded in Florence today."

People gasped, looking at each other. Sal forgot his role as a translator as he rose to his feet; he had family in Florence. Helga and Frederick looked at the others with confusion until finally Zoe explained.

Chef Martin continued. "It is very sad. And of course people were hurt, some dead. Innocent people." He shook his head sadly. "These are bad times we live in.

"So we have a change of plans for tomorrow. Market day will not be in the village we have scheduled, which is very close to Florence, and so will most likely be impacted by the tragedy there. Instead, we will be heading in a different direction. Unfortunately this alternative market is not as big or diverse as the one we planned to attend, but we will make do. Those of you in Group A will be ready in the Lobby at eight o'clock, huh?"

"Now I think for tonight we will dispense with our critique. Marie says the Villa has set up some televisions in the bar for any of you who want the news. I'm sure there will be some that can translate.

Good night and please offer your prayers for the victims."

Millie looked at Ruth with a white face. "Claire. Claire is in Florence."

"Now Millie, keep calm. There are thousands of people in Florence. It would be unlikely that Claire would be anywhere near the explosion." Then, seeing her friend's anxiety, she gave up. "Why don't you call the hotel? Maybe you can reach her."

When Millie joined her friends in the bar later she shook her head at Ruth's silent inquiry. "I couldn't get through. The lines are totally jammed."

Ruth nodded. "That's what Sal said. He called a friend who will go into the city to check on Sal's family for him."

Millie sat down with the others, watching the pictures on the screen. The pictures were enough; they didn't really need words to explain what they were seeing. Millie worried and fretted, but there wasn't anything she could do. Since her husband had been taken from her so cruelly and senselessly, she had always been overprotective of Claire. She knew it. She tried to be calm, to hide her fear that somehow Claire would be stolen from her, too. But despite her efforts she still became irrational at any thought Claire might be in danger. Claire was now in her forties and she was a sensible, capable woman. She told herself her baby was fine. She would be safe.

And when she finally went up to her room to retire for the night the blinking red light on the phone beckoned to her. She collapsed on the side of the bed as she listened to Claire's reassuring words.

"Hey, Mom, I hope you're having fun. I'm sure you heard about the bombing here. Don't worry, I'm safe.

But it's very chaotic and sad. Many of the museums and tourist attractions are closed now, so I've decided to go out of town for the weekend. I'm not sure where I'll end up, so I'll call you when I get settled. I'm going to try to explore some of the hill towns Marianne Peabody recommended. I'll be back in Florence in plenty of time to travel to Venice as we planned.

"Since I don't know how long I'll be away, I've decided to keep my room here so I can come back when I want. Have a great time at your retreat.

"Love ya'. Bye."

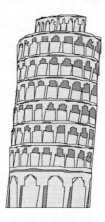

CHAPTER 6

"Millie, you're going to be late," Ruth warned her as she headed for the kitchen.

Millie checked her watch and saw she was right. "I've got to go now, Antonio, but have a good day. I'll look forward to hearing about your shopping trip at lunch. I can't wait to see what your group prepares for dinner. It's always hard to be the first, isn't it?" She waved as she headed for the room which had been assigned to Group C for the morning session.

She was a little stiff this morning and the bruise was tender, but she was determined not to show it. Ruth had already launched into another tirade when she saw the bruise while they were dressing. This morning it was a deep purple, almost black and there were a few more which appeared in places Ruth couldn't see. She admitted it had been foolish on her part to play the hero, but it had worked. So she didn't regret it.

But this morning listening to Ruth scold her, it had reminded her of how she was always worrying about and scolding Claire for putting herself at risk. And now that the shoe was on the other foot, so to speak, she wasn't liking it at all. She promised herself she would remember this the next time her worry erupted on Claire.

"Ah there you are Millie, we thought we lost you." George Binns smiled his greeting. "And did you contact your daughter last night?"

Millie nodded. "Kind of. She left a message on the phone in my room. She knew I'd hear about the bomb and assume the worse. She said everything in Florence was closed, so she decided to visit one of the hill towns. She'll call today to let me know where she is."

"Good morning," Sal Salenesso said hearing Millie's news as he entered the room. "So, Millie, you have heard from your daughter, and I have heard that my family is safe also. So we can concentrate on our cooking, yes?"

"Yes," they responded moving to the front of the room to better see what he was doing.

Sal Salenesso was a local. Ordinarily he worked in a restaurant in one of the large Florence hotels but had agreed to assist Chef Martin at the Italian Culinary Association's request. His specialty was desserts, so naturally he was working with each group assigned to desserts.

He was an attractive man, not too tall and slightly rotund, a testimonial to his skill in the kitchen. He had a very pleasant personality and had made himself popular with the Retreat members.

"Sal, how will Frederick and Helga survive without you today?" Renee asked. "Aren't you their interpreter?"

"Ah, yes but Helga is in the group with Zoe and Antonio. Both have assured me they would see that she doesn't miss anything. And Jacques speaks many languages like a native and he agreed to see Frederick understands everything." Sal beamed. "So I am only talking desserts today."

"I have reviewed your work from the planning session on Thursday and I see you plan to provide a cake, a pudding and a ricotta and cookies for your desserts. So I have assembled several recipes for you to choose from. Then we will do the prep work. This afternoon our session starts at three and we have two hours to complete our desserts." He smiled at their dismayed looks. "Don't worry, we'll make it. You'll see.

"Now, we are selecting three recipes, four including the cookies, and each of you will make a set of each. That will be more than enough for dinner, but I'm sure the Villa's kitchen staff will be glad to help us dispose of any leftovers."

Sal opened his portfolio and removed a stack of papers. "Here are some suggestions for you to look at. I would caution you that you will need to have agreed on your selections by break time in order to finish the prep work before lunch."

A hush fell as they each busied themselves with a stack of recipes.

"Here, Millie, look at this. Doesn't it look good?

Millie took the sheet of paper from George and read the recipe.

Budino di Chocolate, it sounded marvelous. She handed it to Randy. "Check this for the pudding. George and I think it might be a winner. It sounds different."

"This is the cake!" LiAnn's tone left no room to dispute. George looked at it with raised eyebrows and then passed it to Renee.

Renee nodded. "Looks fine to me. Let me see the pudding choice you have, Randy."

"Here's a torte cake that looks interesting," George offered.

LiAnn looked at him sternly then retorted haughtily, "We're doing the Torta Soffice di Mele. We don't need another cake choice."

George shrugged, shuffled his torte recipe to the bottom of the stack and started looking for cookies.

LiAnn having gotten her way with the cake choice was agreeable on the pudding, but then suggested, "I don't mind the ricotto, but let's do a better one than Chef Martin's."

Renee grinned. "So, LiAnn, you didn't like Chef Martin's?"

George glared at Renee. "Don't be a fool Renee. I agree with LiAnn. We don't want to offer the same recipe. We need to have something different."

"Let's not use raisins," Millie suggested. "I'm not overly fond of raisins even when they're soaked in wine. I don't think they're special enough. Can't we use some kind of fresh fruit?"

"I'll check in the kitchen and see what's available." Sal left them.

"You know at the George V, I frequently made a dessert with fresh fruit which I marinated in Frangelica. It was wonderful. I think it would be delightful spooned over the ricotta, and different."

"What is this Frangelica?" LiAnn asked. "I don't know it."

"It's a liqueur. Made from hazelnuts, isn't it, Renee?"

"Yes, it's similar to Amaretto but lighter; it would be very good with fruit." George answered for Renee while nodding his agreement.

Sal returned with the list. "We have strawberries, peaches, plums and cherries available. Do any of those strike your fancy?"

Everyone had an opinion. "Wait I saw a recipe for strawberries." George dug through the recipes in front of him. "Here it is, Ricotta Con Le Fragole." He passed it to LiAnn.

"I think peaches would be good," Renee offered.

"I love cherries." Millie sighed. "It would be wonderful with cherries and we could use a small amount of almond extract in the ricotta and sprinkle toasted almonds over the top to garnish it."

"That does sound good," Randy agreed. "And cherries are more elegant. The season is shorter and they're only available for a small window of time."

Everyone paused to consider Randy's comment. Sal was questioned further about the cherries and finally he agreed to go back to the kitchen to get a sample for them to taste.

"I agree the cherries would be special, but only if they are wonderful cherries," LiAnn pronounced.

And after tasting, they agreed that these cherries were special. So Ricotto, flavored with Almond and covered with sweet cherries soaked in Frangelica would be their third selection.

Now the cookies were the battleground. Millie felt exhausted; making decisions by committee was a wearing process.

But it turned out that the Almond Biscuits were chosen with ease. Made with egg whites and almonds, they would be the perfect accompaniment to their Ricotto Cherry dish.

And they finished fifteen minutes before the break.

As soon as they were released, Millie hurried back to her room to check the answering machine. But there were no new messages.

* * *

The desk clerk looked up with a friendly expression as the men approached the counter.

"We're looking for the American women," the taller of the two, dressed in a brown suit, shod in expensive Italian loafers, said in a gravelly voice.

The clerk misunderstood the gravity of the situation, retorting in a facetious manner, "American women? We have many here, do you have a name?"

The large hand around his throat dragged him forward over the counter so his toes barely touched the floor. It was hard to breathe but he was afraid to jerk or pull away because of the knife. The sharp point was pressed uncomfortably against the skin below his right eye. He was so scared he thought he was going to wet himself.

"The American women! Two of them. Checked in yesterday!" The voice was terrifying.

Confusion was clear on the clerk's face; he was desperate to give the right response.

"Two American women! One has red hair," the second man offered. He didn't dress to match his friend. His attire consisted of khaki pants, tee shirt and a red

nylon jacket, but his expression was grim. He meant business.

The clerk trembled, still not moving. He stopped gasping for air long enough to say, "Yes, yes." But he didn't nod, the knife was still there.

The tall man released his neck at the same time the knife disappeared, "So? What room? Are they in?"

The clerk glanced at the cubbyholes where they kept the keys and nodded.

"Give me the key."

He started to protest but one look at the men changed his mind. Silently he retrieved a key and handed it to the tall man, the number 722 clearly marked on the tag.

The tall man handed it to his companion and said, his eyes never leaving the clerk, "I'll just wait here with our friend. You take care of this."

They both watched the man enter the elevator, the doors shut behind him and the floor indicator slowly moved to number seven.

The clerk didn't know what to do. The tall man stood off to the side watching him carefully. He accepted the keys from two sets of departing guests, nodding nervously at their exclamations about the brightness of the morning. He didn't encourage conversation with them, just hoping they would leave without asking a lot of questions he didn't have the ability to answer. Meanwhile he wondered what was happening on the seventh floor.

Room 722 was at the far end of the hall from the elevator. The man didn't bother to knock. He fitted the key in the lock, turned it and then slammed into it so hard that the little safety lock broke and the door swung wide. The two women looked up. Their shocked expressions quickly turned to horror as the large gun in his hand silently jerked. First the red-headed woman who was leaning over her backpack fell, red blossoming on her breast, then the other woman, the one with the mousy brown hair, whose head exploded before the scream emerged. He left without even checking the corpses. No need; he knew they were dead.

When the elevator opened on the lobby again he nodded at his companion as he headed for the door, his gun tucked back in his waistband, hidden by the red jacket. The tall man followed without a further glance at the clerk.

The desk clerk stood mutely, shaking, thinking about what to do. He knew he didn't want to go up to the seventh floor. He knew it wouldn't be good.

* * *

Claire sat quietly thumbing through a fashion magazine. Since she was unable to read Italian she was reduced to looking at the pictures when she wasn't surreptitiously glancing Kristen's way. It was all she could do not to interfere but she wasn't Kristen's mother, so how could she protest even when the beautician kept cutting and cutting and cutting. And Kristen seemed to be fine with the amount of hair strewn around her. At last the scissors were put away; the razor came out to trim her neck and around her ears. Finally the beautician squeezed something from a tube, rubbed her hands together and then worked it into Kristen's hair, or what was left of it. With some adroit movements of her fingers she was finished. Kristen's hair was as short as a boy's cut, and the hair on top of her head, a little longer than the rest, had been spiked. And Kristen was smiling as she fitted her dangling earrings back in her ears.

"So, what do you think?" She asked gaily.

Claire didn't want to tell her, so she stalled, looking at her friend carefully. "I wouldn't know you," she said slowly.

"Really? That's great! Here, now what do you think?" She fitted a pair of glasses on her nose. The frameless, blue tinted lenses gave her an even more modern look.

"You look like one of the models in this magazine I was looking at."

Kristen smiled big. "Precisely. But I look different, don't I?"

Claire had to admit she did.

"Now are you sure you don't want to have yours done?" Kirsten was serious; she didn't seem to notice the shiver that ran through Claire as she firmly shook her head.

"It wouldn't do me much good. I don't have a handful of passports with different names. And besides, no one is looking for me...." She paused a moment, thinking. "Well, except for my mother, maybe." But she hoped not. She was counting on the message she left for her last night forestalling any anxiety on her mother's part. With the bombing on all the television channels, her mother was sure to hear about it. And when she couldn't reach Claire she would naturally panic. It had been so easy to purchase a phone card and call the Villa Tuscany. Unfortunately she wasn't able to reach either her mother or Ruth. But, as the Villa Tuscany was a five star establishment, each room had its own voice message system. Claire just left a message so her mother wouldn't worry, and that way she didn't have to lie to her directly. It was a very satisfactory solution.

"Now what?" Claire asked Kristen.

"Well, we've got time to kill and it's too early for lunch, so how about we see some of Siena?

"What does that guidebook of yours recommend?

That's how they ended up at the Duomo.

"Kristen, this church has two Michelangelo statues, several of Bernini's works, some Pisano and even a Donatello. Most museums would spend a fortune to add them to their collection, if they even had a chance to bid on them. And here they sit for everyone and anyone to see."

They entered the vestibule of the church with anticipation. But they no more than got through the door before the floor, the beautiful, intricate, detailed marble pavement took their breath away. Claire spent the next couple of hours hunched over, examining every detail. She only nodded abstractedly to Kristen's comments on the Michelangelo statues unable to lift her eyes long enough to examine them. Never had she seen anything as wonderful as this vast floor. It was mind boggling. She hoped to burn it into her memory so she could remember the details for years to come. But in case her memory wasn't good enough she bought a lot of postcards and even a book with detailed pictures. When Kristen finally lured her out of the Duomo with promises of food, she went reluctantly, vowing to herself that she would be back, perhaps tomorrow or another time, but she would be back to look some more.

They ate in the fashionable Il Campo. But not at one of the trendy, expensive outdoor cafes spread along the perimeter of the great paved piazza, but with the dozens of office workers and students. This group bought their lunches, as they had, from one of the small delis; then sat in the sun, eating their lunches perched on the various stairs, fountains, benches, and even sitting cross-legged on the pavement of the piazza.

Claire had finished her Panini, a sandwich like affair with thin dry ham on a crusty buttered roll. Now she was starting to peel her orange.

"Yuck. What's the matter with this orange?" she asked Kristen.

"Oh, you haven't had one of our oranges yet, have you? It's a blood orange. It's red inside, not orange, but it tastes very good. Try it."

Claire took a small piece. It was tasty despite its blood red color, so she lost her hesitancy immediately.

"Claire, I'm a little surprised you don't have a cell phone. Haven't you entered the twenty-first century yet?" Kristen teased.

"Oh, I do. I just didn't bring it. People told me I'd have to make arrangements to have it work here, and it seemed like too much trouble for what little use I would get from it.

"What about you? It seems that everyone here has one attached to their ear most of the time. Shouldn't you have one?"

"I don't know that many people. I don't need one and when I make my weekly report I always use a public phone. It's safer."

They let their gazes wander around looking at the others eating and sunning there. Then Kristen continued, "I guess your bookstore is making it?"

Claire nodded. She had left the library while Kristen was still working there to transform the outdated bookstore her great uncle left her into the trendy Gulliver's Travels Bookshop. It had been a very risky venture for someone who had spent the first half of her life in a safe, conservative job. But, in spite of the reversals from the dot-com crash of Silicon Valley and the following tragedy of 9/11, the business was still solid.

"I love running the store. I love being my own boss and doing what I want. Well, of course, I have Mrs. B, Theroux and Tuffy-Two to consider."

She saw Kristen's confusion and laughed. "Mrs. B is my assistant manager. She's somewhere between fifty-five and eighty-five and she's lived. She's traveled everywhere, done everything and loves working in the store, schmoozing with the customers and pushing me in directions I'm sometimes too cautious to go. And Theroux is the cat, who moved in and made the store her own. She tolerates us and allows the customers to fawn over her when she feels like it. And then there's Tuffy-Two. Some friends gave me a West Highland Terrier puppy last Christmas. I'm afraid he has taken over our lives. Even the cat has taken him in hand. In fact I'm a little surprised Theroux hasn't taught him how to use her litter box."

"Gee, Claire it sounds wonderful. I know everyone thought you were having some huge mid-life crisis. They thought you were going to ruin your life by leaving the library after all those years. But I didn't. I thought with all the time you had in the library you probably needed a change."

She sighed. "And of course I've learned how easy it is to completely change courses in life. Sometimes it only takes a small step to send you in a completely different direction."

They both fell silent pondering the strange turns of fate.

The sun, the muted noise on the piazza and the food made Claire realize how sleepy she was.

"Kristen, I think I could use a nap. What do you think?"

She agreed, so they dumped their garbage and headed back to their hotel.

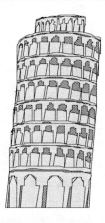

CHAPTER 7

Kristen was first to notice the surge of pedestrians moving with them up the narrow curved street to the hotel. "What's going on?"

Claire had been concentrating on getting up the steep street without losing her breath. She was very tired. Visions of victims and the blown out buildings crowded her mind every time she had shut her eyes, which had robbed her of a sound sleep last night. Now she looked up and saw the people crowding the street ahead of them, going the same way they were. It was strange.

"Oh, my god," Kristen breathed, as they rounded a curve giving them a view of the crowd amassed in front of them. Police cars and emergency vehicles were clustered in front of a building which looked suspiciously like their hotel.

The crowd was being held back by determined policemen holding out their arms. Something was obviously wrong.

"What's going on?" Claire asked, frightened.

Kristen shook her head and motioned Claire to follow her into the edge of the crowd. She asked lots of questions as they worked their way forward until they could see it was definitely their hotel which was cordoned off. Finally, near the front, she found someone who seemed to know something, and the rapid-fire Italian went on and on until Claire wanted to scream at them. At last Kristen turned back to Claire and whispered, "That was one of the maids. She said two men forced the desk clerk to give them the room number of the two American women. They were very specific; they wanted two American women, one with red hair."

Claire's eyes widened in horror.

"And..., what happened?" She wasn't sure she wanted to know.

Kristen swallowed hard. "He gave him the key. One of the men stayed with the clerk and the other went up in the elevator. When he came down they left."

"And...?" Claire felt a scream in her throat and forced it back. "What did they look like? Ask her what they looked like."

Kristen turned back to the woman and spoke again; Claire wished she could understand.

Just then a ripple went through the crowd. People pressed forward craning their necks to get a better glimpse of the activity near the door of the hotel. A collective gasp came from the watchers as the gurneys came out, one after the other, each draped with a sheet over what could only have been a body bag. The attendants loaded the gurneys into the back and then the ambulance moved silently down the street, the crowd opening a path for it to pass.

Kristen turned and slipped back down the street with Claire right on her heels. They didn't stop until they collapsed in the chairs at a table in a sidewalk café just outside Il Campo. Kirsten ordered two espressos and the hovering waiter disappeared.

"There doesn't seem to be much of a question here." Kristen was grim. "Two Americans? One with red hair? How did they know? How could they have found out so soon I wasn't in the building they bombed in Florence?"

"Was it him? Did she say?" Claire's heart was pounding so rapidly she could hardly breathe.

"One was tall, good-looking, dressed in a nice brown suit, shiny with flashes of green. And the other was wearing casual clothes and a lightweight red jacket."

Now Claire was truly afraid. "This is really serious, Kristen. Someone wants you dead."

"Not hard to guess who, is it? I guess 'Daddy' still has contacts in the old country." She looked around at the other people sitting in the café. "But how did they find me?"

The waiter brought their coffees and the bill. Kristen laid a few coins down, swallowed the espresso in one gulp and said, "I've got to be moving on. It won't take long for them to find out they made another mistake and this town will be easy to search."

Claire shivered; she knew Kristen was right.

"I think the best thing to do now is for you to go back to Florence and go about your vacation as if you had never found me. I'll hole up somewhere until my contact people can find a safe place for me to go."

Claire thought about that for only a moment before shaking her head. "I can't. I can't just let you go without knowing you're safe."

"Claire, don't be silly. You need to make sure you're safe. Besides, what can you do?" Her gentle smile took the sting out of those words.

She shook her head stubbornly. "I don't know but I'll do my best. You know... the two heads bit. And two pairs of eyes watching. And don't forget if I hadn't found you yesterday, you would have been just one more casualty in Florence."

"Claire, they've identified me. They know where I am. They know I have red hair. They're looking for me and apparently they don't care who gets in the way."

Claire stared at Kristen a moment. "That's it! Kristen, they think you have red hair! They don't know. We have an advantage right now." Claire brightened at the thought.

She carefully studied her friend. Kristen's spiked brown hair was growing on her. Actually with Kristen's fine bone structure the style somehow made her look more feminine rather than butch. She certainly didn't resemble the red-haired woman Claire had followed yesterday. For that matter, she looked entirely different than the blonde, freckled face student who had worked in San Francisco. She wasn't even sure she would have recognized Kristen in Florence if she saw her like this.

"Where should we go?"

Kristen shrugged. "Don't know. Let's get on a bus and see where we end up."

Claire nodded, glad Kristen had accepted that she was going with her. "Let's go."

The creaky bus lurched along the hilly roads, stopping frequently to accommodate passengers. Claire was fascinated by the people getting on and off—family groups with assorted members, people going to and coming from shopping burdened with assorted bundles and bags, school kids with heavy backpacks, even on Saturday, and business people with newspapers and briefcases. This was obviously a well traveled route for the natives.

The bus's destination was Pisa, and when they arrived, they wandered around long enough to see the famous Leaning Tower, which really did lean at an impossible angle. Not far from the Tower they got on another bus. They took this bus only as far as the train station where Kristen approached a window for tickets.

"Where are we going?"

Kristen indicated a train resting on one of the tracks. "Genoa. There's our train. We're in third class." She pointed at the car in front of them. "Choose a seat."

The railroad car looked similar to the BART trains she had ridden in San Francisco. She sat down on the molded plastic seat and held her backpack on her lap. When the train started moving the gentle sway of the car rocked Claire to sleep in spite of her anxiety, or perhaps because of it.

"Claire, Claire, wake up. We're getting off here."

Claire, groggy with interrupted sleep, struggled out of her seat and lurched after Kristen, surprised to find they had arrived at Genoa so soon. But when she really opened her eyes on the station platform she saw the signs reading La Spezia and was really confused.

She grabbed Kristen's arm. "I thought we were going to Genoa."

Kristen kept moving purposely forward, saying over her shoulder, "I changed my mind. I was looking at your tour book and realized we could get to the Cinque Terre from here. Why not? It's off the beaten track. It should be jammed with day-trippers coming to walk the cliff trails, and it's so tiny we'll see anyone who doesn't belong. It sounds like a good place to hole up until I make contact again. What do you think?"

Claire's brain was starting to function again, and she could see the sense in Kristen's logic. And of course she had heard of the Cinque Terre. It was a quite well known off-the-beaten-track destination. She followed Kristen past several tracks to a little old fashion type train setting there as if it was waiting for them.

This train clacked and clicked along a track that wound through tunnels and then hung over fabulous seascapes. They rattled through several villages, but when they emerged out of one tunnel to stop on a small platform before entering the next tunnel, Kristen got up and nodded to Claire to follow her. They stood on the platform until after the train disappeared into the far tunnel, then looked around them. The train platform dissected the little village. The road went under the platform. Up the hill colorful buildings were stacked tightly until they reached a highway at the top of the village. At least that's what Claire's guidebook said. The road going down twined through the village with structures on top of structures, crowded closely, most with laundry hanging out of windows flapping in the sun, until it ended abruptly in the piazza at the water's edge. There they could see fishing boats, bottoms up, resting for their next venture into the sea, umbrellas and tables clustered around some restaurants and some local boys noisily playing soccer amongst it all. Their shouts and cries carried up the hill and were easily heard on the platform now that the train had gone.

Vernazza was a postcard perfect village, really just a cluster of colorful buildings perched on the cliffs over the sea. It looked more like a movie set than a real place but the villagers were moving about in pursuit of their business and the tourists were evident.

"The book recommends a couple of the pensions up the hill, if you want to try there first?"

Claire nodded. Kristen had been pouring over the book so she was the expert here. They made their way down the stairs and then under the platform. From here they could see the road curling steeply up to the left while on the right a series of steps led high up the hill, threading behind homes and climbing further yet.

"My god, how do you suppose they carry their groceries up there?" Claire commented.

"That's probably why they shop everyday. Then they only have a few things. Or maybe there is another way up there, some road or alley coming down from the highway across the crest of the hills."

"Wouldn't it be heaven to live in a place like this? Do you suppose they forget to notice how beautiful it is?" Claire exclaimed.

Kristen shook her head, concentrating on a handwritten sign in Italian posted on the side of a building. She looked up to her right at the little zigzagging path snaking up the hill. "This sign is advertising a room and bath in a private home up there." She pointed up. "What do say we check it out instead of one of the pensions?"

Claire nodded, then followed Kristen up the steep path, turning in behind some of the buildings until they arrived at a building set high on the hill, the tiny front yard enclosed from the path by a short hedge which protected the recessed doorway.

The landlady, a middle-aged woman wrapped in an all encompassing apron was friendly, apparently pleased at the thought of rent money. She stood back gesturing them to come in.

"Claire, come on. Let's look at the room."

Claire crowded in the foyer behind Kristen. The large kitchen stretched across the right hand side of the house and a wizened old lady, clad completely in black sat at the table, hands clenched around the cup before her. Her eyes were bright and shrewd as she examined Claire and Kristen. Nothing would escape her scrutiny, Claire thought. But they must have passed her inspection as they moved to the stairway, because she returned Claire's smile with a nod.

The room was tucked in the top of the building, up four flights of stairs. The landlady bustled cheerfully to the window, showing no signs of heavy breathing from climbing the stairs, and opened it wide to let in the sun and the breeze. The white stucco room was large and airy. The huge bed covered with a down comforter looked like a comfy nest. Claire had to restrain herself, she wanted to fling herself on that bed and forget everything that had happened in the last two days.

The bathroom was tiny, hardly bigger than a closet, but clean. The toilet shared the shower space and, unlike the hotel in Florence, had a shower curtain to protect the rest of the bathroom from the spray.

Claire nodded her agreement to the question in Kristen's eyes and went to the window to look out over the village while Kristen paid for the room and handed over their passports.

"I'm going to wash out my dirty laundry, then close my eyes a minute before going out again. Okay?"

Kristen nodded. She had already sunk down on the bed, claiming the side by the door as her own.

"I need to make contact as soon as possible..." and she was asleep.

Claire quietly did her wash, hung it out the window as everyone else in the village seemed to do and then lay down herself. The quiet and fresh air worked their magic and she, too, fell into a sound sleep.

* * *

Every meal at the Villa had been wonderful but tonight was special. First the appetizers, Group B had provided a selection of roasted cozze (mussels) in garlic and cream, bruschetta, toasted rounds of bread heaped with fresh mozzarella and topped with chopped tomatoes and basil in olive oil flavored with garlic and the final selection was zucchini flowers stuffed with sausage.

"Taste the wine," Ruth urged Millie. "I picked this one."

Millie rolled it around on her tongue. It was a Pinot Grigio. The flavor blended with the appetizers. As a matter of fact everything was so tasty she had to restrain herself so she'd have room for the main course. And of course, she knew what was coming for dessert. Thank god, Chef Martin had announced they would forgo the pasta course tonight to ensure everyone could adequately enjoy the contributions from each of the groups.

"Save room for the main course," Steven admonished from across the table.

"So, Steven, what's on the menu?" Randy leaned around Zoe who was sitting between him and Steven.

"You'll see. But it's good. Trust me on that. Right, Zoe?"

Zoe nodded, looking pleased, but didn't elaborate.

"Coniglio Arrosto Morto, rabbit cooked in wine and stock," Antonio, sitting on the other side of Randy, announced with a flourish. "And..." he nodded to Sam down the table further.

Sam slowly rose to his feet and said in a surprisingly loud voice, "Bracioline Affocate, Drowned Veal Escalopes, and..." he gestured to Helga at the other end of the long table.

"Pesce Spada Con Patate," she said perfectly then, struggling with the English words, "Baked swordfish with Potatoes."

The rest of them applauded her efforts. Then Antonio finished it off. "And these are served with Passato Di Fagioli, Bean Puree, Beitole Con Pinoli, Swiss chard with Pine nuts and Pomodori Fritti, Fried Green Tomatoes. We hope you enjoy."

The wait staff came out of the kitchen with the laden plates, and more bottles of wine were produced. Millie could see this meal was going to go on forever.

"Save room for dessert," she warned Ruth, "You'll be sorry if you don't."

Ruth nodded; she was really enjoying this Retreat.

Millie tasted everything very carefully, trying to detect every spice in each dish. After dinner they would all get copies of the recipes used for all the dishes, but only after having the detailed discussion and critique of the meal. She had already discovered that many Tuscan dishes were deceptively simple, relying on freshness and quality to produce wonderful flavors.

"These are very good, especially the veal. But our group can beat this," George said from the other side of Ruth.

Ruth drew back, taking exception to his statement. "Well George, you haven't tried Group B's main course yet. I think you'll be hard pressed to surpass us. Those appetizers were only an indication of the talent we have in our group."

"Huh oh, I think I may have thrown down the gauntlet. Millie, what do you think?"

"I think Group C is undoubtedly the best here. I'm sure by the time we leave, Ruth will agree with me, reluctantly perhaps, but she will be truthful. Won't you, Ruth?"

Ruth shook her head. "You wish." She took another bite of the veal. "This is really good. And the rabbit! I never cook rabbit and now I wonder why. I think I like it better than chicken. What do you think?"

"Don't eat too much or you'll be sorry," she warned her friend again.

"Nag, nag, nag..." Ruth laughed. "Don't worry; I'll have plenty of room for your dessert."

George winked at Millie and turned to LiAnn on his other side.

Finally it was time for dessert. Millie was excited as she expected the other members of the group were.

They had decided to have three of their five sets of deserts placed on the table for people to admire. And the Villa staff would plate the other two. As they were serving three deserts to everyone, the small servings of each would mean two sets would be more than enough.

Millie looked critically at the plate set in front of her. The serving staff did a good job of making each dessert attractive with the others on the plate. They poured a light, sweet Moscato d'Oro wine which complimented the desserts perfectly. She watched with satisfaction as the diners tasted the desserts.

"Oh, this custard is wonderful."

"It's Chef Martin's ricotta, but it's different. Taste it."

"How did you get the layers in the custard? I love this," Ruth asked her. But Millie shook her head, refusing to answer.

Millie eyed the custard. It was inverted just before serving so the caramelized sugar, which had liquefied in baking, puddled around the rich chocolate custard resting on the hazel nut crust. She tentatively tried a bite. She sighed with pleasure finding it tasted as good as it looked.

When everyone was positive they could eat no more the tables were cleared and coffee was served while Chef Martin led a lively discussion of the dishes served. Everyone had an opinion, a comment or a suggestion, some more than others. LiAnn was very outspoken in her comments, but Millie had to agree she made some very good points. Frederick and Helga both contributed even withstanding the language barrier. Steven, too, had a lot to say. Of course in his business you'd expect he would. But they all agreed they had produced a fine meal. Chef Martin congratulated them and led them in a round of applause.

"Now remember, tomorrow is pasta day. Chef Geno will be joining us with some of his best offerings. And tonight there will be jazz music in the main salon."

The group dispersed, many adjourning to the Main Salon.

"Did you get a message?" Ruth asked when Millie joined her at the table off to the side of the room.

Millie nodded. "I didn't talk to her, just another message. But at least I know she's safe.

"She went to Sienna. Says it's lovely and the Duomo has the most exquisite marble floor. She said she would call again but didn't expect to reach me."

Millie was relieved. Just then the cocktail waitress came by, so Ruth ordered another Gin and Tonic while Millie ordered a mineral water with lime.

The Main Salon was situated between the lobby and the bar. It was fairly full as not only the members of the cooking retreat were here but other guests staying at the Villa and even some people who had come for dinner were staying for the music. For a while they just sat there enjoying the music and watching the people. But when the jazz combo took a break Ruth announced she was joining some of their classmates to continue their poker game.

"Got to pay for the trip, you know." She winked at Millie as she left.

"Just be quiet when you do come to bed, I need my beauty sleep," Millie retorted, content to sit for a while longer and finish her mineral water.

"Can I buy you another of those?" Chef Martin asked as he pulled out a chair. "What is it?"

"Mineral water and no, thanks, this will do me."

He made a face. "You're drinking mineral water in the middle of wine country?"

"Don't worry, I've had my share of wine. I'm not used to having a different wine with every course and, by the time we finished dinner, I was feeling it."

He chuckled. "So was everyone." He looked up and smiled as the waiter put down his drink, then turned back to Millie. "Looks like you're one of the few left. Are you a jazz buff?"

She nodded. "Kind of. Not an expert, I just enjoy it when I get the chance. And I won't be here for long. It's already past my bedtime, but I just can't get up the energy to move."

He laughed, and then he looked at her carefully. "I just can't believe you had the strength to knock me over yesterday. I truly appreciate it. I think that only you and I know how close I came to having a terrible accident." His voice was low and steady, conveying his appreciation.

Millie felt the heat as the blood rose to her cheeks. "Really, Chef Martin, it was nothing. Wait, I don't mean that it was nothing, just that anyone would have done the same thing if they had been where I was and had seen what I saw."

He looked at her solemnly and then shook his head. "No, no I believe you are mistaken. There were many people there and no one saw it but you. And, even if they saw what was happening, not everyone would have had the courage or the foresight to act as quickly or as effectively as you did. I am truly very grateful to you." He smiled and she felt her toes curl. "And when we are not in class, please call me Jean."

She nodded happily. Then changing the conversation to a more pleasant subject she inquired about his pending trip to the Culinary Olympics.

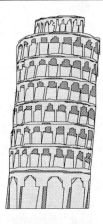

CHAPTER 8

Millie and Ruth shared a breakfast table with George and Jacques. They were all a little subdued this morning.

"Too much rich food and wine," Millie suggested.

"Not for me. It was that poker game, which didn't end until the wee hours," Ruth retorted.

Jacques nodded in agreement, but truthfully he was the only one who looked bright-eyed this morning.

Millie considered him, thinking sourly that youth will win out. "Did you win?" She asked Ruth, knowing how much she loved to win at cards.

"Not much. No, my friend, there is the winner." She nodded her head at Jacques. "That sweet innocent face, his shy grin, and we all fall for his bluffs. Well, no more! You'll see at the next game, my friend. We're all on to you now."

Jacques just smiled and from George's expression Millie guessed he had been one of the big losers.

"I've decided to go to church this morning with Jacques. There is a Mass at eight-thirty he says, and the bus will leave a little after eight o'clock. Want to come, Millie?"

Millie considered, thinking while in Rome... But then she shook her head. "I think I'll take a walk. The fresh air will do me good before we're cooped up in the kitchen again."

"That does sound good. Do you want company?" George asked tentatively.

"Of course, love it."

They headed out through the gardens, admiring the profusion of healthy herbs and the row after row of lettuces. They found a path at the end of the vegetables just as the desk clerk had told them and followed along the vineyards as it sloped gently downward.

At the fork they veered away from the fields and into the trees. Here the path led through a heavily wooded area. The cool dampness was wonderful; the air had an earthy smell. Shortly after taking this path they encountered Sam and LiAnn.

"Good morning. Isn't it a lovely morning?" Millie was enthusiastic; the walk had already perked her up.

Sam nodded, LiAnn spoke. "How are you this morning? Have you had breakfast yet?"

George nodded. "How's the trail that way?"

"Nothing much there," LiAnn said. "But there is a little fork up ahead that might be interesting to explore." She smiled her inscrutable smile. "We're heading back for breakfast now."

Further down the trail George shook his head and said, "That LiAnn is something, isn't she? She's always moving around, poking her nose into everything. She can't just be part of the group. And yesterday her insistence on that cake was annoying. I mean, it's supposed to be a group process."

Millie nodded. "Well, you do know she is the revered matriarch of a very large family. And, as the Chinese traditionally honor their parents, I think she is law in the family and so she probably just expects the same from everyone." Millie chuckled. "I'm sure it never occurred to her that others may consider themselves in charge. No, she is the director."

Then Millie laughed out loud. "Did you happen to see her face when she found out we would each have to make a set of desserts? I could see it was a struggle for her. Maybe it's her age. God only knows how old she really is."

Millie thought a moment, then shook her head. "No, I think she usually gives the orders and then only directs the action. It was hard for her to actually make the dishes."

George nodded thoughtfully, agreeing with Millie's conjecture.

"And George, truthfully, the cake was very good. And it was attractive with the layered apples on top. And it went wonderfully well with the Ricotta and the Budino, so it was a very good choice."

"Ah, Millie, I expect you're the peacemaker in your family. It was good and it did work well with the other desserts, but I can't give her any credit for that as we hadn't decided on the other dishes at the time she decided on the cake." He smiled. "But I guess I'll cut her some slack. You're right. She is an old woman who has accomplished a lot in her lifetime. I guess she's entitled to be a little autocratic."

Millie nodded, thinking George was a very nice person.

"This must be the fork she spoke of. Want to take it, or go the way she did?"

Millie looked at the fork and then shook her head. "It looks like it goes back up toward the vineyards; let's stay on this path in the woods where it's so pleasant."

They walked for another twenty minutes until George warned they needed to turn around or risk being late to morning class.

The way back was almost like taking another trail as they saw different things coming from the other direction.

"Oh look, George. Are those mushrooms?" The white fungi nestled among the tree roots in the damp earth.

George looked at them closely then shook his head. "I don't know. They look like mushrooms, but I wouldn't want to be the one to try them. I'm afraid I don't know enough to say."

"Well, they look beautiful, but you're right. The safest way is to buy them at the market. You know I have a wonderful recipe for a mushroom medley I use with roasted meat and serve with polenta." And they finished their walk talking about favorite recipes.

"Hey, you two, look at this?" Marybeth Lewis called to George and Millie from the corner of the garden.

They joined her and saw the profusion of zucchini flowers on the vines in front of them.

"No wonder they had all those flowers available for us to stuff for appetizers last night. I thought we were just incredibly lucky." She rose to her feet and dusted off her hands, looking around the garden. "Don't you just love this? It makes my small herb garden look a little dowdy." She pointed at another row of basil.

"That basil makes me want to cry. I hope we're going to use it today in our pasta class."

"Speaking of..." George looked at his watch.

"Oh, dear, we'd better hurry." Marybeth led the way.

* * *

The early morning fog had already dissipated by the time Kristen and Claire arrived at the waterfront. It took a while to choose from the bewildering array of pastries at the bakery and then they ordered coffee and orange juice from the café next door. They selected a table on the piazza in full sun, the umbrella still closed. The table sat invitingly just above the little strip of exposed wet sand. Today there were few boats sitting on the quay. Sunday was apparently not a day of rest for fishermen. Sitting back with legs outstretched to catch the warmth of the sun, they enjoyed their breakfast while they watched the drama of life in the village. Mass let out in the church at the water's edge. Its doors opened onto the piazza and worshipers spilled out. Some clustered around the priest at the door, some moved in clumps through the piazza. Some were hurrying to begin their day, some were reluctant to leave, calling to friends, enjoying Sunday as a day of rest.

Claire smiled at the nod from one of a group of woman who could have been cloned, they looked so much alike. She recognized one as the old woman who was the mother-in-law of their landlady. The black-clad women moved slowly, almost painfully through the piazza, chatting quietly amongst themselves, waving their hands in accompaniment to their words, only their eyes moving swiftly, darting here and there, absorbing everything.

Claire commented to Kristen, "Did you notice their feet?"

No wonder they appeared to walk painfully, their knobby toes and heels were bursting out of the cuts made in their low heel shoes to accommodate their misshapen feet.

"Do you think that's from a lifetime of climbing these hills?"

Kristen shrugged. "Maybe, or maybe arthritis from the dampness of the sea. Or it could be from spending their youth cramming their feet into fashionable Italian shoes."

Claire shook her head, unable to imagine these traditional old women wearing short skirted garments and high heel shoes that were the fashion in the 40's or 50's.

"Look at those day-trippers. Fashionable shoes will certainly never give them problems with their feet."

The group of five young people outfitted with backpacks and water bottles were clad in shorts and tee shirts, each with a sweater or lightweight jacket tied around their waist and all were shod in clunky hiking boots. They watched the group gaily tromp across the piazza and up the street, only to move purposefully between two buildings. It didn't take long until they emerged above the buildings on the trail moving up the cliff on their way to the next town.

At the same time Claire noticed people going behind the church and, by leaning way back, she could see there was another trail on this side of the piazza. She pulled the guidebook from her backpack and after a minute said, "The trail over there," her head nodded toward the hill beyond the house where they were staying, "goes to Cornigia and is rated difficult. It takes two hours. But the trail up behind the church goes to Monterosso de Mare and it's only an hour and a half. It's an easier trail. Or, if we wanted, we could take the train down to Manarola or Riomaggiore for lunch and take one of those walks back this way. They're both rated easy and take less than an hour."

Kristen nodded. "Sounds like a good way to spend the afternoon. But let's wait a while until I make my next call. We've got plenty of time and I'd like to check around here a little bit and maybe walk up to the top there." She pointed to the other side of the piazza where a tower of some sort loomed high on the cliff overlooking the sea as well as the village.

Claire looked at her with disbelief. "Up there?"

Kristen nodded. "Sure, we could take our time. It can't be too bad. There's a restaurant up there. I bet it's a gorgeous view."

Claire wasn't convinced any view would be worth the climb, but she knew wherever Kristen went she intended to be right there with her until she had seen her transported to safety.

But right now they weren't going anywhere. Sitting on the piazza, breakfasting in the sun amidst other tables full of tourists she decided to have another Latte while she finished the last pastry. She could almost forget what had brought her here and just enjoy the day.

Finally finished, they wandered around the village, peeking in the church and a few of the shops which were open for the tourists. The restaurant where they had dinner last night was closed, but their waiter was outside hosing down the cement under the tables clustered around the door. He recognized them and waved with a friendly smile when they passed.

"If you're serious about climbing up to the tower, let's do it before the caffeine jolt wears off."

Kristen laughed and headed for the steep set of stairs narrowly cutting through the buildings.

It wasn't as bad as Claire expected, because the stairs twisted and turned constantly changing the view and even sometimes allowing tantalizing glimpses of the sea. When they arrived at the base of the tower they could see all the way down the coast.

"Look, Kristen. That must be the trail I read about." They could barely see the little figures moving across the jagged cliffs apparently heading for the next village which was hidden from them by the distance. Turning they looked across the piazza, but the coastal view that way was blocked by the large hump of land rising behind the church. From here the village looked unreal. They watched as people boarded a boat on the quay and it swung out of the small harbor heading north.

"I didn't know they had boat service here, did you?"

Kirsten shook her head. "Maybe instead of taking the train this afternoon we should take the boat to one of the other villages. That would be fun and we'd get a different view."

When they headed back down they paused at the little restaurant, whose terrace hung over the point. It was up far enough to escape the spray of the waves and had an unobstructed view of the turquoise sea.

"Let's check the menu. This would be a great place to have dinner tonight and watch the sun set."

Claire, originally reluctant to come up, now found she wanted to come back. She wished she had her camera, but that wasn't one of the items Kristen told her to put in her backpack. Then it occurred to her that she could buy one of those little disposable ones. She was sure they would have them in the little store they passed.

Returning down the stairs Claire noticed how the stairway they were on connected with other stairways and paths snaking through the thick maze of buildings, some even heading up in the direction of the hill where they were staying. She resolved that when they went back up the hill they would try to cut through this way and see if they could find another way through. Maybe it would connect to that little train track they saw this morning on the hill. Their landlady had told them it was used during harvest time to transport the grapes from the vineyards on the hill. They hadn't seen the vehicle but could imagine from her description the train-like motor, pulling a line of crates on wheels filled with grapes.

When they reached the piazza again Claire headed for the harbor. "Let's check on those boats."

Kristen followed willingly and after a long discourse with the man at the ticket booth she made a purchase.

When she joined Claire again she said, "We could leave on the next boat but I really need to call in before I do anything else. So I couldn't get a ticket until two-thirty. I guess on Sunday this is a popular excursion. But, we're on it for Riomaggiore, we can have a late lunch there and then walk as long as we like. We'll just take the train back when we've had enough, okay?"

After eating all those breakfast pastries Claire was willing to wait for lunch. They came to the little shop she had seen. "Wait a minute. I need to buy a bottle of water. And maybe I'll get one of those disposable cameras. If we walk on one of the trails I think I'd like to take a few pictures."

The little shop seemed to be crammed with a little bit of everything, so when Claire emerged she had both her water and a camera. She blinked in the bright light noticing a train had just stopped on the platform up the hill. They watched it disgorge its load of assorted people. The day-trippers were easily recognizable by their hiking clothes and boots. The family groups, dressed in Sunday best, were probably coming for lunch, or maybe they had relatives in the village. And the tourists were struggling with their baggage while consulting their maps and books for directions to the pensions. Amongst the few other people, who looked as if they were residents returning from somewhere, were two men, who didn't look as if they belonged.

Claire reached out and grabbed Kristen's arm, dragging her into the shadow of the building they were passing.

"Kristen, it's him!"

"Him? Him, who?" She stretched her neck to see.

"No, no stay back. It's the man I followed in Florence; the man, who had the large box strapped to the back of his bike; the man who parked his bike behind the art store!"

Kristen sucked in a mouthful of air, then said, "Are you sure? Where?"

"He just got off the train. See there? He's with that guy in the red jacket.

"And, yes, I'm sure. Do you think I would mistake that suit? I'm sure it's a one of a kind. He was wearing it that day of the bombing."

Kristen studied him, taking care to keep well back in the shadow. The taller of the two men was wearing a brown suit of some kind of shiny material that flashed green when the light hit it. He was way overdressed for the sleepy fishing village. Even from this distance he stood out from the others. The second man, shorter, more square was wearing casual clothes with a red, light-weight windbreaker over his shirt. He looked like a day-tripper or even one of the locals dressed for his day off. The two men conferred, took a long look at the down side of the village, then went down the stairs, under the tunnel and up the hill.

"They're looking for us, aren't they?" It was a rhetorical question. Kristen knew the answer.

"I think they're going to start at the top and work their way down."

"Oh, no, I've really got us in a pickle. We're trapped. There won't be another train for an hour, but there's no way we can get on a train without them seeing us. And the boat has already gone. Damn, I wish we had been on it."

"No, that wouldn't have been good either. We'd have come back at the end of the day and walked right into them," Claire told her.

Kristen's voice quivered slightly, the only sign of her fear. "I need to make my call. We need help."

She moved furtively across the street to the pay phone fishing in her backpack for her phone card while she watched up the street in case the men started back down their way. She had inserted her card and was just poking in a series of numbers when

Claire reached over and pushed down the connector, cutting her off.

"No! Wait! Don't call. Don't you see? They know we're here. They didn't just accidentally arrive in Vernazza. They're here looking for us. They must know we're here."

Kristen's eyes widened.

Claire continued. "But how could they know we were here? How did they know to look for us in Sienna yesterday? For that matter how did they find you in Florence?

"You've used different passports. And you look so different I can hardly recognize you. There is no way they could have known where we were unless someone told them."

Kristen turned so white her freckles once again popped out like polka-dots. Claire put out her hand to grab her, thinking she might collapse.

She whispered, "Me? You think I told them?"

Claire nodded. "Not intentionally, but it's the only way. No one knows who I am or my connection to you. They can't be following me. So it has to be you. It's you they want. And you have been calling in each day to dutifully report where you are. And then the next day that guy shows up and someone gets killed."

They stared at each other with horror.

"Did you tell them you changed your hair?" The guilty look on Kristen's face was all the answer Claire needed.

"But that can't be. These are the people who are trying to keep me safe. They need me to help them convict Sonny."

"Apparently not all of them are. Trying to keep you safe, I mean."

Claire's words were too much for Kristen. Her knees gave out leaving her clutching the post supporting the telephone. She lost her composure, wailing, "But I have to be able to trust them." She looked at Claire, tears in her eyes, suddenly calm again. "You're right! How else could these guys be tracking me?"

She took a deep breath, panic close to bubbling over. "I just don't know what to do."

Kristen's fear was contagious. Claire's own heart was beating so hard that for a moment she couldn't even hear the noise around them. She took three deep breaths.

Breathe in deeply, hold, release. Breathe in deeply, hold, release. On the third release her heart was no longer pounding in her ears and she had remembered something.

"Kristen, what is the code we have to use for a call to the States."

Kristen looked at her strangely, probably wondering who she needed to call at such a critical time as this, but gave her the number without question. "Use double zero then one before you put in your area code and number."

Claire left Kristen's phone card in the slot and punched in the numbers she had memorized at Jack's insistence last September. She was hoping they would work.

Jack Rallins, her friend with the mysterious connections, had come to her rescue twice before, once in London and then in Washington D.C., where he thwarted a mugger who tried to use a knife on Claire. Later, before they parted at the end of that visit, Jack had insisted she memorize this number. He said she just seemed to attract danger, and he would feel much better if he knew she could get help if she had a "problem". They both understood that "problem" meant if her life was in danger she should use this number. Of course, Claire never expected to need it; she was only humoring him in gratitude for his support.

Now, waiting endless moments for the connection, she glanced up the hill wondering where those two men were. Wherever they were they hadn't yet appeared in their line of sight. Finally, she heard the ring.

"Hallo?" The youngish female voice threw her.

"Hello, hello who is this?"

"Hallo, yourself. Who were you calling?"

Claire's heart started racing again, but she managed to keep her voice steady as she replied, "Is Bernie there?"

"Hold on one minute please."

It could have only been seconds, but Claire felt as if the silence stretched forever.

"Hello, who are you calling?"

"Bernie. I'm trying to reach Bernie."

"Who's calling, please?"

"This is Claire Gulliver and I need to talk to Bernie."

"Ah, Miss Gulliver, I'm sorry Bernie is not available right now..."

With a terrible sinking feeling, Claire's hand was already moving to disconnect, but she paused as the man quickly continued.

"...but I see that we have implicit instructions to respond to your inquiry. Is there something I can help you with?" The older male voice sounded genuinely concerned.

Confused, reluctant but not knowing what else to do, Claire admitted, "I have a problem and Bernie said if I had a problem I should call."

"Right, good idea! Perhaps I could help. Would you like to tell me about it? Where are you, by the way?"

"Right now? Well, I'm at a pay phone in a little village called Vernazza on the Coast of Italy."

"Would you give me the number on the phone in case we should be disconnected?"

Claire read off the number ignoring the questions in Kristen's eyes.

"Good, good, now what seems to be the problem, Ms. Gulliver?"

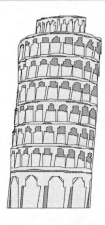

CHAPTER 9

With all of them in the kitchen at one time it seemed to be too many people. It wasn't only their class of fifteen and Chef Martin, Sal and Wanda, but Chef Geno and even Marie Verde were in attendance today. Sal and Wanda had prepared three different work stations for the demonstrations this morning. Using the first, Chef Martin had demonstrated the basics of pasta. He had produced a fresh marinara sauce, which he then modified to make several different sauces from the same base. He then put together an egg pasta dough which he used to make linguine, bowties and even rigatoni, using a pasta machine to press out the tubes. The participants were amazed at the variety of dishes he produced from the same basic ingredients.

Now, at the second work station, Chef Geno was making gnocchi which he was going to use with the pesto sauce he had already made out of the beautiful basil they had seen growing in the garden.

Millie moved to the side to get a better view of what he was doing.

"Now remember, quick and gentle to make tender gnocchi." His hands worked quickly, mixing the flour and egg into the mashed boiled potatoes. Then he turned the dough onto the board to quickly form ropes of dough before cutting each rope into little pieces.

It looked so easy while he was doing it. Randy winked at her. He had told her earlier he had never had any luck making edible gnocchi. Tough and gluey was his description. She knew he was planning to try again while the experts were in attendance during their hands-on session this afternoon.

As she watched, LiAnn slithered through the bodies, managing to squeeze in front of Frederick and Helga, who stood at the very front intent on the process Chef Geno was using to mark his gnocchi with a pattern. Surprised to find LiAnn suddenly standing in front of them, they smiled graciously, stepping back a bit to give her room to see. Millie thought about George's complaint of LiAnn while on their walk. He was right, LiAnn was always roaming around. Earlier Millie had noticed her flitting about the other work stations while the rest of them clustered close to Chef Martin in order to hear his every word. And while she had no idea where LiAnn had been during this demonstration, it was clear she now wanted to be in the front row.

Millie realized, with a pang of guilt at having judged LiAnn: well, of course she wanted to be in the front row. As tiny as she was she wouldn't be able to see anything over the heads of the others, especially since they were all wearing their big droopy hats. And no wonder she roamed about so much, she probably got claustrophobic being closed in a group by the larger, taller people. She told herself she needed to be a kinder person, but then she forgot about LiAnn as Chef Geno offered them each a bite of his delicious gnocchi and pesto.

He nodded graciously to acknowledge their applause. Chef Martin suggested they take a ten minute break before the next demonstration, which was appreciated by everyone.

"Well, they must have heard you, Marybeth."

"Oh, the basil? Yes, it was wonderful. Fresh young basil makes all the difference."

"I loved the gnocchi," Ruth spoke out from one of the stalls in the ladies room. "But I'm usually reluctant to order it because, frankly, so many places serve chewy tasteless globs and hope their sauce will cover their mistake. And when that happens I am disappointed with the whole meal."

"Well, you need to visit my restaurant someday. I guarantee you'll get wonderful gnocchi. In the fall and winter I serve a pumpkin gnocchi, which is very popular."

Ruth washed her hands, smiling at Marybeth. "That's almost enough enticement to bring me East." Then she looked at her. "Say, who are you partnering with this afternoon? I had promised to work with Jacques, but maybe I'd rather learn how to do pumpkin gnocchi with you."

Marybeth laughed. "No way! I'm working with Michael and we're using one of Chef Geno's recipes. Lucky for you I won't tell Jacques you were going to dump him over a recipe."

Ruth shrugged. "It was worth a try."

"Well, my pumpkin gnocchi's not secret, so you can get one of my books or send me a letter and I'll send the recipe."

Ruth brightened, nodding as she left with Millie. "If I get the recipe, Millie, you can make it for me, can't you?"

"Ruth, you can cook as well as I can," Millie reminded her friend.

"Yeah, but I don't like doing it nearly as much as you do."

When they went back to the kitchen someone had placed several stools in front of the work station they would be using. Millie was happy to accept one of them as she was feeling the effects of the long hours of standing. She saw that not only she and Ruth were sitting, but Sam and LiAnn. Steven had offered his stool to Zoe and to Marybeth, but both had declined so he sat as well as Helga and Jacques. The others, tall enough to see over them were milling about behind those seated.

"This is going to be good," Michael whispered in Millie's ear from behind. "This is one of Chef Martin's specialties. I order it every time it's on the menu."

"Tortellini dell'erba e degli spinaci con salsa di noci," Chef Martin proudly announced. "Or, as we call it in the States, herb and spinach tortellini in walnut sauce."

They leaned forward eagerly, watching him blanch and peel the walnuts then grind them to a fine paste. He added the bread, which he had soaked in water and then squeezed dry, the garlic and salt and then slowly the sour milk as the food processor made it into sauce. Finally, the consistency deemed just perfect, he strained the sauce through a sieve into a bowl and set it aside.

"Keep this at room temperature while you work on the tortellini." He looked up and smiled at the group, each feeling he was smiling at them.

"Now we will make the filling for the tortellini."

He processed the fresh baby spinach to a smooth paste and added the herbs he had chosen. The fragrance released by the food processor filled the air, heightening their anticipation. They watched him add the ricotta and parmesan cheeses, the eggs, the garlic and salt and pepper, then with a final burst it was finished. Everyone was handed a tiny taste while the filling was stored in a waiting bowl, and Wanda whisked the dirty dishes away from his working space.

Ruth and Michael had a short conversation about the herbs, but everyone kept their attention on Chef Martin, waiting for the next step.

Chef Martin upended the bowl of flour in a heap on the surface in front of him. Taking his fist he made a crater in the top of the mountain of flour. "Water and wine. Wanda, what kind of wine are we using today?"

"Pinot Grigio, Chef Martin. Some left from last night's dinner."

"Wine was left? Impossible!"

They laughed. Considering the amount of wine consumed last night, it did seem unlikely. Chef Martin appreciated their laughter.

"Any white table wine will do. Do not use a cooking wine!" he admonished. "If you're going to use wine, use something good enough to drink." He took a sip of the wine. "Perfect," he pronounced.

He poured the water and wine into the crater he had formed in the flour and then using a fork he began dragging the flour from the edge of his crater and mixing it into the liquid. The crater became larger as the dough in the middle got bigger.

His fork took more of the flour and then he paused, looking puzzled. He looked closer as he pulled his fork through the flour bringing a lump of something to the edge.

"Eeeey-iiii!" LiAnn let out a screech, jumping off her stool and running to the back of the group.

The rest of them jumped. Millie almost fell off her perch, but George standing behind her grabbed her and steadied her.

Chef Martin looked up, his confusion changed to anger. He face flushed and he looked around. "Chef Geno," he screamed. "What in the hell is in my flour?"

They all craned their necks, their curiosity peaked.

Chef Geno bustled up from the back of the group where he had been observing the demonstration. He looked at the white lump on the board. A dead, flour-encrusted mouse lay on the table top.

The horror on his face quickly spread to the faces of the watchers. They had all tasted the pasta earlier as well as the gnocchi, both of which were made from the same source of flour.

Chef Geno shook his head, trying to deny it. He looked around at the shocked faces and then bellowed to his assistants on their side of the big room. It didn't matter how many of them crowded around shaking their heads; it was a fact that the flour had been contaminated.

Then things became even more confusing. Apparently anything made from flour in that container would have to be thrown out and, since it was close to lunchtime, it would be a big problem for the kitchen. Some dishes would be removed from the menu; others would be quickly made once more in time to serve. Then, Sal explained the exterminators would be brought in to check everything. The old adage "if you see one there must be more" was taken literally by the people in this kitchen.

Chef Martin was beside himself. After he conferred with Chef Geno and Marie, he dismissed the class early for lunch. "We will be delaying the hands-on session this afternoon until three o'clock to allow time for the kitchen to be put back in order. I apologize for this, but as you all know, when you're working in the kitchen, and when the kitchen is in the country, well..., anything can happen." He shrugged but, no matter how philosophical his words, he was obviously angry.

"You know, I'm not very hungry for some reason," Millie told Ruth.

"Me either." Ruth made a face. "In fact I'm feeling a little green."

They looked at each other, then both said, "Let's take a swim."

They laughed as they headed for their room to change.

* * *

Aaron tapped his pen on the desk until he got Craig's attention. He gestured to the phone and, when Craig nodded, he turned his attention back to the story he was hearing. He occasionally wrote a note, but was confident that Craig was setting in motion the complex machinery that was their forte. Hours and days, sometimes even weeks went by in excruciating boredom before their unique skills were needed. The boredom was as big a challenge to the group as the problems were. They needed to be ready, always. They never knew when they would be needed, or where they were needed, or even what kind of problem they would get. And while usually they dealt only with the professionals in the company, who were assigned throughout the world, on occasion, such as this, a call came in from an amateur who had been given their number for protection. Of course, 9/11 had impacted their unit. Their calls were up, their problems seemed more complex, but they were up to the challenge.

Their building, innocuous from the outside, contained all the latest electronic equipment on the inside. They were located in plain sight in an Industrial Park in the suburbs of New Jersey, far away from their headquarters for safety. Their operatives were the best, the smartest, the most imaginative problem solvers. These people knew how to cut through red tape everywhere to affect their rescues.

A bank of computer scenes on the near wall flashed into focus. The first held a map of Italy with the small village of Vernazza marked in red. As he watched, Marla, working on a computer two desks over, was locating their operatives near that area. They appeared as blue dots on the map, all but two were an alarming distance away.

Aaron nodded at Marla, knowing she would turn her attention to the two operatives closest to their target. She accessed their current assignments which flashed on another screen. Meanwhile, Claire was just about finished with her story. So Aaron started with his questions. Beginning with who it was Kristen was contacting and at what phone number. Then he wanted to know how long it was since they had seen the assassin and what her estimate was for the amount of time it would take for him to get to her. And then he asked about escape routes from the village.

Claire had a hard time keeping her voice even as she explained that all the boats were full until two-thirty and that they didn't dare try the train as the train platform would have them in full view of the entire village until it left. It was too dangerous.

"Buses? Rental cars?"

"No, you don't understand. There is a highway of some sort, way up at the top and maybe we could get a bus there, but there is no way to get up there without passing the two men who are searching for us." Claire's voice was trembling.

"Okay, keep calm. We'll get you out of there, I promise!" Aaron hoped he was telling her the truth.

He covered the mouthpiece as Craig and Jason approached him.

"We need some time. Can you get them on one of the trails? By the time they get to the next village we can have someone there to meet them," Jason told Aaron.

"Claire? Are you up to a little hike?" he inquired, seeing Jason's nod as he pointed to a map he had placed in front of Aaron.

"We'd like you to take one of the trails, perhaps the one to Corniglia. Do you think you can do that? Can you get on that trail without being seen?" He paused a moment for Claire to respond.

"Okay, this is what we'll do. You take the trail to Corniglia and we'll have someone there by the time you get there. Don't go back to your room, just leave. We can *collect any of your stuff later. And tell Kristen not to worry about calling in, we'll make contact for her.*

"Okay, don't worry about recognizing our people; they will be accompanied by uniformed Italian Police Officers. You'll know who they are. Now when you hang up, go right to the trail and try to stay out of sight. We don't want these guys on the trail behind you."

When he hung up the four people eyed each other. Marla said what they were all thinking. "We'd better not screw this up. I wouldn't want to have to explain it to Bernie when he surfaces."

"Hell no. He's trusted us. We're going to take care of this," Craig asserted. "We've got James Martino in that area. I think he's our best bet. Are you able to make contact with him, Marla?"

The four gathered around the big central table they used so often in planning their rescue operations. They didn't have much time; they would have to move swiftly.

* * *

Claire hung up the receiver, removed the phone card and handed it to Kristen. "They want us to get out of here. We need to take the trail to Corniglia. Someone will meet us there. We need to leave now."

"But what about my call at one o'clock?"

Claire paused and looked at Kristen with a grim expression. "I think when they don't get that call someone there is going to assume their killers were finally successful."

Kristen gasped, then recovered and nodded. A determined gleam came to her eyes, she said, "Let's go! I think the trail starts on the other side there between those buildings. That's the way the day trippers went earlier."

There was a tiny sign with an arrow pointing in and the name Corniglia on the side of the building. The space was tight, just a corridor between the buildings, only enough room to walk single file. They hurried, nervously glancing over their shoulders until they turned a corner and could no longer be seen by a casual glance from the street. The lane twisted and turned as it moved upwards between and behind the tightly packed buildings forming the village. They stopped to catch their breath on the trail high above the house where they were staying. Here they could see right down into the village. Here they were higher than the tower perched on the cliff over the sea.

The village was so beautiful, so peaceful. Claire could see the old ladies in black, sharing a bench across from where their trail started. And she could see him now, the brown suited guy and his friend in the red jacket. They were striding purposefully out from under the tracks, heading down to the piazza.

"Maybe we're being paranoid," Kristen said hopefully. "Did you ever think they just might be tourists? They may not be assassins looking for us."

Claire glanced at her and saw how hard she was trying to believe it.

They watched as the men approached the women on the bench. They had no way of knowing what words were exchanged, but one of the women clearly pointed across the street where the path cut through between the buildings and then pointed up to where they were standing. Both men turned and stared while Claire and Kristen were pinned to the path as immobile as frightened rabbits.

The men nodded at the women and moved into the street. They conferred and separated. The man in the red windbreaker headed back up the hill while the brown suited man disappeared between the buildings.

"Paranoid? I don't think so," Claire said. "Come on, we need to move fast. We don't want him catching up with us."

Then as they moved briskly around the bend in the path, "I wonder where the other man was going."

Their path was now in full sun and dusty. It wandered down the coast, sometimes through terraced grapevines planted on either side, sometimes running along the cliff, high above the waves crashing on the rocks. Occasionally, hikers coming from Corniglia passed them and once Kristen asked two young men about the trail ahead.

"Good, very good," they told her. "Just follow the red and white markers and, if you've brought your suits, there are a couple of great places to swim."

The other young man seemed eager to join the conversation. "Or if you didn't bring your suits there's a nude beach near Corniglia." This suggestion was delivered with such a lecherous look on the young man's face that Kristen laughed in spite of her worry about the threat coming behind them.

She promised she'd consider a swim, waving as they moved on. It wasn't long after they passed the young men that they reached a point in the trail where they could see it hugging a cove and then stretching back around the cliffs far on the other side. From this point they could see a few little figures moving both ways, those in front of them going to Corniglia and those heading their way from Corniglia. And there was a lone figure wearing something bright red.

Claire halted abruptly the little hairs on her neck standing up straight. She didn't want to believe it, but she felt certain. "Look Kristen. Is that the man who was with Brown Suit?"

"Maybe." Kristen shaded her eyes, making a telescope out of her fingers in order to see better.

"Could be. Maybe that's where he was going when he left Brown Suit in Vernazza. Maybe he took the train to Corniglia so he could come the other way and sandwich us between them.

"Pretty clever, these assassins." Her attempt at humor didn't work. They were both too worried to be amused.

They looked at each other, wondering if not saying out loud, how far behind them Brown Suit was. Their brisk pace meant to put distance between them and the danger following them now looked like it was only moving them faster towards a new danger in front of them.

"It doesn't seem to make a lot of sense to keep rushing this way only to end up meeting him." Claire looked at the long trail in front them, searching in vain for a dissecting trail. "Maybe we should go back a ways and try to climb up through those vineyards. Maybe we could find a road."

"I think the vineyards are too far back. They were pretty close to Vernazza. We might meet up with Brown Suit before we get there..." She too was looking around. "Claire, did you notice a little way back that section of path that veered toward the cliff? It was cordoned off."

Claire hadn't noticed it.

"It was just before we met those two guys. I'm wondering if it was the original path. Maybe they closed it so people wouldn't walk so close to the edge of the cliffs. Maybe we should go back there and see where that path goes. It would get us off this trail for a while and then after Brown Suit passes we could get back on the main trail and make it back to Vernazza in time to make the boat for Riomaggiore."

Claire realized it might work. They had no other options, so she nodded her agreement and they headed back the way they came. Their pace picked up so they were almost running. They weren't sure how close Brown Suit was and they wanted to get off the trail before he came around a bend.

"There it is. See up ahead that clump of rocks?"

Claire saw the clump of rocks but couldn't detect the trail until they were almost on top of it. It hadn't been used for a while as was obvious from the weeds breaking through the worn path almost obliterating the trail. And while Claire didn't read Italian the sign on the barricade was clear the trail was closed.

"Come on, Claire, hurry." Kristen was tense. She ignored the sign, leading the way, confident her plan would work.

Claire, close on Kristen's heels, climbed over the barricade and around the rocks used to block the trail. On the other side the trail was wide and only slightly sloping downhill until it turned around a bulge and was hidden from the trail above. They paused here looking around them. From this point they could no longer see any of the trail either coming from or going to Vernazza which they hoped meant that they couldn't be seen either. They moved comfortably along walking abreast. Claire drank some of her water and then shared the bottle with Kristen. They had been on the trail for almost an hour. Claire was tired, mostly a result of the heat and the stress, but so far the hike hadn't been too bad.

Almost in answer to her thoughts the trail they were on narrowed, dipped down and then around another bend it climbed steeply. Halfway up a steep cliff the trail faded. Here it was covered with loose gravel and sand. It looked treacherous, obviously the result of previous landslides.

Kristen started confidently across before Claire could even open her mouth to suggest caution. But when Kristen reached stable ground on the other side without incident, Claire, with her heart in her mouth and refusing to look down, followed. She breathed a sigh of relief when her feet were once more firmly planted on the hard, wider path on the other side. She hurried after Kristen, who had disappeared around another turn.

This trail was much more rugged than the one they started on. This trail wended its way on the very edge of the cliffs. Some places the trail seemed cut impossibly into the cliff and it was a sheer drop to the jagged rocks and water far below. Claire could understand why it had been closed and the other trail, cutting inland along a safer route, opened.

"This must run into the other trail up here somewhere but I didn't see where it did before we decided to turn around, did you?"

Claire shook her head, realizing they might not want to merge with the main trail as they might come out just where Brown Suit and Red Jacket met.

It turned out there would be no danger of that happening, because abruptly the trail ended. They both stood and looked at the deep gouge in front of them which was probably formed when part of the cliff fell into the sea, taking the trail in front of them and quite a bit of the hillside.

"I guess this is why it was closed."

"It looks like it happened quite a while ago." Claire backed up, wondering how secure the section of the cliff they were standing on really was.

Kristen followed her backwards, maybe having the same thoughts.

"Well, nothing to do but go back to the main trail. Hopefully, Mr. Brown Suit has passed."

Claire nodded, heading back, this time in front.

They were making good time, striding with the confidence of having already been over this trail, so when they came around the bend and came face to face with Brown Suit and Red Jacket they were stunned.

But for only for a moment; then Claire, with a flood of adrenaline rushed forward, not giving Brown Suit a moment to prepare his attack. His face was frozen in a look of astonishment as she raised her leg and kicked out with all her might. He was more agile then she expected, jumping back out of the way so her foot missed his knee completely. Her momentum, unchecked, threw her off balance carrying her dangerously toward the edge of the cliff. That's when Kristen grabbed Claire's backpack, yanking back until she got another hand on Claire's upper arm, pulling back enough to counterbalance her. As Claire and Kristen both straightened up their eyes were drawn back to the drama developing on the trail in front of them.

When Brown Suit had leaped back to avoid Claire kick he had put himself squarely back on that portion of the trail covered with loose gravel. His highly polished Italian loafers, now marred and dusty, were not meant for trail walking. They started sliding on the treacherous surface. He tried to regain his balance but only upset more debris as his scrabbling feet sought a purchase in the loose sand. Red Jacket, just behind him, tried to steady him, but Brown Suit was now panicking, his arms flailing as he flung himself against the side of the cliff, clinging to some plants rooted in the wall of the cliff. But he only succeeded in pulling them out from the earth, adding more dirt to the slide that was starting.

The frantic activity of the men was too much. Red Jacket turned and tried to lunge for the more stable ground behind him, but Brown Suit grabbed him.

All four of them watched with disbelief as the ground reshaped itself, gravel and rocks sliding with more intensity. The men struggled to maintain their footing on the fast disappearing trail. Claire and Kristen on solid ground backed away. Claire would never forget Brown Suit's face; his initial predatory look had changed to one of terror, before he and Red Jacket were swept off the cliff along with a good portion of the trail.

Claire and Kristen had mutely retreated around the bend, praying that the slide would stop before it reached them. Finally silence seemed to echo in their ears. Claire collapsed into a heap on the trail, her knees just gave out. She clasped her arms around them, rocking back and forth, saying, "I don't believe it. I just don't believe it."

Kristen slowly lowered herself to the hard path and stared out to sea. She too was stunned by their unexpected reprieve.

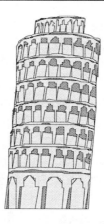

CHAPTER 10

Millie spooned some of Randy's gnocchi with shrimp in a light cream sauce onto her plate. She hoped it was more successful than his self-professed gluey usual. She examined the bowl of rigatoni she and Antonio made. They had relied heavily on the taste of the pasta choosing to only toss it with olive oil, herbs, bits of bacon, chopped tomatoes and chunks of blue cheese. It looked very attractive. She was hoping for kind criticism from her fellow students after the meal. She moved down the table making room on her plate for each of the pastas offered and then filled the rest of it with the green salad. There was no risk that there wouldn't be enough to eat. Chef Geno and his staff appeared to be determined they each get more than their share of food.

Tonight's dinner was a pasta buffet including all the dishes the students prepared this afternoon. The Villa provided salads, the breads and a couple of appetizers. The desserts were already sitting out and Millie could see the desserts her group had made last night were included with several new selections. That pleased her as she wanted to try the Budino again. She had wondered how it would hold up after an overnight in the refrigerator.

As Sunday dinner was meant to be more casual, multiple tables for six were set up instead of the long table. Each table was gaily set with red and white checkered tablecloths, casual dinnerware and clunky diner type glassware for their wines. It seemed like a party.

"I can't believe how fast time is going. This class is almost over," Millie commented joining Ruth, who was sitting at a table with Stephen, Zoe and Michael. She nodded to the waiter who was hovering, ready to pour her wine, and spread her napkin on her lap just as Randy approached.

"Room for one more?"

"Please join us," Zoe invited graciously.

"Time does seem to be moving very fast," Stephen said in response to Millie's comment. "And is everyone satisfied with the content?" He looked around at the others sitting there.

"Well, I've got my money's worth with that dish." Randy pointed to the gnocchi on Millie's plate. "Have you tried it yet?"

She shook her head and picked up a fork full. She chewed it carefully, savoring it in her mouth. "Wonderful," she pronounced.

Randy beamed. "Hell, yes! It's wonderful. And it was easy."

Everyone dipped into the gnocchi.

"I love this."

"I'm going to try this."

"What's the secret?"

"Quick and gentle, just as Chef Geno said. That's how you get tender gnocchi. Who would have known?" Randy puffed up with pleasure.

Stephen looked at Ruth and Michael. "What about the two of you? Neither of you are chefs, or wannabe chefs, so has it been worth the money and time?"

Michael laughed. "What is this article number 746? Are you working tonight, Stephen?"

Stephen actually blushed. "Busted. Well, I thought a couple of the airline magazines might be interested in an article about the Retreat. You don't mind, do you?" He looked around anxiously, but seeing no one was concerned he relaxed. "After all, I'd like to recoup some of my costs."

Michael nodded. "Well, I've had a great time and we still have two days. The hardest part for me was keeping up with my group. I'm not used to working in a professional kitchen and I admit my skills with a knife are almost non-existent. But everyone has been very understanding."

Ruth nodded. "And it's even more amazing when you consider that Michael, Jacques and I are all in the same group so Marybeth, who is super, and Frederick have to carry the load."

"Well, our group is coping with me, LiAnn and Millie. George and Renee are our anchors, right Millie?" Randy said. "I guess that's why they set the teams up the way they did. Smart!"

"Oh, my God! Did you try this?" Zoe pointed to the ravioli on her plate. "I think it's stuffed with lobster. What do you think, Stephen?"

They all tried it and discussed the stuffing as well as the sauce. Then Stephen steered the conversation back to their impressions of the Retreat.

"I love it. And except for the mouse in the flour today, everything has been super. It's been so well planned." Zoe was more enthusiastic than Millie remembered seeing her.

"Ugh, that mouse was ugly. Does that really happen in kitchens?" Ruth was still put off by the incident.

"Of course! That's why they have kitchen inspections and certifications around the world. But truthfully, I was very surprised it would happen in this kitchen. The Villa is five stars. Or was! It won't be if Zagat finds a mouse when they visit." Stephen nodded sagely.

"I almost fell off my stool when LiAnn squealed." Millie smiled. "I didn't think she could move so fast."

"I think we were all more startled by her scream than the mouse," Randy commented, "But I happened to pass her and Sam after we were dismissed and he was sure giving her hell for something. I couldn't tell what, because it was in Chinese." He chuckled. "But no doubt she was in trouble and she was looking pretty chastised."

"I can't believe it. Sam hasn't said word one since we started classes. I just assumed LiAnn rules in that family," Millie said with surprise.

Randy shrugged. "I don't know but I know when someone is getting a thorough scolding when I see it, regardless of the language."

"Actually, I was upset by the mouse, more because of the effect on Chef Martin than anything." Michael, as always, was defending his hero.

"He's a star and twice he's had problems with his demonstrations. Someone hasn't been doing their job prepping for him. That should never happen to a chef of his stature."

"And don't forget the little accident at the winery. If Millie hadn't pushed him out of the way, the forklift would have run right into him instead of the conveyor belt," Stephen reminded them.

"What? What are you saying?" Ruth demanded. "Is something funny going on?"

"Hardly funny," was Michael's terse reply.

Ruth waved her hand. "You know what I mean. Do you think these incidents were related somehow?"

Michael stared off into space for a moment, and then shook his head. "No. Really I don't. The incident at the winery was really strange, but we have no idea how they work. It might just be a sloppy operation. And the other two incidents are probably just the result of a busy kitchen and the impact of all of us on it. But, hopefully, that is the end of strange events. You know Chef Martin is going from here to the Culinary Olympics and he doesn't need to be carrying a load of worry with him to distract him. He needs to be fresh and ready."

Stephen nodded, agreeing. "You know he's really a nice guy. He did get me into the Olympics as a member of the press. So I'll be going there directly from the Retreat. My paper is excited about having an on-site report of the competition. So much so they're willing to foot the expenses. And I'm sure I'll get enough material for several more articles." He beamed. "Life is full of opportunities."

"That does sound exciting." Millie's face reflected her enthusiasm. "I hope you'll let us all know when any articles about the Retreat or the Culinary

Olympics come out, so we can be sure and get a copy to read."

"Of course. Let me have your e-mail addresses before we leave and I'll send out an announcement."

"I'm going back for seconds." Zoe announced. "Can I get anything for anybody?"

Randy pushed away from the table. "Me too, I have some favorites I'd like just a bit more of."

Ruth and Stephen got up too, leaving Millie and Michael still at the table. "Are you going to the Olympics?" Millie asked.

"Naturally, who else would lead the cheering section?" He laughed, explaining further, "there are a lot of us groupies who go to every event. It's kind of like being an ice skating fan, or following gymnastics. In fact, I'm meeting some of them in Cannes before the Olympics so I will be leaving here before Chef Martin and Stephen. But I'll catch up with them in London in time for all the action."

"I envy you; I'm sure it will be exciting. Will it be on the Food Channel?"

"No, not yet, but several magazines will be reporting it and of course if he wins it will be in the U.S. papers. It is exciting."

"Well, I think I'm going to check on the desserts. Please excuse me." She left the table anxious for her sweet.

* * *

"Oh, my god, I thought for a moment I was going over the edge." Claire shivered. "Thanks for grabbing me."

"What was that, anyway?" Kristen questioned.

"What was what?"

"I mean, what were you doing? Karate? Kick-boxing? You moved so fast you scared me, them too, I think."

"Well, Brown Suit couldn't have been too scared; you saw how fast he moved." Claire shook her head with disgust. "I learned that at one of those women's self-defense programs. They said move fast and aim for their balls. If that doesn't seem possible, go for the knee.

"I wasn't sure I could kick high enough to reach his crotch, so I went for the knee. I just wasn't expecting to miss. He sure moved fast. Maybe he went to one of the same kind of classes I did."

She raised her head off of her knees and looked at Kristen with surprise. "But, I guess it did work. At least it works when your attacker is on an unstable path in slippery shoes."

She thought a minute. "Maybe that wasn't the right thing to do. If you hadn't grabbed me I would have gone over the side. That sure wouldn't have helped you."

"Claire, get real. You saved our lives. I was just thanking my lucky stars you insisted on coming with me. Otherwise it would have probably been me at the bottom of this cliff instead of them."

"When I came around that part of the trail and looked up to see them there, I thought I would faint. Sometimes when I get scared I just freeze. One time I blacked out completely. But they scared me so much I guess my instincts just took over. I swear that grin on Brown Suit's face took me beyond terror. I felt so ferocious I think I could have wrestled them over the edge with my bare hands."

She looked at Kristen and managed a small smile. "Fortunately, I didn't have to test that. And now I just feel like a limp dish rag...and I have to pee really, really bad."

Kristen laughed. "Don't think you'll find a toilet around here, but there was a clump of boulders down there a ways. That should serve you."

Claire slipped her backpack off her shoulders and set it on the ground. Then using it as a lever she struggled to her feet and then stood for a moment to test her knees before moving cautiously down the path. When she reappeared she seemed more like her usual self.

This time instead of sitting on the dirt path she selected a large rock half buried in the cliff to perch on. "Well, Kristen, we don't have to be running from Brown Suit any more, but I'm sure whoever sent him will send someone else as soon as they realize what happened."

Kristen nodded; she knew she was running from something bigger than Brown Suit and his friend.

"But our real problem is getting off this trail..." Claire continued.

Kristen blanched. "Oh, shit!" She said it with real feeling. "I've really got us into it this time. How are we going to get back to the main trail? We're trapped here now, aren't we?"

"Well, I sure didn't see a way off it, but maybe we should walk it again. We need to look carefully; perhaps there is some place where it is possible to climb out. Either up or down. What do you think?"

Kristen stood up and turned toward Corniglia. "Let's go, time is wasting."

When they returned to that wide space in the trail again they were very hot, and discouraged. Claire sought out the same stone she had used before which was in the shade of the bulge of the cliff. Now the sun was lower in the sky and the heat seemed to be attracted to the cliff. She removed her backpack and rummaged through it. "Do you have anything to eat in yours, Kristen?"

Kristen, sitting cross-legged, Indian style, on the trail in part of the pool of shade started doing the same and came up with three energy bars and a little packet of trail mix. Claire had a package of Swiss Chocolates and part of a bottle of water.

She took a slug of water and passed the bottle to Kristen, accepting an energy bar in return.

"We could be here a long time."

"What about your friend? He was sending someone to meet us in Corniglia. Surely they'll come looking for us when we don't show."

"I hope so."

It was depressing. They sat there for a while and then began talking to distract themselves from their distress.

"Kristin, I don't understand how you ended up in Europe. I didn't think the Witness Protection people placed their people outside the United States."

"I don't think they do. But I'm not really in their program yet. I'm being held by the U.S. Attorney's Office, and the Witness Protection people are just monitoring me. They have the system already in place so it was simpler and safer to be under their management until after the trial. Then I will go on the program. They'll develop an identity for me and a history. Then I'll be placed some place under their jurisdiction, in the States."

Claire nodded. "So how did you end up in Florence?"

"I negotiated." She nodded her head. "I told them I had already had my life ruined, so it was the least they could do for me while I hid out." She shrugged. "I didn't really think they'd go for it but they did. I had always wanted to take some art classes and my Italian was good. Of course living here these past months has certainly helped with my language skills. I call in to the Program in the States regularly and I have my emergency kit." She patted her backpack.

They were staring morosely out to sea, now too discouraged to even talk.

"Did you hear that?" Claire wondered if she was hallucinating.

There, she heard it again. She got up and moved around the bulge in the cliff to the little bit of trail now abruptly ending in the gash of fresh dirt and stones of the slide area.

"Hello," he called in an accent that could only be American. Close behind him, peering over his shoulder was a man in combat fatigues of the Italian Police.

"Are you Claire Gulliver?" the man called.

"Yes. Who are you?"

"I'm James Martino. Bernie sent me."

Claire felt limp with relief. "Thank God, Kristen. He's come to rescue us."

"Is there a way through at the end of the trail?" he asked them.

"No, we're trapped. We came over here." She gestured to the break in the trail. "But the two guys chasing us caught up. When they came over this part they loosened a slide." Her eyes just naturally looked over the edge into space.

She shuddered. "They're down there somewhere. But we ended up trapped." She heard the anxiety in her voice and took a deep breath. Now was not the time to lose control, she told herself.

"Okay. Okay, don't worry. We're going to figure out how to get you off that ledge. Was there anywhere behind you where you could get down to the water or climb up over the top?"

This time Kristen chimed in. "We went back and checked again. We didn't see any place that would work. That's why we're still sitting here." She sounded a little cross, but Claire thought she had the right to be after the past couple of days.

The man called James nodded, then turned and spoke with the guy behind him. The policeman then spoke rapidly into a little radio attached by a strap to his shoulder, but he was too far away for Kristen to catch any of his words.

"My friend here says they are good at search and rescue. They do it all the time on these trails. His friends will be here soon."

They heard it before they actually saw the helicopter. Then it swept over the top of the cliff and came down about level with them hovering over the sea. The wind from the blades blew them back against the cliff. They could no longer hear anything. Slowly it moved away, the noise and wind headed down the coast toward the big slide area.

"They're looking for a good area to stage the rescue, "James yelled at them. He turned and spoke to the man with him who was speaking into his radio once more. After a while James yelled again, hands cupping his mouth to help project his words.

"They're going to have to lower a basket for you. There is a wide space back about two hundred yards. They think they can do it there."

Claire nodded; she remembered the place he was talking about. They moved back over the trail to where the helicopter hovered. There the trail was very high above the ocean and wider. And the cliff rose only about ten feet above the trail so the helicopter could hover without worrying about the drafts flinging their chopper against the cliff.

Claire and Kristen arrived in time to see a contraption on cables lowering a man in fatigues slowly down to the trail level. They both grabbed the harness to help steady him as he landed. They were so glad to see him they both looked kind of weepy, but perhaps that was only the wind from the helicopter propeller blowing dust in their faces. And really there wasn't any time for sentiment. Words were useless with the chopper hovering above them, but their rescuer's hand signals were easy to understand.

Claire didn't want to go first. She really didn't want to get in the thing that looked somewhat like the basket swing for toddlers on the playground. The whole thing was suspended from cables placed to keep it from turning over. The policeman was adamant and when Claire tried to defer to Kristen, Kristen motioned her to get in. Claire reluctantly climbed in, sliding her legs in the holes as if stepping into shorts. The policeman arranged the harness over her shoulders, strapping her in, stepped back and waved to the chopper. Before Claire could protest she was smoothly pulled up in the air and then swung away from the cliff. She didn't dare look down. She didn't want to see how far up she was. Her legs and feet dangling made her feel like she should pull them up out of danger. Suddenly she thought she had to pee again, but she didn't have time to even think about it as she was quickly winched up into the belly of the chopper. Soon hands were grabbing her, pulling on her and her feet were planted on the floor of the aircraft. The solidness of it felt wonderful.

One of the policemen led her away from the door, strapped her into a seat and gave her a bottle of cold water.

Pretty soon there was a flurry at the opening again and Kristen appeared. She joined Claire, gratefully chugging her own water bottle.

One more time there was activity at the open door and the man, who had come down to help them, was now on board. The helicopter banked sharply to its side and moved away from the cliff.

The aircraft was now moving alongside the cliff, lower than the trail. When they hovered a moment, the men clustered around the still opened door pointed excitedly and Claire realized they must have located the bodies of Brown Suit and Red Jacket. Then the chopper glided into a turn rising above the cliff before lowering itself to the ground.

Claire flashed a look of her relief toward Kristen. She couldn't wait to get out. But they didn't, instead James and the policeman climbed on board and the chopper rose in the sky again.

James grinned at them and stuck his thumb in the air before putting on some headphones with a mike which apparently enabled him to talk to the others who were also wearing headphones.

Claire had no idea how long they flew. It was so dark where they were sitting she couldn't read her watch. But she could see through the still open door the sun was going down. The droning of the motor seemed to chase all coherent thought from her head. They were safe and someone else was worrying about where they would go. So for the moment she was content.

Again the chopper hovered then slowly descended. The lurch when it sat on the ground stirred a bit of activity. Two of the policemen unfastened her and Kristen's seat belts and guided them to the door. This time there was a ladder hanging out, and they followed James down to the ground. It looked to be a large field gone fallow. James motioned to them and ran hunched over out of reach of the rotating blades. They followed.

Then turning they waved to the men crowded around the door as the helicopter rose into the air again. Turning sideways it flew off.

The three of them stood until silence descended once more. It wasn't quite dark even though the sun was down and everything was gray and shadowy.

"Hey there, James. You're later than we expected. Hope you didn't run into any trouble." The man behind the powerful flashlight beam emerged, grinning.

"We didn't, but the ladies here had a bit of a problem that took a little working out. I think it was solved rather satisfactorily." James looked at Claire. "What do you think?"

"I think we owe you a lot of thanks..." she started but stopped when James just walked away following the man with the light over the uneven ground.

At the edge of the field was a small house. James flipped the switch to turn on all the lights. And after they followed him into the cottage, he introduced the man with the light.

"This is Will; he's a colleague of mine. Now, if you'd be so kind as to put your backpacks on the table; empty your pockets of everything, and take off your shoes." He grinned at their stunned expressions. "We just want to make sure you're not carrying a bug. After all we wouldn't want to accuse someone of selling out and find that you inadvertently advertised your whereabouts through a little tracking devise planted on your person, would we?"

It made perfect sense, but Claire couldn't imagine where they could have picked up a bug. And they hadn't. After Will and James went through everything in the backpacks and Will used some instrument to search for signals, they asked them to take some of their clothes from the backpack and change out of the ones they were wearing so they could examine those closely.

"So, most likely you're right, Claire. Someone in the Witness Protection program has to be the culprit. You haven't contacted anyone else during this time, have you?"

They both shook their heads, then Claire remembered. "Well, just my mother. But I didn't talk to her. She's at a cooking class at the Villa Tuscany and, since I couldn't reach her, I left a message on the answering machine in her room. But I didn't tell her where I was. Wait." She thought a moment. "I told her I was in Sienna but didn't tell her about Vernazza. That's right." She looked to Kristen for confirmation.

"What's her name, and do you have the phone number and room number of where she is staying?"

Claire gave it to Will, who wrote it down. Nodding, he said, "We'll check it out. We don't want to leave any loose ends.

"Okay, folks. Let's get going."

"Where are we going? I thought we were already here."

James and Will smiled as they shook their heads. "No, this isn't safe enough. The chopper dropped us off only a little ways from here. This would be too easy for someone to track us. But, of course, we needed to make sure you weren't bugged. Now we can head for the safe house."

Claire and Kristen grabbed their backpacks and checked to make sure nothing was left behind and followed the men out the door. James turned off the lights while Will hurried to the old barn set behind the house. They watched him open the doors, disappear inside and then he drove out in the dark sedan. Claire and Kristen wedged themselves in the back seat while James went back and closed the barn doors.

The dense blackness of the countryside was cut only by the lights of the car. Will obviously knew his way around as they took a bewildering number of country lanes. Only twice did they approach a little village, but each time he turned on the perimeter road to avoid driving through the center.

After the first few minutes on the road, James had explained that Will and his wife, Emily, ran the safe house where they were heading. Then a hush fell on the occupants of the car as each seemed occupied with their own thoughts.

Finally Will turned into a little lane and approached a house in the middle of nowhere. He hit a button on the visor and the garage door opened for them. They scrambled out of the car and followed Will through the side door emerging into a kitchen/family room combination filled with good smells.

That's when Claire realized how hungry she was.

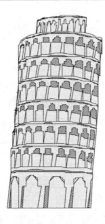

CHAPTER 11

Emily wasn't at all what Claire expected. She was slender, wearing comfortable jeans and a yellow cotton sweater which had seen better days. And she was barefoot. She was probably Claire's age but it was hard to tell. Her dark hair could have been natural or might have had help keeping the gray out and her eyes were gray. She seemed pleased to have them here.

"Oh, I'm so glad I cooked today. How did I know someone would be here to share it?" She moved to the stove, removed a lid and stirred the pot. A tantalizing aroma reached Claire.

Not waiting for an invitation, Claire hung her backpack on the back of the closest chair at the table and sat down. "I'm starved. And I don't know what's in the pot, but it smells heavenly."

"Wow, that's for sure." Kristen joined her, then, "Oops. I need to wash up."

Will led Kristen away while James sat down. "Emily, this is Claire. She's had a rough day, haven't you, Claire?"

Emily looked at Claire and smiled. "Well Claire, you're welcome here and safe. We've never lost a guest." Her smile lit her face.

Emily moved around the kitchen confidently and soon there were glasses and a pitcher of wine on the table, followed closely by a large loaf of crusty bread and a crock of butter. By the time Kristen joined them, Claire had already eaten the large hunk she had torn from the bread on Emily's directions and drank half of her glass of a very pleasing red wine.

The comfy kitchen looked like something designed to be featured in *Italian Living*, if there was such a magazine. The terra cotta floor and rough stucco walls were offset by the aged, rough wood used for shelves, beams and cupboards. One large shelf stretched over the windows above the huge sink. This held brightly painted Italian pottery, an assortment of pitchers, platters and serving dishes which would have made Claire's mother drool. The wide window sill held a variety of small planters filled with herbs, while the glass fronted cabinets on the side held a colorful collection of dishes. The kitchen included modern conveniences, yet still had the look of old country. The generous butcher block cooking island separated the kitchen from the eating area, but still allowed people at the table to feel a part of the kitchen activity. The table was a wooden oval surrounded by a variety of worn wooden chairs. Beside the table was a bank of windows. In the darkness Claire could only dimly see they looked out on the courtyard, and imagined in the daylight it would be very pleasant sitting here. At the other end of the common room was a large fireplace, flanked by two comfortable looking overstuffed chairs. This part of the room was comfortably crowded with a couch, a wooden chest serving as a coffee table, a TV, and a cabinet/bookshelves unit crammed with books and magazines. The hall where Will had led Kristen to the bathroom was at the end of the room and near it was the vestibule with the front door.

"I guess I could wash up a bit too. That way?" She pointed and headed down the hall to find the small closet under the stairs which now contained a toilet and tiny sink. It was a clever use of space in a house built before modern conveniences were available.

"...but who do you work for? I mean what do you do? Do you just sit around and wait for someone to call you? Who pays for that?"

James slouched in his chair, wine glass in his hand. "We're government employees. And no, we don't sit around and wait for someone to get in trouble. But if they do, we've been known to respond."

"Anyone? I mean Claire just called. And the next thing we know the Italian Police Force is coming to the rescue with you. Why would you do that for Claire? Or for me? I can't believe the government thinks I'm important."

"Whoa, wait a minute. We thought you were a major witness on a big racketeering case." He sat up and spoke sharply to Will, "Get the car out, we'll just take them back."

Emily sputtered, unable to contain her laughter, so she spoiled James' joke. The shock on Kristen's face was dissolving just as Claire entered the room catching the end of the joke.

It felt good to laugh. It relieved the tension that still gripped Claire and Kristen. After the laugher faded all talk was suspended so they could give their attention to the meal Emily had assembled. She had put a large platter of pasta on the middle of the table. It looked like rigatoni, covered generously with a fragrant red sauce and grated cheese. She took two large spoons and tossed it in front of them.

Claire felt faint with hunger when the enticing smell reached her. It was all she could do to mind her manners and wait for an invitation to eat. They were already shoveling the pasta into their mouths when Emily put the large bowl of salad on the table and took her place at the end where she could easily access the kitchen if she needed. It didn't take her long to fill her plate; she seemed as hungry as the rest of them.

Finally sated, plates and serving pieces removed, Emily placed a large platter of cheeses and fruit on the table. After refilling the wine pitcher she sat down again looking from Kristen to Claire expectantly. Now they told their story. Emily and Will were an enthralled audience.

"Oh my gosh! Weren't you scared to death?" Emily asked with a visible shiver. "I know I would have been. And I know I wouldn't have thought of kicking his knee out from under him. That was so brave."

"Like me. I just stood there, frozen. Thank God I moved fast enough to grab Claire and steady her before she went off the trail. Then the cliff just disintegrated before us.

"Well, at first I was just glad. You know? It didn't bother me a bit to see them slide into space, but then we realized we were trapped. That was really depressing. Just when we thought we were saved, we found ourselves stuck."

Kristen looked sad. "And now that I'm out of danger I remember that look on their faces as they went over the edge. They were desperate but there was nothing for them to grab. They knew. You could see it on their faces. They were just people after all."

She sat up straight, her look now determined. "But I have to remember that they were scary, bad people. I think about those poor American women in Sienna, and then I think they got their just reward." She shivered. "Can you imagine how long that fall must have seemed?"

"Probably not long enough," was James opinion.

Claire just nodded. Sitting here in the warmth of this kitchen, with their stomachs full and their wine glasses filled, it was hard to remember how frightened they had been.

Kristen still had questions about their rescue. "So, James, explain once more how you managed to get a helicopter and a whole bunch of Italian policemen to help you rescue us. It sounds more like a movie plot than real life." She looked at Claire. "Don't you think, Claire?"

"Well, Kristen, I guess you just don't know who you are traveling with."

Kristen looked sharply at Claire then with confusion at James. "What do you mean? I've known Claire for years. We used to work together at the San Francisco Library. I remember when she inherited a bookstore from her uncle and decided to turn it into a travel book store. So I do know her. Are you saying she works for you?"

She turned and looked at Claire. "Is that why you attacked him? Are you really a secret agent, trained to kill?" She was seriously confused.

Claire laughed. "Hardly. I'm just who you think I am. Retired librarian turned bookstore owner. If I was a government agent, let's hope I would have been more successful at landing that kick."

She said sternly, "James, what are you talking about? You're confusing everyone."

James shrugged. "Everyone in the Company has heard the story, Claire. We know you saved the Vantage flight from Guiness. You're one of our heroes. I guess you could say you're a spooky heroine." He chuckled at his joke.

Claire felt the heat in her cheeks. "But I was just saving myself."

Will shook his head. "I don't buy that. No one else noticed. And even if they noticed most people would have just shrugged off their suspicions rather than make a big fuss and risk looking foolish. You didn't. And you saved everyone on that airliner."

The looks of admiration from Emily, Will and James and disbelief from Kristen made her even more uncomfortable. "Look, I don't want to appear ungrateful for what you did for me." She sighed, her breath catching in a little hiccup betraying her distress. "I just don't want to get into all that right now. It was only a year ago and between that and the incident in Washington, I've had more than my share of violence." Her eyes turned to Kristen as she explained, "That's how I met Jack, my friend who gave me the number to call."

Her gaze went from Will to Emily to James, as she chided, "I thought all this stuff you guys did was secret. How does everyone know about London?"

Will and James were embarrassed. Emily was sympathetic. "You poor thing. Please forgive us. We're kind of isolated here and we tend to glom onto any excitement we can. And you know it's a small group, so the stories do get around and around."

"But this situation isn't about me," Claire said firmly. "It's about Kristen. I'm just incidental, along for the ride, so to say. I just happened to recognize her in Florence. I just happened to confront her at a portentous moment, which caused her to be out of that building when it exploded. And that saved her life.

"She is the target. She is the one needing protection."

Emily nodded turning her gaze on Kristen. "Kristen, let me try to explain better. We work for the Company; you probably heard it called the CIA. We have people all over the world. And no, we don't leap into action for just anyone, because most people wouldn't even think to ask for our help. And we do work for the government and we each have assigned responsibilities. While we're on location, we are on duty 24/7; most of the time we deal with pretty mundane stuff, but we try to be ready for anything.

"And, because we all know how dangerous this life can be for any of us, we're all quick to respond to the Crisis Center whenever a need arises. They are there for us. We know they're going to do whatever is possible if we need help, and sometimes they do the impossible. They make sure we're safe. We all appreciate that.

"So you see, the fact that Claire had the number meant she would be protected. Her friend apparently knew her well. He assumed she would need help sometime and made it possible for her to get it."

James glanced at his watch. "Oops, just about time to call in."

He and Will pushed their chairs back.

"What are you going to do?" Kristen was concerned. "Who are you calling?" Her anxiety was appropriate considering her belief there was a mole in the Witness Protection group.

"We're calling the Crisis Center. We need to make plans. You can come with us if you want. Actually, it would be best to have you there."

Kristen was on her feet in a flash following behind the two men. Claire sat where she was, willing to let the others figure out what their next move would be.

"Emily, I'm not much of a cook, but I'm a whiz at cleaning up," Claire offered.

While they were loading the dirty dishes in the dishwasher Claire told Emily about her mother's dream to turn her retirement into a second career catering to people who didn't have the time or skills to cook. "She's currently attending the annual Italian Culinary Retreat at the Villa Tuscany. A friend came with her and they're both going to meet me in Venice on Wednesday afternoon."

"Oooh, how lucky she is. I've heard of that program. It's very prestigious. It's meant for serious cooks and chefs who want a refresher. It's not like all these cooking vacations that have become so popular. Those are for anyone who wants to brag to their friends and eat well on their vacation. But the Retreat is expensive as well as exclusive. Your mother must have a reputation in the field."

"Or her ex-boss has connections," Claire responded. "Well, actually my mother is a great cook, but of course mostly she was cooking for the two of us. I'm sure we couldn't eat enough to allow her to really develop her skills the way she wanted. I guess that's why she wants this second career. She probably should have had twelve strapping sons to feed. If she had she'd be tired of cooking by now."

Emily nodded. "I hear you. Living out in the country like this we can't just decide to go out to dinner. So we have to cook every meal and it can be a burden if you're not in the mood to cook. Fortunately Will is a good cook. So if I don't feel like cooking, he gets in the kitchen and surprises me with something elegant. Or when neither of us wants to cook we pull something out of the freezer and nuke it."

"Aren't microwaves wonderful? I'm ashamed to say most of my cooking is done in one. If it's not a frozen Lean Cuisine, it's popcorn. But it works equally well on both of them." But, now looking around the homey yet efficient kitchen, she speculated as to whether or not a kitchen like this in her little bungalow in Bayside might not tempt her to use it more often.

* * *

"Did you hear from Claire?" Ruth asked as she came through the door.

"No." Millie looked anxious. "I don't know if she went back to Florence or what. I'm so worried. I tried to get her at the hotel, but she wasn't there."

"Millie...," Ruth said with some force. "You know how capable Claire is. And she's careful. Just don't worry. She'll call when she gets a chance."

Millie nodded. It was easier to say don't worry than it was not to worry. "I thought you were going to play poker with your buddies. Kind of early for you to have lost all your money, isn't it?"

"We didn't play. Not enough people. Sam wasn't around. Jacques went down to the village with Randy to play some video games. I had a drink with George and Marybeth, but then I decided to have an early night." She yawned. "I'm not as young as I used to be. I can't take all these late nights. And I don't even get an afternoon nap." She grimaced. "It's not on the schedule."

Millie smiled. She understood completely, although she never expected to hear Ruth admit it. Usually Ruth liked to party to the end and she never wanted to give an inch due to her advancing years. But obviously the previous late nights were catching up with her.

"Maybe I should try to call Claire again at the hotel in Florence."

Ruth shrugged. "I doubt you'll catch her. Just wait, she'll call and leave a message for you when she gets time." She saw Millie's expression and gave up. "Whatever you do, please do it quietly because I'm going to bed." She took her pajamas into the bathroom with her to get ready.

* * *

"Hey, Aaron, what's up?" Jack was tired, he didn't feel like talking to Aaron; he felt like falling into bed for at least twenty-four hours. But Aaron was a good guy and had saved his bacon on more than one occasion. So here he was calling, just as the message requested.

"We heard from a friend of yours today. Claire Gulliver."

Suddenly Jack was wide awake and charged. His heart was beating too fast. He didn't know why Aaron heard from Claire, but he knew it wasn't good.

"Is she all right?" He forced his voice to remain steady so as not to betray the anxiety he now felt.

"Yes, yes she's all right. She is now anyway."

"Where is she? I thought she was tucked safely away in some small town in California. I'm guessing I'm wrong about that or you wouldn't be asking me about her."

"Well, she is tucked safely away, but certainly not in California." Aaron paused. "Actually, I'm surprised to hear from you so soon. Your contact said you were involved."

"Yeah, well it's winding down. I have a few days break before finishing up the odds and ends." Then he went back to the subject which interested him more. "So where is Claire, and what's she up to now?"

"Well, she's in Italy. She seems to have gotten herself into a situation."

Jack nodded. One thing he knew about Claire was she had an uncanny way of getting involved in 'situations'. "But she's all right?"

"Oh, yes. She's fine now. Our people there worked some of their magic. They've got her tucked away in the countryside. She called in earlier today." He proceeded to fill Jack in on the details of Claire's escape and subsequent rescue.

Jack couldn't believe Claire was in Italy. He hadn't seen or talked to her since September in Washington D.C. Right after they parted, the events of 9/11 caused him to be deployed immediately. Since then he had no time to think about Claire, his daughter or any other personal concerns.

Well, that wasn't entirely true. He had sent Claire a couple of postcards when he had a chance to have colleagues mail them from various exotic locations far from where he was actually assigned. But he hadn't talked to her. And he hadn't had any of her letters forwarded to him for months. So he certainly hadn't expected to hear she had turned up in Italy. And especially he didn't expect to hear she was in trouble.

"She what?" Jack felt the tiny hairs on the back of his neck stiffen as Aaron described Claire's attack on the man pursuing her. "She doesn't know Karate. Hell, she usually faints when she gets scared."

"Well, not this time. She said she was so scared she didn't think; she just acted."

Jack nodded his head; that was his Claire. Well, she wasn't really his Claire, he just had hopes. Unfortunately, his plans for retirement had been put on hold for a while, which had also put any plans he had of developing his relationship with Claire on the back burner. Suddenly he was so frustrated he wanted to slam his fist into the wall. But he didn't. He was used to being in control and showing a calm unruffled persona in the most aggravating moments. It had only been seven months since she had survived the incident in D.C. and here she was in trouble again. What was it about that woman?

"So, Aaron, you're sure this has no relationship to anything Guiness is doing?" His immediate concern was that the villain of the past hadn't once more reared his ugly head. He listened while Aaron responded. Then satisfied that Aaron knew who was involved and why he asked, "So what are you guys planning to do about this?"

He nodded, listening to the plan Aaron outlined; he agreed it was good. But when Aaron described how he planned to use Claire and Kristen to flush the mole and capture the assassins, he cut in, "But not Claire! You don't need Claire for that, right?"

Aaron was silent for a moment, thinking. "I guess you're right. We don't need her but I'm not sure we can convince her of that. She's very protective of her friend. She's very much the mother hen." Aaron's voice clearly communicated his skepticism of his ability to separate Claire from Kristen.

"Well, you said she was supposed to meet her mother in Venice on Wednesday. Believe me; she'll want to be there so her mother won't worry. And I understand it doesn't take much to worry her mother. Claire will go to great lengths to avoid upsetting her." Jack was confident.

"Look, Aaron, I really appreciate what you've done for Claire, what you're doing; but please, do me another favor and send Claire on her way. You can convince her she has already done more than enough. Tell her she'll jeopardize the operation. Promise to let her know how it all comes out. She'll believe you. I promise."

They talked for a while longer. Jack suggested Aaron replace Claire with a police woman to make sure Kristen was protected. Then after they talked a while more Jack promised to check in the next day. After hanging up the phone Jack sat down on the bed in his bleak hotel room and ran his fingers through his dark hair. "Shit!" That was exactly how he felt about it.

He didn't feel like sleeping any longer, but he would. The next few days were going to be much busier than he originally thought. He lay down, staring at the ceiling, as he concentrated on relaxing each portion of his body, feeling the tension seep out. He admitted to himself, the smile on his face was entirely due to the fact he was going to see Claire again, soon.

* * *

Claire was ensconced in one of the comfy overstuffed chairs near the fireplace, dozing, when Will, James and Kristen noisily entered the room. Claire sat there for a moment, letting the words swirl around her until finally she began to understand what they were talking about.

"It will be perfectly safe. I promise we can protect you. But we'd like to pick up the assassin. I know he's just hired juice, but it will be an insult to the Don, you know?"

"And if we can turn him we can use him to testify against the mole we identify..."

Claire listened carefully; she knew she was missing a portion of the plan which had probably already been discussed.

"You're going to use Kristen as bait to trap the mole?" She was incredulous. "That sounds way too dangerous. Kristen, what are you thinking?"

Kristen looked at her and then shrugged. "I have to Claire. Someone is selling me out. I'll never be safe until we discover who it is and remove them."

"Well, there has to be another way." Claire looked at Emily, then Will, finally settling her gaze on James. "This is too dangerous! She isn't one of your trained agents. She doesn't belong to your Company. She's just a person who was in the wrong place at the wrong time. She's already had her life ripped apart because of it. She doesn't need any more danger."

"Claire, Claire, really, we've talked all that out. Believe us it's the best, fastest and ultimately the safest way. Kristen agrees. We're going to have someone with her and someone guarding her. She'll be perfectly safe. I promise."

"Well, we'll see. I'm going to be there too." Claire was angry; she thought this plan was too dangerous.

"No, Claire. We want you to go back to Florence, pick up your bags, check out of your hotel, even settle up for the bike and then continue your vacation as you planned. I believe you're scheduled to go to Venice where you will meet your mother, isn't that correct?"

"Yes..., "Claire admitted grudgingly, "but I can't just walk away leaving Kristen still in danger. I have to know she's safe."

"Claire, I'll be okay. It's a good plan. It will work. And afterwards the Witness people will place me somewhere safe until after I testify. And then, while I can never have my old life back I can at least build another one without always looking over my shoulder."

Claire wasn't convinced. So they went over the entire plan once more, discussing each detail. In the end she had to agree; she had no more arguments and they were all so certain it would work. They were the experts. This was their business. And by that time it was so late she couldn't think straight. So she would just pray it worked. And James promised her he'd send someone to Venice to tell her what happened.

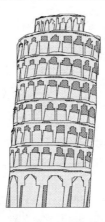

CHAPTER 12

"Good morning."

Only Emily and Kristen were at the table when Claire got to the kitchen.

"Well you were dead to the world when I got up. I guess you caught up on your sleep." Kristen smiled.

Emily went into the kitchen for the coffee pot, and filled the cup sitting in front of Claire. "I made a frittata. Can you eat some?"

Claire nodded. "Please, it sounds wonderful. Has everyone else eaten?

"I just finished. And Emily says Will and James went out early."

"Where are they?"

Kristen shrugged. "I don't know, but I'm sure they'll be back soon because they want me to call in."

"You haven't changed your mind, have you?" Claire asked hopefully.

Kristen shook her head. "It's the best way, Claire, really!"

Claire had to accept it. "What will you tell them about how you escaped?"

"We decided I'll just pretend we didn't even know they were there. I'll tell them we felt too hemmed in there. Because we felt trapped we decided to move on." She smiled at Claire pleased with their plan.

"Well, won't they want to know why you didn't call sooner? You were supposed to call in yesterday, remember?"

"Yeah, I remember." Kristen frowned. "I'll say I couldn't get to a safe phone so I waited."

Claire nodded. It could work. She sighed; she would have to trust James, Will, and the people at the number she phoned, to make this work. After all, it was their business.

The frittata was full of mushrooms, spinach, green onions and cheese. Claire managed to eat every bit of the generous slice Emily had served her. In addition she fortified herself with a hunk of bread spread with a soft mild cheese and several pieces of fruit.

Finally, sated, Claire sat back noticing the newspaper Kristen was scrutinizing. "Is that today's?"

Emily nodded. "They deliver it daily down at our mailbox. It helps us keep in touch with the world."

Kristen laid the section she was reading on the table and pointed to a very small paragraph at the bottom of a page. "A terrible accident happened yesterday. Two tourists from Rome were found at the bottom of the cliffs between Vernazza and Corniglia. The names are being withheld until the next of kin can be notified."

She looked at Claire.

Claire blanched but managed to keep her voice steady. "How terrible. I wonder what happened."

"Those cliffs are treacherous. Many day trippers underestimate the danger," was Emily's terse comment. Then, seeking a happier topic, Emily and Kristen quizzed Claire on what she had seen and done while she was in Florence and what she planned to see in Venice.

"Really, you should go to one of the glass factories on Murano. Don't take one of the tours offered by the showrooms. They get you there and then hold you captive until you buy. Just take the vaporetti, that's what they call their water buses, to the island. It's one of their regular routes. I forget the number, but ask, someone will tell you. Then you can explore the island on your own. You'll enjoy it. And I think you'll find the town is quite pretty, much different than the grand palaces of Venice." Emily was enthusiastic. "I wish I was going with you. I love Venice."

Kristen nodded, agreeing. "It's different from Florence. I went on holiday soon after I arrived in Florence. It's small, contained. The only modes of transportation are the water buses and your feet. You can't even use bikes because all the little bridges over the canals have steps that render bikes useless."

"Well, there are the water taxis..." Emily said.

"Don't even think about taking a water taxi!" Kristen was adamant. "They are way too expensive. As are the gondolas unless you have someone special you want to cuddle with, otherwise, stick to the vaporetti.

"Look, when you get off the train just stop at Travelers' Information and find out what number vaporetti you need for your hotel. They'll give you a map of the city and directions to find your hotel. It's a little hard to find addresses in Venice as the streets wander and are apt to change their names. The city is not laid out in grids like most cities. But there are signs and arrows everywhere directing you to key places such as San Marco Square or the Rialto Bridge, and it doesn't take long to get your bearings."

"Is it safe?"

Emily nodded. "It's probably safer than any other city in Italy. It's contained, you see. That seems to keep crime to a minimum. Still traveling alone can be tricky. Don't wander down dark lonely streets; stay where the people are at night. During the day you'll be very safe. Don't you agree, Kristen?"

"Yes, but considering your visit to Italy so far, it wouldn't hurt you to stay indoors after dark. After all, your mother and her friend will catch up with you Wednesday. Then you could safely wander about after dark."

She sounded a lot like Claire's mother. Before Claire could say anything they were all distracted by the return of James and Will. The house filled with noise as they helped themselves to coffee and joined them at the table.

"How is everyone this morning?" James was in a good mood.

After a few pleasantries were exchanged he got down to business. "Well, it's all arranged. Kristen, we'll want you to call in and then we're off.

"Claire, Emily is going to drive you into Florence, go with you while you retrieve your baggage and check out of the hotel. She'll take you to the shop where you rented the bike and make sure that's all taken care of. Then she'll take you to the train station and get you on the right train for Venice."

"Wait, wait." He forestalled her objection. "You know we all agreed last night that this was the best course of action."

She nodded reluctantly, still not comfortable about being excluded.

"We have a specially trained agent, a woman, on the Italian Police Force who will be Kristen's companion. That way we'll have the maximum protection right at her side. Based on your past experiences, we don't expect much to happen until tomorrow morning. It apparently takes them a little time to get their assassins in place after you call in." He looked at Kristen, carefully watching her reaction. "But, we will be prepared for anything, anytime. We won't relax until we have the mole and the Witness Protection people have you tucked safely away once more."

Kristen nodded. She looked a little scared but determined; she was ready.

What could Claire do but agree. "But remember I'm going to be on pins and needles..."

"We promise we'll get a message to you Tuesday, and let you know what happened." James so solemnly crossed his heart that Claire could only grin at the silly gesture.

"You better," she warned.

"Come on, let's make that call."

"I'm going too." Claire followed, then glancing over her shoulder she saw Emily was right behind her. No one wanted to miss this.

* * *

"What's with LiAnn today? She's in a pissy mood," Randy whispered to Millie as he sliced the mushrooms they were going to sauté to serve on top of the crisply fried squares of polenta for one of their antipasto selections.

Millie shrugged. She had noticed, too. How could she have not when LiAnn almost took her head off for no apparent reason? "She must have had a bad night," was her only comment.

And maybe that was all it was. Today, LiAnn's face was so rigid her age lines appeared deeper making her look ancient. And Millie had noticed she wasn't able to control the tremor in her hands while she was working. It had struck her how frail LiAnn really was, so she resolved to help her unobtrusively which only resulted in LiAnn loudly and tersely telling her to get lost. Her cheeks burned in embarrassment remembering the incident. LiAnn's rudeness had really been unwarranted.

"Millie, can you help me here?" Renee asked, turning out the dough he had mixed, which they would roll around the little Wild Boar sausages.

Millie quickly washed and dried her hands eager to help roll out the dough and encase the sausages. "Are you sure all these will reheat without losing their freshness?"

"We're not even going to bake these until just before serving so they'll be fine. And I've used the crispy fried polenta before, so I know it reheats easily. The grilled eggplant and sweet peppers stay at room temperature marinating in garlic and oil, so we don't have to worry about those. We made good choices here."

"Those look good enough to eat already, Millie." George smacked his lips. "We're doing very well, right on schedule. I'm just about to grill the vegetables. Randy is almost ready to sauté the mushroom medley. Renee, when you finish here do you want to help him? Where's LiAnn?"

He looked around. "Oh, there she is, slicing the chilled polenta. Millie perhaps you can help her finish up there?"

Millie and Renee nodded. George was playing head chef for them today. It was his turn. They needed a leader so one of them played that role at each of their activities to make sure everything got done efficiently. They covered the pans of sausage rolls and Renee carried them into the big walk-in refrigerator to keep until the kitchen staff would put them in the oven to bake before serving tonight.

Millie joined LiAnn. "Should I start frying these, LiAnn?" she offered.

"No, I'm going to fry them," was her abrupt reply. She must have realized how she sounded because she said in a more normal tone, "Please, if you could finish slicing these, I'm just about ready to start." She indicated with her head the large deep pan of oil heating on the back burner of the stove.

"Of course." Millie stepped up to the table, anxious not to upset LiAnn again. She looked carefully at the rectangles LiAnn had cut, making sure she duplicated her efforts.

"Stop!"

Millie paused, her knife in mid-cut, thinking someone was talking to her.

"Wait, don't do that." George actually grabbed LiAnn and pulled her away from the stove.

"Take your hands off of me." The fury in LiAnn's voice was startling. Everyone turned toward her, but George didn't let go.

"The oil is too hot. Can't you see the smoke? If you put the polenta in now it would sputter and pop and most likely bubble over. It would be very dangerous. We could have a bad grease fire. You might even have been burned."

LiAnn stopped struggling. She looked at George, her gaze inscrutable.

Randy stepped around George and took a towel which he wadded up and used to hold the handle of the pan as he carefully moved it to another burner, one that was not lit.

Renee looked at the flame which had been on under the pan. "My God, who turned the flame up so high? George is right! The polenta contains a lot of moisture which makes it bubble and spit. LiAnn, if you put it in oil that hot, for sure it would have bubbled over. The oil could have even ignited if it reached the coals in the grill." He pointed to the charcoal grill next to the burner where the pan had been heating.

Luckily George had been standing there grilling the eggplant and peppers and noticed how hot the oil had become. "George probably saved you from a nasty burn."

LiAnn nodded her head and stepped back from George. "Thank you, George. But who turned up the gas? I set it on low, and I checked the temperature with the thermometer just a short time ago. It was 350°. That is the correct temperature, is it not?"

"Well, it's not 350° now, and it's been off the flame for a minute or more." Randy looked at the thermometer in his hand. "It would have been very dangerous. When it cools down we'll light the burner once more and carefully monitor it. Then we can finish the polenta."

LiAnn nodded her head meekly, moving over to help Millie finish cutting the polenta.

Millie thought LiAnn had turned the flame too high herself, even though she wouldn't admit it. It was probably just a senior moment; one more example of LiAnn's day going amok.

They finished their chores in the kitchen without further incident. LiAnn had declined to fry the polenta, obviously still shocked at her close brush with disaster. So George good-naturedly finished up with Randy's help.

When Wanda came to check on their progress they showed her the prepared food and handed her the written instructions for the final preparation to pass on to the Villa's kitchen staff. They were all pretty pleased with the results of their morning by the time they joined the others for lunch. They were looking forward to the afternoon when they would visit the Villa's wine cellars and select the wines that would be served tonight.

* * *

"Hi Mom. Sorry I missed you again, but I guess you're pretty busy. I hope you're having fun.

"I'm back in Florence, but checking out in a little bit and will be off to Venice. I'm looking forward to it. I loved my little sojourn to the hill towns. I'm so sorry about the bomb in Florence, but it resulted in a nice change of schedule for me. I visited Sienna and then the Cinque Terre. They were both beautiful and if you ever come back you need to include them on your itinerary.

"I won't call you again unless I have a change of plans. Otherwise, I'll meet you at the train station in Venice. Look for me near the Travelers' Information sign. I can't wait to see you and hear all about the Retreat.

"Tell Ruth hi for me, and I'll see you Wednesday."

* * *

Venice's Santa Lucia Station looked like all the others Claire had seen on this trip. She followed Emily and Kristen's instructions and made her first stop the Traveler's Information desk.

The clerk's English was good. The words he used were correct even though his accent was confusing. However, he was sincere in his efforts to make her understand. So she left the train station fairly confident she could find her way to Alloggi Riva, the small hotel where they had reserved a room. The first hurdle was getting on the vaporetti number 82 with her wheelie bag. The vaporetti was a boat and, like all boats, it dipped and swayed as people got on and off. And while the wheelie bag was compact and much easier to wheel rather than carry, certain activities such as lifting it into the overhead bin in the train and now getting it from the dock into the body of the vaporetti made Claire wish she had packed lighter.

A kind man reached out and pulled the bag on board. Claire smiled her thanks murmuring "Grazie."

Abruptly the boat moved away from the dock and Claire clutched a rail to keep from falling. Suddenly she realized she was in Venice. The little boat chugged from one stop to another, sometimes stopping on one side of the wide canal, sometimes across the canal on the other side. People got on and off with a casual skill that Claire envied. She didn't take a seat when they became available preferring to stand next to her bag, so she would be better prepared to disembark when they arrived at her stop.

And when they finally reached her stop, she almost missed it because she was so busy looking around. When she found herself on the dock she was breathless, but her suitcase was beside her and her backpack hanging securely on her back.

It was late afternoon and the sun was beating directly overhead. She felt terribly thirsty and wondered if she had time for a drink at one of the inviting sidewalk cafes lining the waterfront. She glanced at her watch and decided she would make time. She was on vacation and besides Emily had called the hotel to ascertain they would hold the triple room until she arrived.

She took a seat at a table at the outside edge of the group of tables where she could keep her suitcase next to her out of everyone's way. She had drunk almost half of the frosty orange juice she ordered before she noticed a huge ocean liner was docked down the wharf to her left. No wonder there were so many tourists here. She had heard cruising was a wonderful experience, but had never had the pleasure. Well, she thought, Some time, perhaps. Actually, with her urging, her mother had signed up for a cruise to Alaska with her church group. Unfortunately, that cruise was scheduled for the same time as the Culinary Retreat, so the church ladies were onboard but Millie had to change her booking to a September cruise. Claire shrugged, feeling no remorse for her role in her mother's aborted cruise. The Culinary Retreat was too good an opportunity to pass up. And, as Millie was retired now, two trips in her first year would be good for what ails her, and if nothing ails her, they would still be good for her.

She carefully checked her map and then bravely started out once more in search of her hotel. She followed the signs for Rialto Bridge, frequently crossing canals, lifting her bag up the stairs and then hauling it down the other side. She was grateful she had the foresight to stop for a drink, because it seemed a long time before she located the hotel. In fact, she suspected she might have been traveling in circles because all of the bridges were starting to look familiar.

Alloggi Riva was a small place, recommended by Marianne Peabody. She said it was centrally located, comfortable and very clean. And the lobby created a good first impression with open windows looking right onto the canal flowing beside it. Senora Sorenson was very welcoming and her English, while basic, was good enough to explain that the nun sitting with her was Sister Marie Terese, her sister as well as a nun. There had been a death in the family, so Sister Marie Terese was on bereavement leave. Sister Marie Terese had no English but she was trying to learn. She smiled cordially at Claire.

Senora Sorenson bobbed her head at Claire's attempt to express her sympathy. "No, no. We do not grieve. What is death but a part of living? Our aunt led a long and fruitful life. We will miss her, but we have been blessed with her presence for many years."

Claire nodded, thinking it a very healthy way of regarding the death of a loved one.

Despite the twenty or so years Senora Sorenson had on Claire, she picked up the wheelie bag as if it weighed nothing and led Claire up the steep stairs. Claire was embarrassed by her shortness of breath by the time they reached the top, because it didn't seem to bother Senora Sorenson at all. But when she pushed open the door and Claire stepped into the room, she forgot about the stairs. The large room was sparsely furnished with three beds, two chairs, a small writing table and large corner windows which overlooked the meeting of two canals. The pleasant room was cheerful and airy. As she watched, a gondola and a barge loaded with boxes came to the corner from opposite directions. The barge tooted a horn and the gondola gave way. It was a wonderful view.

Senora pointed out the features of the room and then left Claire to get settled. She promptly pulled one of the chairs to the window and sat down to watch the action for a while, thrilled that Venice was every bit as good, if not better than she imagined.

* * *

"What do you mean? Tell him to send someone else, someone with some guts. How hard can it be to take care of her? I can't believe she's still there.

"The trial starts in less than sixty days. Sixty! I need to know they won't have any witnesses to testify against me." His voice changed from bullying to *pleading. "Pop, why can't you send one of your own guys? Then we'd know it was done right."*

"Don't worry, Sonny. I'll take care of it. I took care of the others, didn't I? You keep calm, stay out of trouble and you'll soon be free. Trust me."

Sonny nodded. "Pop, I know you're gonna take care of it, but this place is driving me crazy. I gotta get out of here. I've been here too long. I know, I know I hadda stay put while you took care of all the witnesses. But now I'm going bonkers; now I just want out. Please, just get rid of her for me." He didn't realize his voice had slipped into the whinny pleading tone he had used to get his way since he was a kid.

He hung up the pay phone slowly. He ignored the others in line, who had been waiting patiently for their turn, concerned only with his needs. He was confident no one would object; they all knew what happened to anyone who crossed him. Three thugs with strong ties to his father were in here with him. They saw to it that Sonny was protected. They made sure he continued to be pampered in the way he had always been, albeit in a more confined manner.

Sonny turned away and headed for the exercise yard still thinking about the trial looming on his horizon and how the incompetent Italians had botched the simple task of eliminating the last witness.

He had been here way too long. They had arrested him more than a year ago. This facility was never meant for long term incarceration. Almost everyone here was waiting for trial, so there was a sense of anxiety amongst the residents as they worked out their strategy while fitting into the daily routine. When he was first sent here and his lawyers had begun a constant stream of actions and motions intended to delay his trial, specifically to give his father time to make sure that all damaging witnesses had been removed, he was willing to be patient. And they thought they had been successful, and so the trial date had been set and he began to look forward to his freedom once again. Then they learned about the secret witness who had been closeted away.

Sonny reached into his pocket for a cigarette, pausing in the lee of the building to protect the match flame while he lit up. He inhaled deeply, letting the smoke drift lazily out his nostrils while he looked around for his guys. He didn't see them in the corner of the exercise yard they had claimed as their own. He moved forward, wondering where they were.

The secret witness had been a nasty surprise. Suddenly it didn't look as if beating this rap was a sure thing.

Kristen, he remembered, was a babe. And he recalled how well she danced. He had been putting the moves on her since he first saw her. Now he admitted grimly she was hot, but she certainly wasn't worth the chance he would fry. No babe was.

California had the electric chair. That thought gave Sonny pause even though he admitted he had never thought of it before his arrest. Somehow, it had never occurred to him he would be held accountable for his actions.

No, Kristen was expendable. She needed to disappear and stay gone. He didn't know what she saw, but it must have been good enough for them to fake her death and spirit her away. It took a lot of money for his father to even learn of her existence say nothing about her whereabouts, then he started calling in favors to make sure she was taken out. But so far nothing had worked and the trial date was getting closer.

A shadow swept over him and he looked to his right and saw Ben Hoa silently keeping pace with him. He showed no reaction, keeping his cool demeanor as his eyes swiveled to his left and saw Huey Chou. They had him boxed in and were moving closer to him. Sonny swiveled his head, looking for his own guys, at the same time preparing himself to be jumped. He knew why they were here. They told him more than once that they owned the candy store. They worked for the Vietnamese Triad and thought they had the exclusive right to the prison drug trade.

Sonny had ignored them. They were nothing! He would do his own dealing just as he had outside. And he knew his father would protect him.

But now he was alone. Neither his father, nor his father's men were near. As he was being crowded into a narrow area near the wall he realized these guys were deadly serious about protecting their territory.

"What's going on? You guys wanna talk?" He tried to sound reasonable. He gasped; the burning sensation in his belly was sudden. He didn't have time to panic, the knives came from all directions and momentarily he was past noticing anything.

* * *

"Hi Sam. Where are your card playing friends?" Millie asked when Sam wandered into the small piazza where she sat with her book.

He shrugged. "Don't know. I hope they're not playing without me."

"I don't think so. Ruth says you're the one with all the money."

He smiled. "Ah, your friend Ruth is quite a woman."

Ruth had told her that of all the players, Sam was the real card shark. He used his aged look and his somewhat vague manner to throw the others off his game.

"Say, Sam?" She decided to say something. "Is LiAnn all right?"

He looked at her with surprise. "All right? What do you mean?"

"Well, I just thought she was acting a little funny today." She didn't think it prudent to tell Sam about the bad mood LiAnn had been in all day or how grouchy she was, instead saying lamely, "I wondered if she was feeling okay."

Sam shrugged again. "Oh, LiAnn gets in her moods. I hope she didn't offend anyone, sometimes she can be pretty demanding, especially if things aren't going the way she wants. It's usually the family, you see. She always worries about family and frankly she worries too much over things she should just let be." He looked at Millie with a twinkle in his eye. "If she was a true Zen she'd just go with the flow."

Millie nodded; she couldn't fault LiAnn for worrying. She was guilty of that herself and she only had one child. "I'm sure that must have been what it was."

George entered the piazza with Stephen and Zoe. "There you are Sam. How about some cards? Only four handed today, because Ruth and Jacques are fixing our dinner." He looked at her. "Unless Millie wants to play?" He was hoping new money would be added to the mix.

She laughed. "Not a chance. I'm hanging on to my money; I've heard about your games." She buried her nose in her book again as they took up their customary places in the shaded corner.

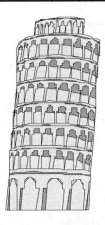

CHAPTER 13

Millie looked around the lobby and spotted Randy and Renee. She waved and walked over to join them. "Are we ready for our outing?"

They grinned back at her, obviously looking forward to their adventure.

George came up with LiAnn. "All set. Let's find Chef Martin."

"I've got the list." Randy, in charge of their shopping excursion, held up his piece of paper. "Let's hope we find everything we need, or we'll be making last minute modifications to the menu."

It was a beautiful morning. If there had been any low hanging fog on the hills it was long gone now. Instead the light was peachy colored, the sky was startling blue and the hills green with early grass or darkly lined with green vines. It was a pleasant drive, but they were anxious to begin their shopping; their dinner tonight depended on the items they would purchase. Finally their van pulled into the small village which hosted market day each Tuesday. The village square was swarming with people, converted recreational vehicles and bright canvas covered stands. They could see a large variety of food stuffs. In addition, there were clothes, household goods and luxury items of every type available for sale.

"It's best if we secure the meat and fish first," Chef Martin told them. "Refresh me, what's on the menu?"

"Stuffed cabbage rolls, Braised lamb shanks with mushrooms on polenta and Fillet of Turbot stuffed with spinach and shallots in a Hollandaise sauce."

Chef Martin nodded his approval. "Well, if we don't find Turbot we like, we can substitute another fish without too much problem. I would think there will be plenty of lamb this early in the year. I saw a butcher yesterday who might have what we want, if I can locate where he's set up today. The problem will be quantity. How many do you want?"

Randy conferred with Renee and then said, "We need at least twenty-five, possibly thirty, if they have them."

Chef Martin thought. "I think you're over-estimating. Remember, serving three entrees means you will serve smaller portions of each. If you crack the shanks into two or three sections you can serve a portion instead of a whole shank. Let's say we could do it with twelve, huh?"

"I wouldn't want to run out." Millie was hesitant.

"Ahh, the dreaded 'not enough' syndrome. Don't worry, you'll have plenty. I'm guessing there will even be leftovers. But first we need to find the lamb shanks."

He led them confidently into the market. It reminded Millie somewhat of the outdoor market she had visited in Florence with Claire and Ruth. But while that one sold items to satisfy the tourists' appetites, this was aimed for the locals' needs. She was surprised at seeing how the big RV's were modified into modern, compact shops on wheels. They parked in the market stall and lifted the side of their vehicle to form an awning to protect the customers from the weather while they examined the displays of goods. Inside the vehicle they had freezers, cold boxes, lights and any of the tools needed for their trade. She saw poultry vendors with cases of eggs as well as chickens, ducks and geese. There were cheese vendors with dizzying assortments of cheeses, each only too happy to provide a taste if the customer desired. There was a dairy shop which sold milk, cream and butter. One man sold only mushrooms, both fresh and dried. And there were numerous farm stands. The farmers didn't use the fancy shops on wheels; their tables of goods were covered with canvas awnings to protect their vegetables from the searing sun or the occasional rainstorm. Sometimes their truck was backed right up to the stand, so they could sell right off the truck. As vast as the market was it was plain to see that it was only temporary. Tomorrow there would be no trace it had even existed, but next Tuesday it would be here again.

Under Chef Martin's guidance they made a complete tour of the food selections in the market to identify the offerings before they began to shop. He told them it was a good way to make sure they bought the freshest at the best price. And one of the most important elements of the school was the price. For each session they were required to not only provide the recipe, the ingredients and the steps in making the item, but also the price of the dish for the menu. It was an exercise that kept them all keenly aware of what their ingredients cost.

They were having a good time, chatting amongst themselves as they evaluated each vendor's offerings. LiAnn was a different person today, alert, energetic and happy. Millie thought it was almost as if she had taken some mood-altering drug. Rather than question the change she was just grateful she would be working with today's LiAnn instead of yesterday's version. This afternoon in the kitchen, Millie would be the acting Head Chef. She was relieved that responsibility wouldn't require her to coax LiAnn through one of her moods.

They were lucky to find a fish monger with fresh Turbot. They spent some time discussing if they wanted to buy fillets or whole fish. Chef Martin stood to the side allowing them to make the decision. LiAnn thought whole fish were too much work. Randy thought they would pay for a lot of waste. But Renee insisted they would have perfect fillets only if they filleted them. George nodded his agreement. That was enough for Millie. If the two professional chefs wanted to fillet the fish, she was going to agree with them. And after they had purchased the fish Chef Martin nodded his approval of their decision before leading them on to the butcher shops.

They found a butcher, who had the equivalent of five lambs, but they decided that twelve shanks, cracked in three pieces would be plenty as Chef Martin had suggested. They carefully selected the shanks they wanted and waited while he cracked them to their specifications. And the same man agreed to grind the beef they wanted for the cabbage rolls. While he was preparing their order Randy sent LiAnn and Renee off to purchase the cabbages and sauerkraut. Then, he sent Millie and George off to buy spinach and leeks.

"Let's meet in twenty minutes at that little café we saw near the entrance." Then he called out to Millie, "And mushrooms. You and George get the mushrooms for us, will you?"

They nodded their agreement moving purposefully into the crowd.

"George this spinach is beautiful. Look how fresh it is."

At George's nod she filled two bags, still operating on the assumption that more was better.

At the next stand George found leeks which would meet his standards and examined the display of mushrooms carefully.

"Wait, let's get the mushrooms at that rolling store we saw near the front. They had a huge selection of both fresh and dried. I think we can get a nice variety there."

The vendor's disappointment at the loss of the mushroom sale was somewhat appeased when they purchased the leeks. Then they moved toward the front of the market. The mushroom selection was extensive and, while the price was higher than the other vegetable vendors, they both agreed the quality justified the price. George was loaded down with bags having insisted he would carry them all. Millie was right behind him when she glimpsed the display of colorful Italian pottery behind the mushroom vendor.

"George, look at the gorgeous pottery; let's take a few minutes to look."

George groaned. "You've got to be kidding."

"Don't be such a spoil sport. It's too good a chance to pass up. Look, there's the café and only Chef Martin and Randy are there. You go join them and order me a cappuccino. I'll be there in just a minute."

She hurried; she wouldn't dare keep them all waiting while she shopped, but she just had to stop. And it really only took her ten minutes to purchase two platters, a rectangle shaped baking dish and a large pitcher. And five of those minutes were spent while the vendor wrapped the pottery. When she got back to the café, struggling with her awkward bundles, the others were all there enjoying their coffees.

"Wow, how are you going to get that in your luggage?" Randy asked.

Chef Martin and Renee laughed at her stricken expression when she realized it wasn't going to fit.

"It was such a bargain I couldn't resist." She now realized she was going to have to carry the pottery home. Then she brightened. "Maybe the Villa will ship it for me. Do you think?"

"Probably, they have agreed to ship the binder of recipes for those who ask them," Chef Martin conceded. "Now, Randy, let's go over the shopping list one last time and make sure we've got everything you'll need."

Randy read off the items and they responded.

"Mushrooms? I wanted to pick out the mushrooms; I know just what we need." LiAnn had that look again.

Millie afraid her good mood was coming to an end, hurried to explain, "They're beautiful, LiAnn, trust us. We bought them at that RV over there." Millie pointed. "They had a wonderful selection. I'm sure you'll be pleased."

George nodded. "We did get a great selection. You'll see when we get back."

LiAnn accepted it, but clearly she wasn't happy. She struggled to be part of the team, but it didn't seem to suit her nature. She wanted to do what she wanted to do, and she wanted them all to follow her directions.

While they finished their coffees Randy went back to find the Villa's van and ask the driver to come around to pick them up. Their purchases had accumulated into quite a load and Randy had suggested the van could come to them easier than they could get to the van.

* * *

The vast square was filled with groups of tourists clustered around tour guides holding colorful umbrellas high, despite there being no clouds visible. Then a guide would dart toward one of the sights, the group following right behind them, struggling to keep up, heads swiveling to see everything as they moved this way and that through the piazza. Just then the bells on top of the tall tower started to ring and caught Claire's attention until they had finished striking eleven. She sighed; the day was moving very slowly. Earlier she had gone into the Basilica, which was very ornate and decorated with lots of gold, but the crowds of tourists discouraged her from staying long. She didn't want to feed the pigeons on the piazza as she saw many of the tourists doing. She remembered Ruth's encounter with a pigeon in Florence and, while she had dropped some laundry off this morning, she felt she didn't have enough clean clothes to risk the pigeons. She was able to get a good view of the outside of the Bridge of Sighs and spent some time finding the best camera shot.

Now she decided it was time for a snack. She had been warned the Venetian breakfast would consist of hard rolls and coffee, so she wasn't surprised. But her stomach felt betrayed. She wandered down the edge of the piazza to the wharf and sat down at the same café she visited yesterday when she got off the vaporetti. Now she could see another cruise ship was docked. This one was gigantic. No wonder the tourists were thick. She ordered herself a coffee, orange juice and something called a 'toasta'. Happily it turned out to be the equivalent of a grilled ham and cheese sandwich. It was just what she needed to make up for her skimpy breakfast.

She glanced at her watch again but it wasn't even eleven-thirty. When would she hear what happened to Kristen? Her imagination was driving her crazy with all sorts of scenarios she hoped were not even close to the truth. She didn't know how she was going to get through the day. James had promised her a message and she was sure it would arrive, but she just didn't know when or even how it would be delivered.

She sipped her coffee while she went through the little guidebook she carried determined to stay busy and keep her mind off unpleasant thoughts. She noted the bell tower on the piazza was called Campanile di San Marco, and you could take the elevator to the top for a terrific view. Remembering the crowds in the piazza she decided to forgo that pleasure. Maybe tomorrow or the next day she could go with her mother and Ruth. She studied the book. What she needed was something away from the square where tourists were less likely to roam.

She saw the listing about the Peggy Guggenheim Collection. That would be interesting until she noticed it was closed on Tuesdays. However the Accademia was open. She decided to visit it and then ride around the entire island on the vaporetti, which would help her become familiar with the layout of the city.

She walked slowly towards the Accademia, looking in shop windows, watching the pedestrians. Then she slowed to a stop, turned around and looked at the shop she had passed. She wondered if she had the nerve. She remembered how Kristen's extreme haircut had grown on her until she had finally admitted it looked young and fresh. She smiled. It would take more than a new hairstyle to make her look fresh, but on the other hand she didn't want to turn into a Ruth. While Ruth wore the latest in clothing fashion, she kept her hairstyle and makeup the same style she used as a young woman. It looked a little garish, but that was Ruth. Now she decided she would just look in and see what they could do. After all she was on vacation and, if she didn't like the results, she had time to change it back.

* * *

Claire was overwhelmed by the display in the Accademia. Room after room had been filled with a dazzling collection of Venetian paintings, but unfortunately, they had all run together. She couldn't remember one outstanding one, rather a colorful blur of a different time; a different life. Standing here near the entrance she was reluctant to go back into the present day of Venice. She needed some time to transition from the Venice she had been inundated with from all those paintings inside. While she stood there she was startled to realize the attractive woman reflected in the glass covered bulletin board was her. She looked critically, turning this way and that. Her hair looked good. It was hard to accept she paid someone to make her hair look like she had just gotten out of bed. Still she knew from the magazines it was top fashion these days.

Then a notice caught her eye. *Concerto* was in big letters. It was in Italian, but she could see it was scheduled for tomorrow night at the Basilica Dei Frari. She thought she recognized the name and, thumbing through her guidebook, found she was correct. It was a church she had marked to visit because of the art works it housed. She found her pen and noted the date and time in the guidebook. She thought it would be fun to go and see the church and its art works while hearing some music. She thought her mother and Ruth would like that. And it would be a different way to spend their first night in Venice. She chuckled, thinking how shocked they both would be to see her new look.

Finally, she was ready to enter the world again and wandered down to the dock to catch a vaporetti.

She rode the entire vaporetti route twice. The first time she just looked at everything, enjoying the cool breeze, relaxing. The second time around she snapped picture after picture of the palaces, the canal scenes and enjoyed just watching the people get on and off. It was obvious that this was the method of transportation the natives used, although she did see many private boats on the water, so assumed the wealthier citizens had their own. By the time they arrived at the dock closest to her hotel, she was ready to go back to her room for a rest and to write a few postcards before venturing out for dinner. She decided to ask Senora Sorenson for a suggestion. The place she had tried last night catered to tourists and it was honestly the worst meal she had eaten on this trip. She needed to do better tonight.

The dock was crowded with people waiting to get on the vaporetti at the same time passengers were attempting to alight. Claire tried to move with the crowd, murmuring, *"Grazie,"* *"scusi"* and *"per favore."* Somehow she managed to get on the dock with no major injuries. She watched as the vaporetti pulled away, scanning the faces for one who looked familiar. Then she turned slowly looking at each face still lingering near her, but couldn't identify who could have thrust the piece of paper in her hand which she now clutched tightly. And as no one was passing out flyers or advertisements she knew it must be the message she had been waiting for.

She knew better than to open it there, no matter how anxious she was. It had been slipped to her in such a furtive manner she needed to look at it in a private place. She hurried down the road towards her hotel. Finally she found a secluded spot in a sheltered doorway where she could pause a moment. She looked around once more and found herself alone, so she unfolded the note.

Tonight, 7:30, Restaurant Alla Madonna—near Rialto

This was it! The message she had been waiting for. She glanced at her watch and saw it was only five. She sighed. Two and a half more hours until she knew whether or not Kristen was safe. She carefully folded the note and tucked it into her backpack pocket where she kept the map and headed once more toward her hotel. She had time for a shower, a change of clothes and writing some postcards. But she gave up all thoughts of a nap. She wouldn't be able to sleep until she knew what had happened.

* * *

Millie checked her list of "To Do" items then glanced at the clock. So far so good, tasks were being checked off in appropriate order. She still couldn't believe she had drawn the honor of acting as head chef for today's work. She would have been much more confident acting in that capacity yesterday for the wine selection or even this morning at the market. But today was their final day, and her group was assigned the main course. Not only did they have to select a menu of items which had not been done in the previous nights, but they had to do their choices better than the groups before them. The groups had become very competitive over the course of the Retreat.

She realized she was dallying, letting her worry interfere with what she had to do. And she really didn't have time for it now, she told herself sternly. She went to the far work station where the mushrooms sat. She needed to start prepping them now.

"LiAnn, what are you doing here? You're supposed to be making the cabbage rolls with Randy."

When LiAnn actually jumped at her scolding tone, Millie realized her voice had been sharper than she intended. But LiAnn's guilty look startled Millie in turn. She immediately felt suspicious. She had been a mother too many years not to recognize trouble when she saw it.

"LiAnn, why aren't you working with Randy?"

"I was just checking the mushrooms. I needed a break, so I decided to see what you and George selected." Her manner was defensive, her voice almost whiny.

Millie didn't even question why she was so suspicious. She pulled the large basket of mushrooms away from LiAnn's grasp and examined them closely. They looked fine to her. Idly she picked up a few and saw something strange.

"Wait, I don't remember buying this one." It was a beautiful white mushroom, so perfect in shape it almost looked as if it was a fake. She dug into the pile deeper and saw two more of the odd mushrooms.

She looked at LiAnn and then the accusation came out her mouth as the thought popped into her head. "LiAnn, did you put these mushrooms in the basket?"

LiAnn's face set into an obstinate expression. "What are you saying? There is nothing wrong with those mushrooms."

"I didn't say there was. I just asked, did you add some mushrooms?" Millie used a firm tone. LiAnn was dissembling, if not outright lying, and she noticed she had not answered her question. Millie picked up one of the mushrooms in question in order to examine it more closely.

"For heavens sake, stupid woman! There is nothing wrong with the mushroom." LiAnn snatched it from Millie's hand. "Why are you meddling, you fool? Do you think you're really the boss? Do you think any of us will follow your orders?"

Millie was shocked into silence at the venom in LiAnn's tone.

"There is nothing wrong with this mushroom!" And before Millie could move she popped it in her mouth. Her chewing motion was exaggerated and finally she swallowed the whole mouthful. Her lips spread into a grotesque smile sending shivers down Millie's spine.

"Delicious!" she announced. Then her face changed, her scorn became apparent. "You don't know anything," she announced with contempt. Then, drawing herself up to her haughtiest height, she announced. "I will not work with you. You are an idiot."

With that she turned and stomped out of the kitchen while Millie stood there with her mouth hanging open.

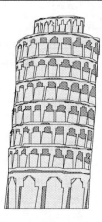

CHAPTER 14

"Millie, I've finished filleting the fish. Renee is rolling them with the spinach and leeks and says he doesn't need my help. Do you want me to start on the mushrooms?" George was at her elbow.

Millie shook herself out of her shocked state. "No. No, I want to talk to Chef Martin about them first. Do you know where he is?"

"Sure, he went into the office with Chef Geno a while ago."

"Would you find him and tell him I need to see him and then go help Randy with the cabbage rolls?"

"Thanks," she called after him. She grabbed the table for support, because her knees suddenly felt weak. She was just realizing the enormity of her confrontation with LiAnn. She didn't look forward to telling Chef Martin she had so offended LiAnn she had caused her to walk out of the kitchen during the last session of class. She looked at the container of mushrooms. Had she been a fool?

She just didn't know.

"Aah, Ms. Gulliver. You needed me?" Chef Martin, as always, was so charmingly formal.

Millie felt tears spring to her eyes. She really didn't want to tell him how badly she had screwed up. She took a deep breath and then, keeping her voice low so the others wouldn't overhear, she explained what had just happened.

He looked incredulous. "She just walked out?"

He then looked at the closed kitchen door as if he expected LiAnn to appear, returning as if nothing was wrong.

"And where are these mushrooms?"

Millie showed him the basket of mushrooms. "I don't recognize these. I'm sure we didn't buy them in the market. It was one of these that she took out of my hand and ate." She was embarrassed by her earlier suspicions. Obviously the mushrooms were harmless.

"George, could you join us here?" Chef Martin waved George over, leaving Randy looking curious.

"George, what are these mushrooms you picked up at the market?"

George looked in the basket and separated the mushrooms into groups of the same kind, naming them as he added them to each pile. The two odd ones he picked up again. Then he looked at Millie confused. "Frankly, I don't remember this one. Is it one you picked out, Millie?"

She shook her head.

George shrugged. "I don't remember these, and I don't know what kind they are."

"Thank you, George. Sorry to interrupt your work."

Chef Martin dismissed him, so George had no choice but to return to the cabbage rolls even though he cast puzzled glances over his shoulder at Millie.

"Chef Martin, I'm so sorry about this. I just didn't handle the situation well. Perhaps if I apologize...," her voice trailed off as Chef Martin picked up the two mushrooms and headed purposefully to the Villa side of the kitchen, motioning to Millie to follow.

"Geno, do you recognize these mushrooms?"

Geno shook his head and then called one of his chefs over. Their conversation was in rapid Italian, and then the other chef picked up one of the mushrooms, turning it over in his hand. He had a look of horror on his face when he replied to Geno.

Geno, looked a little pale as he turned to Chef Martin. "He says it looks like a species called Amanita Virosa." His expression was grim. "Also it is called Death Angel. Where did these come from?"

Millie gasped and might have collapsed except for Chef Martin's hand on her arm holding her up.

"But, Chef Martin...," Millie was close to panic. "LiAnn ate one. What will it do to her?"

Chef Geno looked horrified. "We must find her. She must go to the hospital immediately. It might already be too late," he added grimly.

"I'll go. It's my responsibility. And hopefully we'll find out where these came from."

Chef Geno spoke rapidly to his chef, then said in English for their benefit, "We will collect all the mushrooms in the kitchen. No mushrooms will be served until we find out what happened. Meanwhile, Chef Martin, I will put this one in a bag. If you take this person who has eaten one to the hospital give them this so they can make sure of what she has eaten. Perhaps that way they can identify an antidote."

"But she said it was delicious." Millie still couldn't believe it was poisonous.

Chef Geno shook his head. "Maybe it was, but still deadly. Everyone washes their hands with soap and water. And use a disinfectant. We will take no chances," he ordered sternly; he wasn't going to have a disaster come out of his kitchen.

"George. He touched them and now he's working on the cabbage rolls," Millie realized, frantic.

Chef Martin looked at her. "If he didn't wash his hands before touching the cabbage rolls, they are all to be thrown out. You will have to start over. Do you understand, Millie?

"You are in charge. Give all the mushrooms to Chef Geno for safekeeping. You will have to modify your menu."

She nodded.

Chef Martin left while Chef Geno and his chef picked up the basket of mushrooms.

Millie went back to her side of the vast kitchen area and approached Renee. "Renee, could you stop a moment and join us over where Randy and George are working. We need to discuss something."

They all waited expectantly. Of course they had noticed the conference she had with Chefs Martin and Geno and the subsequent scurry on the other side of the kitchen.

"Where's LiAnn?" George was the first to notice.

So Millie told the story once more and saw by the looks flashing across the faces of her colleagues that they understood completely.

"What is with that woman?"

"Where could she have gotten poisonous mushrooms?"

"What would have possessed her to eat one?"

"Is she all right? Can we do anything?"

Millie shook her head. "Chef Martin has gone after her. He was going to find Sam to take LiAnn to the hospital. And of course, get Marie Verde to go with them for translation sake."

"Millie, remember that day we took a walk?" George waited for her nod. "Do you remember we saw some mushrooms down there?"

She nodded again, understanding his point. "You think she picked them there? Without knowing what they were?"

"Well, you know how positive she is that she is always right. She probably thought they were mushrooms. I bet she never guessed they could be poison, otherwise, I'm sure she wouldn't have eaten one."

Millie felt sick; that poor foolish woman.

Then realizing time was marching on she rallied. "We need to make sure we clean the area thoroughly and then we're going to have to throw away the cabbage rolls and start again."

She saw their protests and shook her head again. "George says he washed his hands before returning to the cabbage rolls, but LiAnn was working on them and she had been handling the mushrooms. We can't take a chance on poisoning people."

That stopped all discussion cold.

"Did she touch anything else?" The heads shook their reply; you could see them trying to digest what Millie had just told them.

"I don't think we have enough beef for another round of cabbage rolls. Maybe we can get some from Chef Geno," Randy said.

"If he doesn't have any beef to spare we could use turkey or Italian sausage," was Renee's suggestion.

George nodded. "I'll go ask. What about the mushrooms?"

"I think we just don't serve them. They were really going to be the garnish to the lamb shanks and polenta; we'll do without. Who will know?"

The others nodded their agreement. George went to the other side of the kitchen to confer with Chef Geno. Renee returned to finish the fish rolls and Randy gathered up the cabbage rolls which needed to be destroyed. Millie cleaned the work station where the mushrooms sat before scrubbing her own hands thoroughly. Then she joined Randy to assess the amount of cabbage and sauerkraut that was still untouched. They were going to have to hustle to finish the dinner in time to get cleaned up for cocktails.

* * *

She retraced her steps, looking carefully for the street Senora Sorenson had described. There it was! But no wonder she couldn't find it. It was but a tiny passage way between two buildings, hardly even an alley. She entered the gloom, shivering slightly with excitement at being so close to the answers to her questions. The alley curved and now she could see the sign. Obviously you had to know about this restaurant, no passers-by would stumble on it by accident. Yet, when she went through the door she found it jammed with people.

"I'm meeting someone..." she started.

"Your name, please."

"Claire Gulliver."

He smiled. "Ah yes, the gentleman has been waiting. Follow me please." He led her through the entire restaurant. Claire could see it was an upscale establishment and she was glad she wore the one dress she had packed for the trip. The maitre'd led her to a tiny alcove which sat apart from the other diners. The man at the table was sitting with his back to her and hearing them approach he stood and turned toward them. She gasped, halting still in her tracks.

The maitre'd looked at her strangely, so she smiled and nodded. "Grazie."

She reached out and clasped Jack's hand. "It is really you, isn't it?"

He looked different. His hair was dark brown, with only a little gray about his ears. His eyes were brown instead of blue and his skin was still weathered, but now had a dark tan hue. All in all he looked like a native, even to the stylish suit and loafers he wore.

But his smile was the same and she relaxed as she took her seat, only then realizing she still clasped his hand. She would have pulled it free, but he wouldn't let go.

"So, you're not safe anywhere, are you?"

"This wasn't my fault. It didn't have anything to do with me." Then she paused, a thought hitting her. "It didn't, did it?"

He shook his head and she relaxed once more.

"I checked. Of course we're always looking for Guiness. And even now when everyone is watching for al Qaeda terrorists, we're still keeping our eyes open for Guiness. It would be just like him to strike now while everyone is watching another arena."

They looked up as the waiter approached. "Chardonnay?" Jack suggested, then nodded his head toward the empty glass sitting in front of him.

As soon as the waiter left Claire asked, "Jack, what are you doing here? I haven't heard from you since we left D.C." Her face fell as she remembered the terrible events which had occurred just days after she arrived home.

He nodded. "Everything changed then. I was gone the next day. I had a complete change of assignment. Everyone is stretched to the limit. I've been in this area for a few months, but now that assignment is winding down. I couldn't believe it when I heard you were here." He paused looking at her. "And in trouble. Again! Luckily I gave you that number to call. But I didn't really think you'd have to use it. I thought you were safe in Bayside."

"Well, I was. Then my mother talked me into joining her in Italy. Just a little trip to idyllic Italy she said. And..., well, you know what happened, don't you?"

"Aaron explained." Then seeing her confusion, "Aaron is the man you spoke to on the phone."

"Thank god you gave me that number. I don't want to think about what would have happened if I hadn't called." She shivered.

"Well, to set your mind at ease, Claire. Kristen is safe, thanks to you. The mole has been uncovered. I'll tell you the details later when we're alone. But I know you'll worry, so this way we can enjoy our meal." He grinned at her. "We do seem to have trouble having a decent dinner together, don't we?"

She laughed softly, remembering their broken date in York and the wild storm in Washington D.C. "I think it's you, because I usually lead a very staid existence."

"Sure you do. I wasn't anywhere near you on this trip until you made that phone call."

She nodded. That was true. She had gotten herself into this mess all by herself. But she wasn't sorry. Because if she hadn't been so determined to make sure the woman she saw wasn't her friend, Kristen, Kristen would be dead now. Goosebumps ran down her spine and she gave an involuntary shiver.

She reached for the glass of wine the waiter had just set in front of her and took a sip. It was so good she took another, and then she felt better.

"This restaurant is known for their fish. I suggest the fish soup, it's famous. Then perhaps this dish." He pointed at her menu. "It's a local fish."

She nodded and the waiter smiled his approval and left. "I'm sure it will be better than last night's meal."

"Where did you eat?"

"Some tourist trap not far from my hotel called The Blue Grotto, the Fish Grotto, or something like that. The food was expensive and inedible."

"That's a shame. Venice has a profusion of wonderful restaurants and you must have stumbled into the exception."

She changed the subject. "I got your postcards. At least I assumed they were from you as they were signed *Bernie* like the rest."

He nodded as he looked at her carefully. "You look good, Claire. I remember your laugh, your sense of humor, often your intelligence, but I guess I forgot how nice you look.

"And you've done something to your hair, haven't you?"

"And do you think of me often?" she inquired.

"Probably more than is healthy for me."

"I thought you were going to retire."

He nodded. "As did I. But when tragedy struck, duty called. Suddenly it was not a good time to worry about my own plans. You know?"

"Well, I'm sorry you're in the middle of it again. I imagine it's very dangerous for you. But speaking as an American, I'm very grateful you're on the job. I know you're good at what you do, and I'm sure we need as many people like you as we can find."

The waiter brought large bowls of steaming fish soup and, while the name sounded plain, the soup was anything but. Claire found she was hungry and eagerly ate smiling at Jack when she met his eyes over her bowl.

She was really glad to see him. Twice before he had miraculously stepped in when she was in a very tight spot. She had begun to regard him as her personal knight. She had first met him on her trip to Great Britain almost a year ago. That was the trip when she had been drafted as the tour leader after her friend, Lucy Springer, had a serious accident and became wheelchair bound, so was unable to go. When the rest of the tour members had been determined to continue on the trip, she, as one of the sponsors, albeit an inexperienced traveler felt she had to support them. Little did she know what problems she would face.

Jack had been the professional tour director supplied by Kingdom Coach Tours in London. Then he had sandy blond hair turning gray, blue eyes and an English accent. And he was cheeky. They didn't get along at first—not openly hostile, but bristling on many occasions. Then as the tour progressed, while they worked together to overcome one hurdle after another, they somehow came to rely on each other. Then they began to trust each other. When they parted at the London Airport, both felt sad their friendship was over. Of course, it wasn't. Because, as it turned out, the trip wasn't yet finished.

She paused, refusing to think about that time. She didn't need to relive all that now.

Then dipping her spoon back into the delicious soup she thought of Jack's appearance in her life last September. She had been invited to Washington D.C. to attend a board meeting at Vantage Airlines. They had wanted to thank her personally for her role in adverting disaster to their company. She hadn't been in town more than a couple of hours when someone boldly attacked her on the Washington Mall.

And the person who saved her life was none other than Jack. He was also in town, albeit for other reasons. However, since he had also been invited to the board meeting he knew she was coming. He had just missed her at her hotel, so had headed down the Mall, hoping he could catch up. He did and just in time.

She had a lot to thank Jack for. And she was relieved he was here in Venice, because when he said Kristen was safe, she could believe him.

"I guess you were hungry."

She looked at her empty bowl and smiled, nodding. "Guess so."

Then she said, "Jack, who handed me that note and how did they find me?"

"We've had someone on you since you left Florence. Didn't you notice?"

She shook her head, thinking back. "No, I didn't see anyone. They must have been good."

"I hope so; their lives depend on their skills. We just wanted to make sure no one was interested in you. We didn't want to make the mistake of protecting the wrong target."

She paled a little, but nodded. She understood. "And was anyone watching me?"

"No, no one seems to be interested in you." He grinned. "Except me of course." The waiter arrived with their plates. "So we'll talk about that later too, okay?"

She nodded happy to turn her attention to the food in front of her.

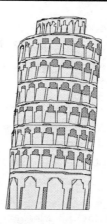

CHAPTER 15

The dining room was noisier than usual. All the participants had dressed in their best, the wine was flowing freely and the mood was festive. Chef Martin had slipped into his seat shortly after the appetizers were served, which relieved Millie's anxiety. George, who sat across the table nodded at her. He too had noticed. Ruth said in her ear, "Relax, everything must be under control if he's back. I'm sure you'll find out later what happened."

Millie nodded and felt the worry finally drop away as she concentrated on the plate before her. The crab puffs were exquisite. She couldn't wait to try this recipe when she got home. At the end of each day they had been given copies of all the recipes served to them, including those used in demonstrations and the ones the Villa provided for breakfast and lunch. Each participant would be returning home with a cookbook for their own exclusive use. And since the Villa was making arrangements to send the bulky binders home for them, they had agreed to pack and send the pottery

Millie bought. Thank god! She didn't know what she had been thinking, buying all that bulky pottery. Well, of course, she knew she was getting some beautiful pieces for a fraction of what they would cost at home, even considering what the shipping would cost. But she hadn't been thinking suitcase dimensions when she made her purchases.

She finished her glass of wine, and the waiter was right there filling it again. The wine seemed more potent tonight. It was probably because it had been a long and stressful day. She decided she best just sip or she'd be out of it before their little graduation ceremony was over. When the waiters brought in the Turbot Rolls with Hollandaise Sauce, Millie eyed the dish carefully to make sure it had been plated according to their instructions. Not only did it look beautiful, it tasted divine. The spinach and leek filling was just right, enhancing but not overpowering the delicate flavor of the fish, while the Hollandaise Sauce they used was the perfect way to complete it. The rest of the group seemed to appreciate the dish. And just as they finished, the waiters whisked away those plates replacing them with dishes of cabbage rolls, simmered in sauerkraut. And then finally, the lamb shanks in rich dark gravy on polenta, their *coup de grace*.

"Wonderful. Superb!" Stephen breathed his approval.

Considering his occupation Millie felt pride swell her head. George winked at her and did a thumbs-up sign to Randy and Renee further down the table.

"Millie, you did yourself proud. What a wonderful combination." Even Ruth was in awe of the dishes.

When the dinner plates were cleared away, the waiters passed around small dishes of peach champagne sorbet to cleanse their palates before the dessert course. And of course, bottles of dessert wine were poured.

Millie took a tiny sip of the sweet wine, then rolling the wine around on her tongue, tossed caution to the wind and took a bigger swallow. If she had a headache in the morning she'd just live with it. After all tomorrow was only a travel day; she didn't need to have her wits about her.

Ruth's Group B succeeded in capping this wonderful meal with outstanding desserts. It was hard to only taste them. Millie's spoon seemed to have a will of its own as it dipped repeatedly into the trio of offerings which had been plated together so everyone had all three at once.

Ruth kept a running description of the preparations going, so all those sitting near her felt as if they had been in the kitchen with her. But nobody minded, because every dessert was outstanding. And while they might not have been in Group B they all wanted to have made these desserts.

Then it was time for the final critique. Everyone was aware that this was the last time they would be together. The comments were enthusiastic and kind.

"I loved the cabbage rolls. But in my country, Croatia, we use paprika to flavor and add color to them."

"Ah, but here in Italy we don't use the sauerkraut. We use a tomato sauce. But I liked this variation."

"The lamb shanks were wonderful. I'm so glad to have this recipe."

"I agree the shanks were divine, some of the best, but I think they needed a vegetable to share the polenta. The plate looked a little bare," Stephen offered.

Michael nodded. "Yes, mushrooms would have been the perfect addition."

Millie nodded seriously, afraid to look at George, not wanting to give anything away by her expression.

Chef Martin stood, held up his hands until everyone quieted. Even the waiters clearing the last of the dishes paused. Absolute quiet fell.

"Ladies and Gentlemen, on our last night of class it gives me much pleasure to turn this over to Rafael Angelino, who you will remember from our introductory luncheon. He represents the Italian Culinary Association, which sponsors this annual Retreat.

Rafael got to his feet, grinning widely. When finally the clapping died away he began, "Thank you all. I have been in constant communication with Chef Martin; with Chef Geno here at the Villa and, of course, with Marie Verde who has spent her time making sure that all events were coordinated perfectly. I believe I can safely proclaim this has been the finest Retreat we have had."

The applause bolstered by cheers and whistles made it clear that everyone agreed.

"I know you have worked hard and I, myself, have witnessed the fruits of your labors at this truly magnificent meal..." again the applause drowned him out and he waited patiently for it to die away.

"It gives me great pleasure to award your certificates of completion and a few tokens of gratitude from the Italian Culinary Association." He held up one of the mushroom shaped hats like the ones they had worn in the kitchen, only these had their names and "*5th Annual Italian Culinary Retreat, Villa Tuscany, 2002*" embroidered in blue on the band which went around the head. And he held up chef jackets, similar to the ones Chef Martin and Chef Geno wore, which were also marked with their names and the Retreat logo.

The participants smiled and clapped once more.

"Oh, we're going to look so good in those it will be hard to stay in the kitchen. When we cook dinner for the Richman brothers and their wives we have to go into the dining room so they can see how good we look," Ruth whispered happily to Millie.

Millie agreed, nothing like some of the trimmings to enhance the dish, or in this case, the chef. She had been planning a thank you dinner for her former bosses since she arrived at the Culinary Retreat, and Ruth had insisted she would act as her assistant chef. She said it would be like final exams.

Then each person went to the front table when their name was called, took their jacket and hat, received their certificate and shook hands with everyone. When it was Millie's turn, Chef Martin clasped her hand in both of his and said quietly for her ears alone, "Ms. Gulliver, I will bring you up to date later. Will you be in the lounge celebrating with the rest?"

She nodded.

"Good, I'll find you."

And she moved on to hug Wanda and thank her for all her support.

* * *

It was truly a lovely dinner. Because they were in the little alcove, they could talk without the worry of other diners overhearing their conversation. While they didn't discuss Kristen or any of Claire's recent experiences they were free to talk about England, last year when they met, and Washington DC where they had been together in the previous September. And they talked about Jack's daughter as well as Claire's bookshop. Claire told him about the Lickman's Christmas present, Tuffy-Two, the West Highland Terrier puppy who had taken over the hearts of all who came to the bookstore. She explained how she had been awarded a VIP Card at Vantage Airlines and the benefits which went along with that honor. And she told him about her mother's recent retirement and her current visit to the Italian Culinary Retreat in Tuscany. They discussed the terrible tragedy of 9/11 and how it had affected their lives as well as the world. They dawdled over their coffees, nibbling the tiny biscotti served to them, but finally it was plainly time to leave.

When they emerged from the tiny alley onto the quay alongside of the Grand Canal, they turned without speaking to stroll past the Rialto Bridge.

"So, I've been very patient. Now tell me what happened to Kristen."

Jack nodded. "She's safe. She called as planned and we had people watching. So after the mole passed the information to his contact he was picked up. They then followed his contact. It led, just as Kristen expected, to Sonny's father, who had arranged through his Italian based family for the assassins."

It was what Claire expected. She knew there was a traitor leaking information about Kristen, but she was still shocked. "Who was it? What did he say? Why did he do it?"

Jack shook his head. "So many questions. It was Kristen's contact. He's been with the U.S. Marshall's office for almost thirty-five years. He was getting ready for retirement and felt the need to pad his nest egg. He had apparently reached a point where he just didn't care anymore. He should have been out of there years before, but...." He shrugged helplessly. "Sometimes people lose sight of their purpose. They get disillusioned. Then they can be very dangerous to people like me. And to people like Kristen who rely on them for their life. So now this man has lost his pension. He won't need it where he's going. He will be spending his retirement in a Federal Prison.

"Who knows how many others he has sold out during his career?"

Jack looked at her carefully. "So once more you were right. Every time Kristen called in to report, her location was passed on to the men who were hunting her. Had she called in again, Sunday from Vernazza, neither of you would be here now to worry about the mole."

Claire shivered. Jack put his arm around her and pulled her close to him until she relaxed again. Then he whispered in her ear, "But, something amazing happened."

She pulled her head back to see his face clearer. "What? What happened?"

He shook his head, his eyes smiled, and then it reached his lips. "Just when you're beginning to think there is no justice in the world something astounding happens."

"Are you going to tell me or just let me dangle here?" Claire was impatient.

"Sonny was attacked in the prison yard yesterday. We heard about it last night. It seems he was bucking the system inside and the man in charge took exception to it. They got him alone and that's all there is."

Claire gasped. "You mean they killed him?"

Jack nodded. "Yep, they got his buddies off on some pretext and then waited for him to show. Sonny was used to doing his own thing. He always had, you see. His old man had always protected him. So naturally he expected to be able to do what he wanted in prison too.

"It didn't work."

"So Kristen is safe?" Claire said slowly, trying to absorb all the ramifications of Jack's story. "She can go back to her old life?"

"Well, she's safe enough now. No one came for her and we know the information about her location got to Sonny's father. So obviously the word is out. We doubt they will pursue her now as there will be no trial. She is no longer a threat to Sonny.

"But I don't think she can just go back to her old life. After all, she died, didn't she? It would be very awkward for her to show up again. No, I think they will help her establish a new identify, to build a new life as they promised. But this life will be much safer, and she should be able to include her family.

"So she will be much better off than she is now, even if it will never be the same as it was before the incident. She has been very brave and very resourceful. Everyone was very impressed with her."

"Can I get in touch with her?"

"Not just yet. They're still keeping her hidden, but I'm sure she will contact you not too far in the future. She seems to credit you with saving her life a few times." Jack grinned widely, looking at her with admiration. "You do have a way about you, Claire."

They walked silently for a while, Claire trying to absorb the story Jack had told her. Eventually, Jack paused and started talking to one of the boatmen clustered at the edge of the canal. Obviously he was fluent in Italian judging by the hand movements which accompanied the rapid-fire words. Claire couldn't understand anything they said, but when the deal was struck she carefully stepped into the middle of the gondola. Holding the boatman's hand to steady herself, she let herself be led to the back where there was a comfortable seat for two under a canopy. She had no more than gotten settled when the boat rocked violently with Jack's passage. He sat close to her, wrapping his arm possessively around her.

The gondola glided quietly through the canal and then turned right into a smaller canal running between the buildings very much like the canals going past her hotel. When the man poling their gondola broke into song, she smiled with pleasure at Jack.

"Thank you. It's perfect."

They slid through the dark water, the still night around them, the notes of the gondolier's song enveloping them. It was everything romantics described about Venice. It was what she saw last night looking out her window before the late night garbage scows started their rounds, which were not at all romantic. It was wonderful drifting along and Jack's kisses were heady too.

The gondolier let them off on the right side of the canal and they headed toward Claire's hotel.

"Nice room?"

"Not the greatest but it's very central, clean and looks out on the canals."

"You could show it to me."

It took a moment for his meaning to penetrate. She looked at him aghast.

"Oh, I couldn't."

He looked at her strangely.

She giggled. "Sorry, that didn't come out right. But you see we'd have to ask Sister Marie Terese for the key, and I just couldn't be brazen enough to drag you with me, ask her for the key and then go upstairs with you. It would just be too shocking for her."

"You're staying in a nunnery?" Jack was incredulous.

"No, not exactly but there was a death, you see. And Senore Sorenson's sister, Sister Marie Terese is staying with her during the mourning period. She is helping out and she is always at the desk." Then Claire stopped and looked at Jack seriously. "Jack, you know I like you very, very much. And of course I find you attractive, you know that, don't you?"

He nodded, watching her carefully.

"But Jack, I have to tell you I'm not sure I want to get seriously involved with you."

He didn't say anything, just waited for her to continue.

"Every time we've been together I've nearly died. So I'm not sure if my heart beats faster from your proximately or from fear. And, while I appreciate what you and your colleagues do to protect the country, I'm not sure people in your business make good mates."

She put her hand up, momentarily halting his protest, and then she continued. "I'm perfectly aware you haven't indicated that you're looking for a mate, but Jack, I'm just not a person who does well with casual relationships. If we were to become intimate..., well, I'm afraid it would be very serious for me. So I think we're not at that point yet, are we?"

"Well, since you put it that way, maybe not." He smiled nervously, but she could see the disappointment in his eyes.

* * *

"Millie, I want to buy you another. What are you drinking?" Randy had more than a few himself, as had most of them.

"Thank you. I'm just having Pellegrino with lime," she told him. She had switched to the bottled water after the first drink. One of the advantageous of getting older is recognizing your limitations and adhering to them.

The waitress soon returned with their drinks just as George and Ruth joined them.

"Randy says you're all going to have a reunion and cook a fabulous meal."

Ruth nodded.

Millie said, "Randy doesn't live far from us. Actually he lives very close to my daughter in Bayside. That's south of San Francisco."

"I, too, am going to cook a great meal, but only to demonstrate to my wife and son what a good investment it was for me to take this class."

"Was it what you wanted?" Millie inquired remembering on the first night George had said he wanted to offer more Italian dishes on the menu at his inn.

He nodded. "My head is swirling with ideas for new menu items."

"Probably just dizzy from all the drinks," was Randy's droll contribution. They all laughed acknowledging there was some truth to the statement.

Just then Chef Martin approached. "Ms. Gulliver, could I have a few moments of your time?" He smiled at the others and led Millie out of the lounge area.

Her heart was beating wildly, wanting to know what had happened to LiAnn, yet afraid to hear. Both LiAnn and Sam were absent from the final dinner and while people had inquired, they had seemed satisfied with the explanation that LiAnn was not feeling well. Of course, Group C knew more, as did Ruth; they would wait anxiously until Millie reported back to them about what she had learned.

Chef Martin led Millie through the lobby and into a tiny conference room. She was surprised to find Chef Geno, Rafael Angelino and Marie Verde already sitting there; all with somber expressions on their faces. Right then she knew her assumption on seeing Chef Martin return to the dinner was false; everything was not all right.

"LiAnn..." she started.

Chef Martin shook his head and Millie felt the blood drain from her face.

"She's...she's dead?" She could hardly get the words out.

"No. No, she is not dead, yet." Chef Martin was visibly upset.

Chef Geno started to explain. "These Death Angels are truly that. She just didn't realize how dangerous they were. Even now she insists she is all right and wants to be released from the hospital." He shrugged; his expression one of pure disbelief. "But these mushrooms attack the liver, sometimes it takes three to four days before the cramps and diarrhea occurs." He lifted his hands helplessly. "By then it is attacking the central nervous system and the kidneys."

"There is no hope." Marie Verde spoke quietly, calmly, her certainty convincing.

Millie felt the room tilt and then Chef Martin and Chef Geno pushed her head down, nearly in her lap. Marie Verde told her to breathe in and out through her mouth. Slowly the room stopped spinning and cautiously she sat up, blinking rapidly trying to process what she had been told.

"But why? Why did she add those mushrooms to the ones we bought? What was she thinking?" She looked at each of the faces hoping for a clue.

Chef Geno answered. "She is not right in the head." He made the universal sign by twirling his forefinger in a circle above his ear. "Her husband says she is determined their grandson win the Culinary Olympics this year. His team came in second during the last Olympics and she was shamed. Rather than being proud of his accomplishments she felt the entire family had lost face.

"You know how some Chinese regard face. It is very important to them.

"Anyway, she apparently decided she needed to make sure Chef Martin didn't win again, so her grandson could. So when she heard about the Retreat she thought she could somehow keep him from competing or at least upset him to the degree he would not be able to perform up to his usual standard."

Chef Martin looked uncomfortable. "It's crazy. It's like that story of the Texas woman who hired someone to kill the cheerleader's mother so the cheerleader would be distracted and her daughter would get on the squad. Remember that story?"

Millie nodded, that outrageous story had been in the papers and eventually made into a movie. Rafael Angelino and Marie Verde were clearly appalled at LiAnn's scheme; it was obvious on their faces.

"Sam Ng said he thought he had talked her out of the notion. But he agreed to attend the Retreat with her. She said she wanted to see for herself how good Chef Martin was.

"He knew she tampered with the ingredients in that first demonstration. Remember the salty ricotta? It upset him, but he didn't think it dangerous. That didn't satisfy her, so she somehow engineered the accident at the winery. He didn't know she did it until he heard about it later and she refused to discuss it. But he says he's sure she was behind it as it was too perfect to be a coincidence."

Millie looked open-mouthed at Chef Martin. She had really saved his life. LiAnn intended him physical harm.

"Sam didn't know where the dead mouse came from, but he knew LiAnn had planted it in the flour as soon as she screamed and ran. He says she has never been squeamish in her life. Her actions were clearly meant to draw attention to the lump in the flour and that told him she was responsible. That's when he told her she had to stop her campaign to distract Chef Martin, but she insisted she was innocent.

"Then apparently on Monday she tried to cause a fire in the kitchen, but one of your group interfered and so it didn't work. That sent her into a rage."

He looked around at all the faces checking to make sure they were following him. "That's when she got desperate. She had only one more day to achieve her goal, you see. Apparently that's when she decided on the mushrooms. She had seen them when she had been out on her early morning walk, so she knew just where they were. She thought she would purchase the mushrooms in the market and then add the ones she was carrying to them so no one would be the wiser. She says these mushrooms are just like ones she has seen in China. She admits they would make everyone who ate them sick, but she's sure they are not deadly. She had not intended that she or Sam would eat them, but when Millie challenged her in the kitchen she became so furious that her plan was once more falling apart, she ate one just to show her contempt. She was willing to be sick just to put Millie in her place." He shrugged helplessly. "In a few days she will change her mind."

Millie couldn't help her tears. Marie Verde pulled a small package of tissues from her purse and offered it to Millie.

"I'm sorry, it's all so stupid. And sad...," Millie wiped at her eyes. "She wanted her grandson to win so badly she was willing to hurt someone, make all of us sick to achieve it? How could she? What will her grandson think of her?"

"Sam Ng blames himself. He says he, as well as the whole family has always catered to LiAnn. They have loved and admired her guts, her tenaciousness, so they have always done whatever she wanted. But recently she has been becoming more and more erratic. He thinks maybe it's her age. Or maybe she's not well. But she thinks she is right. She believes her behavior has been heroic."

They all sat there silently, trying to absorb the horror of what they heard.

"What will happen now?"

Rafael answered Millie's question. "Sam has told her she cannot leave the hospital for four days while she is under observation. During that time they will search for a liver transplant donor. If they find one she may have a chance. However, even with the liver transplant she may not make it as already the poison is spreading through her body. Her children, as well as some of her grandchildren, are on their way here."

Millie remembered talking to the Ng's about their large, scattered family. "Are they sure the mushroom she ate was one of these, these Death Angels? Couldn't it have been a variety of one she knew from Hong Kong?"

Marie Verde shook her head. "The tests were conclusive. It is definitely the Death Angel. We were told by the doctor that people who have eaten them report they tasted delicious. But they died anyway."

Millie shuddered; she couldn't believe it had come to this.

"Ms. Gulliver, we are all in your debt," Rafael announced solemnly. Chef Geno nodded vigorously.

"Yes, yes. Here at Villa Tuscany there has never been a hint of sickness. We take great pains to make sure our kitchen turns out delicious and healthy meals. If these mushrooms had been cooked and served, not only would all these people have died, but the reputation of the Villa, perhaps even the Villa itself would have been destroyed."

Chef Martin looked into her eyes. "What more can I add. You have truly been my guardian angel, Ms. Gulliver. You saved me from injury in the winery at great risk to your own self and now you detected the poisonous mushrooms and prevented them from being served to the class. I thank you for all of us. You are a brave, resourceful woman."

Millie didn't know what to do, what to say, so she just sat there.

"What about the other participants? Will you tell them?" Millie asked dreading having to go back to the lounge and tell her friends.

Rafael shook his head. "I don't see any reason the others need to know."

"But the rest of our group knows about the mushrooms, Randy, Renee and George were in the kitchen when it happened. And my friend, Ruth, she also knows about it. They'll want to know."

The others looked at each other. Rafael looked at Marie. "Can you talk to those four, Marie. You can explain without over-explaining, can you not?"

She didn't look happy about the task but she agreed.

"And will the police question LiAnn? Will there be charges?"

Rafael shook his head saying quietly, "For what purpose. If LiAnn should recover she will be only a shadow of her former self. Quite possibly she would be bed-ridden for the remainder of her life. But, truthfully, there is almost no hope of recovery. She has administered her own punishment."

There wasn't anything else to say. When Millie felt her legs would support her she stood saying to Marie Verde, "Please tell Ruth that I went up to the room and will not be joining them again. I would appreciate it."

Millie hoped she could get to her room without collapsing. She need not have worried because Chef Martin offered her his arm and escorted her gallantly to her door. She noticed his complexion was pasty and he too, looked like he was feeling just about as devastated as she was.

"Good night, Ms. Gulliver, and I thank you again from the bottom of my heart for what you have done for me." And he left her to sort out her thoughts.

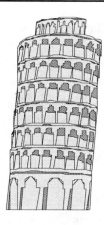

CHAPTER 16

Ruth and Millie arrived for breakfast later than usual. Their packing was done. Millie carried her pottery down to the desk for shipping while Ruth lugged the two hefty binders. Neither of them had slept well. When Ruth had finally returned to their room, Millie, still wide awake despite the late hour, had to repeat the entire conversation from the conference room. Then they had discussed LiAnn's behavior from every possible angle, but they still couldn't understand her.

When they finally went to bed neither slept. They lay silently in the dark still puzzling it out. Unfortunately, as they didn't think like she did, they were never going to understand LiAnn's actions.

Before settling at a table in the dining room, they visited all the other tables of participants to say their good-byes. They collected street addresses, phone numbers and e-mail addresses. They promised everyone they would stay in touch even though they all knew time and distractions would cause them to procrastinate.

"Now don't forget you promised me a visit in Connecticut," Marybeth reminded them. "You can stay with me and even work with me in the kitchen, if you want. It would be so much fun. I'd love to have you, and I promise I have room for you both." She really wanted them to come.

Jacques was very sad at losing Ruth. She had become his friend and his mentor. "But I will come to San Francisco, I promise."

Millie and Ruth agreed they would see him again and probably soon.

Helga and Frederick had left earlier, so they missed saying good-bye to them. But, truthfully, they hadn't gotten close to the couple, mostly because of the language barrier, but also because of their stiff formal manner. Zoe had hugged each of them good-bye in the lobby. Her transportation was waiting for her. Stephen, they knew they would see later. He would be leaving with Chef Martin, since he was going to London for the Culinary Olympics. Michael had said his good-byes to everyone last night as he had left before breakfast this morning to catch his train to Cannes.

Finally they sat at a table and smiled at the waiter who had poured their coffee. "It's so sad," Millie said. "It's only been a week, but it seems we've all become so close. And now we'll be spread all over the globe."

"Ah, but look at all the places we'll have reason to visit."

"Now, Ruth, just because you talked me into coming to Italy, it doesn't mean I've turned into a globe-trotter like you. I like San Francisco. I love my little house, my safe neighborhood. I'm content there. And even though this was a wonderful experience and I'm truly grateful to you and Claire for talking me into coming, I'll be glad to get home. I'm just not very adventuresome," Millie told her friend seriously. "But I am glad we're going to Venice before going home. I've always wondered if it was as beautiful as it looks in the paintings. And of course I'll be glad to see Claire. I wonder how she's doing."

They were just finishing their coffee when Chef Martin stopped at their table and asked if he might sit with them a moment.

"Of course." Millie gestured to the empty chair. "Would you like some coffee?"

"No, thanks, I've had my limit already today." He looked at each of them, then his eyes stopped on Millie's face and he said gravely, "LiAnn's children have begun to arrive. Two arrived this morning, three more will come later today and I believe some more tonight. Early this morning she started having symptoms."

They all were silent contemplating those ominous words.

Chef Martin continued. "Sam tells me she now is beginning to believe we were telling her the truth about the mushrooms."

He shook his head. "He was very upset when I talked to him. And why not? The whole episode is so stupid, so senseless."

Millie paled. So much for LiAnn's determination that she was right about the mushrooms. It didn't work for her this time.

"But how are you feeling, Chef Martin? Will you win the Olympics?" Ruth asked.

"Do you mean will LiAnn's strategy work?" Chef Martin thought a moment then answered slowly, "No, I don't think these little incidents she engineered would have really affected anything." He shook his head vigorously. "No, no. After all, we have all learned to block out problems and worries while we're concentrating, haven't we? Really they were only minor annoyances.

"Of course if the fork lift had hit me, or the mushrooms had been eaten, I would have been stopped. And several others too, I think.

"But you know these Olympics are always very competitive. It never can be predicted who will win. It is really an honor just to compete. I'm surprised LiAnn didn't understand that.

"We are never told what key ingredient has been selected until the competition begins. Then we have to use it to prepare six dishes, including an appetizer, a first course, a second course and a desert. As it is impossible to plan ahead what you will be cooking it really depends equally on luck and skill to win."

He looked sad. "I heard that LiAnn's grandson has withdrawn from the competition because of what his grandmother did. So he now has no chance of winning, and he will probably never enter again. It will always be a painful reminder to her family. So it turns out her determination he win, only succeeded in assuring that he never would."

An awkward silence fell on the table. It was so horrible none of them knew what to say.

Chef Martin looked at Millie. "Ms. Gulliver, I believe you know I have a restaurant in New York City called Jean Claude's?"

Millie nodded as did Ruth. They knew. Everyone talked about it and it was mentioned frequently in the newspapers and magazines. It was where the beautiful people dined.

"Well, every year it has been my policy to accept a few promising students of the culinary arts to intern at the restaurant. Usually they spend three to four months working in the kitchen, hopefully benefiting from their exposure to the work we do, the dishes we prepare.

"As you can imagine the competition for these positions is somewhat intense. We do pay a modest salary to help our interns cover expenses. These people work hard and long hours.

"At any rate, what I'm trying to say is that I would be very pleased, Ms. Gulliver, if you would consider accepting one of these positions."

Millie's mouth dropped open, she was momentarily stunned.

Ruth, too, was amazed, looking from Chef Martin to Millie, speechless.

"Ms. Gulliver, perhaps I haven't described this opportunity appropriately, but rest assured an internship at Jean Claude's would certainly give your reputation a boost. I'm sure it would enhance your standing as a caterer.

"I have been impressed with your work as well as being the happy beneficiary of your competence and quick action. I would like to do something for you that would be of value to you. You understand?"

Millie nodded mutely.

"So, perhaps you will think about this? We have an open slot in the fall. If that is not convenient perhaps we could arrange another time that is." He removed his wallet from his pocket and extracted a business card. He fished a pen from his jacket pocket and scribbled on the back of the card before handing it to Millie. "Keep this and think about my offer. My secretary will be contacting you in a few weeks to pursue this idea. I would love to work with you again."

Then he stood up, smiled at Millie before turning to Ruth. "And I've enjoyed working with you, too, Ms. Clarkson. You have certainly contributed to the success of this Retreat. And I have heard that you have recovered your tuition fees at the card table." They could see the laughter in his eyes. "Good luck both of you and I hope to talk to you, Ms. Gulliver, soon."

He left Millie to scan the card he had handed her.

"What does it say?" Ruth was reaching for it, as excited as if she had been invited herself. "Millie, what a wonderful opportunity this is.

"Now you'll have to consider your clothes. It will get very cold in New York in the fall.

"I wonder if your room will be big enough for company. No matter, when I come to visit I can sleep on the couch or even get one of those inflatable mattresses for the floor."

Then she exclaimed with girlish excitement, "Oh, Millie, we could go up on the train and visit Marybeth. She's not that far from New York City."

Millie shook her head, putting her hands up as if to ward off Ruth's enthusiasm. "Just a minute Ruth, what makes you think I'm going to accept his offer."

"Not accept? Millie, tell me you're not even thinking of not accepting. It is a chance of a lifetime. He's right you know. After studying with Chef Martin at Jean Claude's your success as a caterer will be assured. It's a wonderful opportunity."

"Ruth, this whole thing is getting way out of hand. I just wanted to cook. I thought I could just make tasty, nutritious meals for people who didn't have the time or skill to prepare decent meals after a busy day at work." Millie shook her head with frustration. "Then the Richman brothers generously gave me this trip to the Retreat as a farewell present. They meant well, but truthfully I would have been happy with a gold watch. Now I have this internship offer. It's too much!

"I wasn't expecting to be a big name. I just want the fun and satisfaction of cooking while I transition into retirement. Suddenly I'm being propelled into big name status.

"Frankly, I find it frightening."

Ruth's eyes got big. "Millie, you need to think about this. You need to talk to Claire. Don't make any decisions now. Promise me?"

Millie nodded, reluctantly. Ruth was right. She did need to consider this opportunity carefully. She glanced at her watch.

"Ruth, we've got to get moving. It's almost time for our transportation to the train station to leave and we need to go upstairs to get our things."

So they did.

* * *

"Oh, there she is." Millie waved her hand at Claire as she dragged her wheelie bag across the vast lobby towards the Tourist Information sign.

She threw her arms around her daughter, who, while she now towered over her mother, was still her little girl. "Oh, I'm so glad to see you. Have you been having fun?" Then she drew back and looked at her. "You look different. It's your hair. You did something with your hair."

"I think she forgot to comb it when she got up this morning," Ruth stated as she looked closely at Claire's casual style. "And it's lighter. Claire, you had it lightened, didn't you?" she accused.

"Oh, Ruth, it's combed. Don't you see it's like those styles you now see on all the film stars? They make it look mussed, don't they Claire?" She nodded her head in approval. "I like it. It makes you look more modern, I think. Don't you like it, Ruth?"

But Ruth's attention was fixed on the man hovering behind Claire suspecting he was lingering for no good. "Who's this?" she demanded.

Claire laughed. "I'm glad you like it, Mom. I think it grows on you. I just had it done yesterday. I thought I needed a change. And I am on vacation after all."

She reached behind her and grabbed Jack's hand propelling him forward. "This is a friend of mine, Jack Rallins."

Both Ruth and Millie were surprised into silence.

"Mom, I'm sure you remember me talking about my friend, Jack, who I met on my trip to England. Then we saw each other again in Washington D.C. last September."

Millie nodded, vaguely remembering some mention of this person.

"Well, I ran into Jack on the vaporetti yesterday. Isn't that odd?" She smiled, obviously pleased at the chance encounter, although both her mother and Ruth had suspicious expressions. "He's going to be in Venice for a few days and is going to show us around.

He's been here many times and, as he has been a tour guide from time to time, I'm sure he will help us make the most of our time here."

Jack turned on his charm and soon the women's suspicions melted under the force of his personality, just as the tour members had succumbed to him on the trip through England and Wales. It wasn't long before he had both wheelie bags in hand and was ushering them towards the vaporetti stop, entertaining them with stories of his previous visits to Venice. Claire hugged her mother as she walked beside her, carrying her stuffed tote bag.

"It doesn't look like you have room for much shopping here in Venice, Mom. This bag is pretty full."

"Don't you worry dear; I've learned a great travel secret."

Claire looked at her with expectation.

"What you can't carry, you ship." Her mother laughed gaily.

Claire laughed happily along with her. She was glad to see her mother, and it was obvious she had enjoyed the Retreat because she seemed in such a carefree mood. Claire had some misgivings about her part in convincing her mother to take advantage of the Richman brothers' gift. Her mother had always been such a homebody and she was very reluctant about this trip. She would have blamed herself if it had been a bad experience for her. But now she couldn't wait to hear all about it. And while her mother and Ruth were telling them about the Retreat, Claire, wouldn't have to talk about her own experiences.

* * *

They arrived at the side door of the Chiesa dei Frari (Franciscan Church) early. Jack had said the church itself was worth a visit, and being early would guarantee them a seat for the concert. Claire was disappointed with the church's appearance. It seemed plain after seeing the Duomos of Florence and Sienna. And it certainly didn't compare favorably with San Marco. But, she noticed looking around they were the only tourists in sight. This was the real thing. It was a typical Venice neighborhood. But all thoughts of normalcy fled her mind as they entered the church. The inside was spectacular. It seemed incredible to them that this was just a neighborhood church as evidenced by the table in the back where the Italian equivalent to the Ladies' Altar Society displayed handmade goods for sale. Yet from the back looking to the high altar through the elaborate carved screen, which separated a section which Jack whispered was where the monk's choir sat, they had a clear view of the Titian painting, *Assumption of the Virgin.* Even from that distance it gleamed with light.

Claire shivered in excitement. It was just so wonderful. They worked their way up to the side altar to see the wood carving of *St. John the Baptist* by Donatello and another painted masterpiece by Bellini before taking seats on one of the heavily carved benches in the monk's choir section. Now people were arriving and the space was filling rapidly.

"I can't believe this art is just sitting here," Millie whispered in her daughter's ear. "Where are the guards? Aren't they worried about theft?"

Claire shook her head, she didn't know. At home, treasures like these would be locked away. Even in San Marco's she had seen numerous custodians guarding their treasures, while here this painting was just as it had been installed, in the place of honor over the altar, centuries ago. It was wonderful.

But when the music started they were transported. It was a small section of the Milan Orchestra along with a group of guitarists. And there was a choir and soloists. The audience was held spellbound until finally the music ended and they silently filed out into the dark streets of Venice.

"That is what all concerts should be. That is how all churches should be used. That music and the beauty of that church make you feel there is a heaven," Ruth whispered as they walked through the dark shadowy streets, really only lanes, toward their hotel.

Millie just smiled, nodding, not even wanting to speak, afraid it would break the spell the music had spun over them.

"Jack, thank you for taking us. That was a real treat." Ruth's voice was slightly above a whisper now. The further they got from the church the more the spell was broken for her.

"Don't thank me. Claire saw the notice at the museum and thought it would be a nice experience. We got the information at the Tourist Information Bureau when we came to meet you."

He looked at Claire. "It was great. It's the kind of thing your friend, Lucy, would have suggested if we had been in England."

Claire nodded. "Lucy would have loved it. I hope I can describe it adequately so she'll understand how wonderful it was." Then she shrugged. "Maybe it's another of those things you just have to experience."

"The soprano was magnificent." Millie was still smiling. "Can you imagine being able to sing like that? You know I've always wished I believed in re-incarnation."

"What? Why?" Claire was surprised at her mother's comment.

"Because it would be nice to think that you could come back again." She looked at her daughter as she added seriously, "I would like to come back next time with a voice like that. Wouldn't it be heavenly to stand in that beautiful old church, in front of that Titian masterpiece and open your mouth and have that wonderful voice spill out?"

Ruth laughed. "Well, if I had a choice I think I'd come back as Tuffy-Two."

"You'd come back as a dog?" Millie shook her head. "A dog? What kind of life is that?"

"I think that little dog has it made. What a life! Claire, Mrs. B and all the customers dote on it and Theroux, the cat, protects him. People feed him, walk him, play with him and rub his belly every time he rolls on his back. It looks like a life of ease to me."

They all had to laugh except Jack, who only knew the original Tuffy who lived with the Lickmans in Maryland.

"What about you, Claire? What would you like to do?"

Claire looked at Jack. "You know, I kind of like it just as it is. I know that sounds dull, but truthfully, I love my life. And what adventure I do have is more than enough to satisfy me. Actually, I wouldn't mind a little more dullness."

Jack nodded. "Well, I don't believe in re-incarnation so I don't even think about doing it again. Once is enough for me."

Then they started talking about their plans for the next day. They would be leaving for home the following day, so they needed to get the most out of their day as possible.

Their hotel was just ahead when Jack, apparently reluctant for the evening to end said, "It's really not late. How about trying a Bellini at Harry's Bar?"

"Uh huh, not me. I'm operating on too little sleep right now. I'm looking forward to bed. Thanks anyway."

Millie shook her head, agreeing with Ruth. "You two go on. We're ready for bed. We need a good night's sleep so we can do everything we have planned for tomorrow. Just tiptoe when you come in, Claire."

Claire and Jack watched them enter the hotel and then turned towards the bar. Claire said, "I'm surprised. Ruth is usually ready to party until the last person drops. They must have been up late last night."

"Well, maybe they were just being nice and giving us some time together." Jack slipped his arm around her waist as they moved through the night.

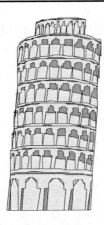

CHAPTER 17

It was quite early, but both Sister Marie Terese and Senora Sorenson were at the desk, smiling warmly, as they checked out.

"Please, you will come again?" Sister Marie Terese said, obviously proud of the words she struggled so hard to say.

"We had a wonderful time." Millie indicated the pile of baggage, boxes and totes near the door. "We shopped too much in Murano."

"Thank you so much for your hospitality," Claire chimed in. "Grazie," she said to Sister Marie Terese.

"Come on," Ruth called from the door. "Jack's here with the water taxi."

It took a few minutes to get everything safely stowed on the taxi and get settled inside the small cabin before the taxi driver made his way through the fog shrouded canals.

"This is a much better idea than trying to transport all this stuff on the vaporetti, Jack. Thanks for suggesting it." Claire had been warned about the cost of the water taxis, but Jack said with four of them sharing the cost it was actually reasonable to travel this way and much more convenient. And as he insisted on paying the whole tab, it was going to be very inexpensive.

Claire tried to drink in the sight of Venice as they passed the picturesque palaces, their outlines now softened by the fog. She wasn't able to resist snapping a few last pictures. She hated to leave. Venice was truly a unique spot and, she sighed remembering the gondola ride in the inky night, very romantic.

"I loved Murano. I know I bought too much, but it was all so beautiful."

"Not all of it. I can live without some of those ornate chandeliers we saw." Ruth made a face.

"Well, you're right. Not all of it. But that one place we found with all that aged glass, which looked like bottles dug up from archeological digs, was fabulous. And I loved all those little colored bottles."

Ruth nodded. "And those wine glasses Claire bought were exquisite. I hope they arrive safely." She didn't trust the mails and had insisted on carrying the pieces she bought on the plane.

Claire shrugged. "They're insured and the shop will make them good if they do break. I think we all have to take a lesson from Jack." She gestured to the one backpack Jack had. He obviously traveled very lightly.

"How do you do that, Jack?" Ruth was curious. "I've seen you for three days now, so I know you're not wearing the same thing each day."

Jack smiled. "Almost. Two pairs of trousers, one I wear. I have a Windbreaker that's waterproof, a jacket that doesn't wrinkle, and three shirts. One of those I wear. Same goes for underwear and socks. And an extra pair of shoes. I have a comb, razor and toothbrush. What else do you need?"

The three women looked at him amazed.

"I think life is much simpler for men," Millie announced.

Ruth nodded. "Must be. I was so proud of myself for only using the one wheelie bag. And even then I cheated by getting one that has a gusset which can be unzipped so the bag stretches to a larger size."

Jack shook his head. "It's too much trouble to get those on and off trains, boats and buses. The backpack is the way to go."

Ruth shook her head. "It'll never happen. Women just need more stuff. But I admire your style."

Claire almost spoke up about traveling with Kristen with only a backpack, but remembered in time and made an inane comment instead. She could understand why Jack traveled so lightly, but Ruth and her mother didn't even know what Jack did. So they didn't understand his work didn't allow for the luxuries they thought they had to have. He only wanted to get from place to place alive. He didn't need travel guides, skin lotion, dress up clothes or swim suits. And she had found out she didn't need them either. But she didn't intend to travel that way again even though she now knew she could.

"And that place we had lunch was perfect. What a find. Did anybody get the name?"

They all looked at each other, then Ruth laughed. "Well, we won't be ruining it by telling everyone about it, will we?"

Claire shook her head, thinking that she might be able to describe its location if she wanted to recommend it. Jack found it for them. He had taken one of the workers at the last glass factory aside and asked him where to have lunch. Finally when the man understood they didn't want to eat at the restaurants along the canal which catered to tourists, he told them about a favorite of the locals. They would have never found it without instructions. It was down the street from the factory, through a passageway between a bar and some other shop, which brought them out into a garden set with tables, some under a roof extended from the building, some out in the blazing sun.

It still amazed Claire how the Italians seemed to love to soak up the sun. She had seen it all through her trip. She would look for the little pools of shade to walk in or sit in, while the Italians sought the sun. Some even had jackets thrown casually over their shoulders as they basked in the rays of mid afternoon, obviously unaware of the risk of melanoma.

They had claimed a table in the shade and had a leisurely, sumptuous, reasonably priced lunch amidst the crowded garden. The hearty red wine was served in little pitchers. The plates of pasta were heaping, the pasta tender and the sauce divine. And the bread, unlike the rolls which they had for breakfast at the hotel, was fresh, light and yeasty. They were happy to while away the afternoon until it was obvious the family who ran the restaurant was trying to close it.

They picked up their purchases, which were being packed for travel, caught the vaporetti and returned to Venice to see as many of the sights as they could crowd into the rest of the day. Claire was happy to find there were no cruise ships moored on the wharf today. Consequently the piazza San Marco was relatively empty and much easier to navigate with only the pigeons to watch out for. All in all it had been a great day.

"Jack, I'm so glad Claire ran into you. You have been a valuable addition to our group."

"Say nothing about my assistance with the luggage." Jack laughed, knowing what he said was true.

Ruth nodded. "The best way to travel would be to have a porter with you. When we came to Venice on the train there was a very old, very smartly dressed lady with many pieces of luggage, who boarded the train outside of Florence. But she had a young girl traveling with her. The teenager was obviously to fetch and carry. She struggled to get the luggage on and stowed, and then she was sent down to the bar car to get her patron a drink. She barely had time to sit before we arrived, and then I saw her trying to unload everything." She smiled. "It looked like a wonderful way to travel to me."

"Unless you were the young girl," Millie commented.

"Well of course, I would want to be the patron. You know, like we all think if we lived in yesteryear we would be the privileged class. No one wants to be the servant, even though that's probably the stock we came from."

They all laughed. Ruth was absolutely right.

"So, Mom, what about this offer of an internship in New York? Did Chef Martin offer it to everyone?" Claire asked, remembering the conversation at dinner last night which had been interrupted by another story.

Ruth and Millie looked strangely at each other and then Millie smiled at her daughter. "No, actually, I think he only offered it to me." She blushed. "I guess he was impressed with my skills."

Ruth laughed, saying cryptically, "I'd say."

Millie frowned at Ruth. "It was very nice of him. I really don't know if he offered a spot to any of the others. He may have. It was very generous of him, but I'm sure I won't be taking him up on it."

That comment initiated a lively discussion with everyone contributing their opinion.

But Millie just shook her head. "I really don't think I need it for the type of cooking I plan to do. But I promise I'll think about it a while before I finally make up my mind."

That would have to satisfy them all as they had arrived at the Marco Polo Airport dock, and here porters were waiting eagerly to help them with their luggage.

* * *

"Millie, I can't believe you haven't said a word to Claire about what happened at the Retreat." Ruth shook her head as she settled into her window seat for the long flight to San Francisco.

Millie sat beside her on the aisle. She had tucked her book, her knitting and a bottle of water in the little pocket in the seat in front of her and had just pulled out the airline magazine to peruse. "It was hard. I caught myself a dozen times. And I appreciate your cooperation. I know it was hard for you with your motor mouth." She smiled gently at her friend of so many years.

"It was. I wanted to tell her. I think she would want to know how close we both came to eating poison mushrooms." Ruth's voice was low so it only reached Millie's ears. The rest of the passengers were still boarding and the airline staff was moving up and down the aisles checking seatbelts and helping people stow their possessions.

"Why? So she would worry? So she would blame herself for talking me into going on the trip?" Millie was adamant. "You know Claire's led a sheltered life. Remember how long it took her to recover from that incident she got embroiled in with your neighbors?" She shook her head vehemently. "No, she didn't need to hear about any of the problems we had."

She peered into Ruth's face. "And don't you go forgetting and blab, Ruth Clarkson, or..., or I'll never forgive you."

Ruth shook her head, sitting back meekly. She and Millie had been friends for a very long time and she knew her well enough to know when she was serious. And she was very serious. Ruth knew they would tell no one about the real adventures at the Retreat and soon they would probably even start to forget what happened themselves.

She reached for her own copy of the airline magazine and turned to the crossword puzzle. That would hold her attention until they were safely in the air, then she would see what movies were going to be shown.

* * *

Claire followed the Vantage Airline representative, who happily carried the large box of Murano glassware her mother had bought. Claire carried her backpack and another bag of purchases she had made along the way. She had offered to take her mother's, so it wouldn't have to be checked. She had already learned when you flew first class with a VIP status, no one gave you grief if your bag was too big or you carried more than the maximum number of pieces on board.

"This way, Ms. Gulliver." The young man respectfully motioned her through the crowd clustered around the door waiting for their turn to board.

Claire felt her face flush. She still wasn't used to this treatment. She felt eyes on her as people obviously wondered who she was and why she was receiving preferential attention. But then she was through the door and down the long corridor of the Jetway, where the young man turned her over to the flight crew, bidding her a pleasant good-bye.

"Have a wonderful trip, Ms. Gulliver. Thank you so much for traveling with us today." And he sounded like he really meant it.

The attendant took her packages and placed them carefully in a bin before ushering her to the generous sized seat in the front of the plane. Last fall Vantage Airlines had awarded her a VIP status for her efforts in saving their president's life. This trip was the first time she had used the lifetime pass and she quickly realized it was more than just free transportation, it included personal, caring attention from the airline personnel every step of the way. It made her feel like she was someone very special. She smiled slightly. Of course she was, but who in the world usually cared. And besides everyone was special, weren't they?

That brought her thoughts back to Jack. They were going their separate ways once again. It seemed to be the story of their relationship. She felt a shiver of pleasure remembering his kisses. The attraction for him could easily escalate, but she held herself back. She didn't really believe all those stories about people who worked for the CIA, because she knew Jack certainly wasn't a cold blooded killer. Still, while he wasn't a glamorous James Bond or even a superman like Bourne, he wasn't an ordinary person.

She thought about his request that she continue to write to him. It seemed silly knowing he wouldn't read her letters for weeks, maybe longer if he was undercover, but she knew she would. She wasn't willing to toss the connection they had away. After all, someday he might retire.

"Would you like a Mimosa?" the flight attendant asked, and at her nod she pulled the tray out of the arm of Claire's seat and set a frosted glass down along with a little dish of warmed nuts.

Claire sipped the refreshing drink, nibbling at the nuts as the rest of the passengers were seated and the plane prepared for departure. She wished her mother was here. Millie would love traveling in first class. But then there would be lies or difficult explanations about Claire's special status at Vantage. No, it was good her mother and Ruth had booked their flights on another airline before Claire even decided to join them on this trip. This way they didn't even know she was in the first class section.

The plane was taxiing out to the runway when the glass and nut bowl were collected and put away. Claire sat back thinking about her mother. She had had a great time at the Retreat. That had been evident. Who knows, maybe she would be willing to take other trips. That would really be good for her. And maybe she'd even accept the internship in New York. After all it would only be for a few months.

Claire relaxed into the plush seat back as the plane hurdled down the runway before tilting sharply, nose up, aiming for the sky.

She didn't like to lie to her mother. She didn't want to hide things from her, but as she explained to Jack, her mother worried and worried. Claire didn't like to give her excuses for more worry. And Jack had been good about it. In all the time he stuck to them like glue in Venice, he never once gave a hint of any of the scary incidences they had shared in their past meetings. She could see both women were very taken with him. She smiled to herself. Now they would both drive her crazy wanting to know how Jack was. Had she seen him? Had she heard from him? When would he be coming to see her?

Well, those were all questions she had herself. She would just wait and see what the answers were.

* * *

Jack stood at the window watching Claire's plane. The motorized Jetway was retracted, leaving the plane isolated on the tarmac for a moment. Then the little tractor with the long pulley contraption on the front engaged and pushed the plane away from the terminal so it could proceed to the runway under its own power.

Once again they had said their good-byes. He wondered if he would ever have the opportunity to develop his relationship with Claire the way he wanted. It seemed like the world transpired to keep them apart. He sighed. Well, he already had his next assignment, but after that, he was determined to pursue a change in his life. He would retire. He would move closer to Claire and he would woo her. She just didn't know how serious he could be.

He smiled. But she would find out.

* * *

"How did you get my name?" The man didn't seem to want to talk to her.

"James Martino suggested I speak to you."

Now she had his attention. He looked at her carefully while he drummed his fingers on his desk top. What he saw was a young attractive brunette. Her hair was very short, very modern, spiked on the top. She wore blue tinted frameless glasses, and she was exceedingly attractive. Her clothes were very casual, the sort you saw all the young people wearing, and her backpack seemed to be a part of her person.

"What about?" he barked, very abrupt; he was a busy man.

"Well, you see, I became involved with James and Will and Emily..."

He nodded, waiting for the rest but not offering any help.

She started again. "Well, you see. I don't have a job. Actually, I don't even have a life..."

He just stared at her.

She shrugged. "Well, since I needed to find a new career anyway, I just thought..., well I wondered..." She took a deep breath. "I thought maybe I could work for you."

His expression was incredulous, then he began reciting all the negative aspects of her request. But eventually he had no more to say and she still was sitting there, calmly, in front of him. Her face expressionless, but her eyes were eager.

He sighed. "You have to go through training."

She nodded.

"It's very difficult."

She nodded, harder this time.

"James sent you, huh?"

She nodded again.

"Hell, why would a nice girl like you want to get involved with this?" But he was burrowing in his desk for some forms. Then he picked up his phone and spoke to his assistant.

When Kristen left his office to fill out the forms, accompanied by his assistant, she felt as if she was as good as in.

The End

If you enjoyed this book, or any other book from Koenisha Publications, let us know. Visit our website or drop a line at:

Koenisha Publications
3196 – 53rd Street
Hamilton, MI 49419
Phone or Fax: 269-751-4100
Email: koenisha@macatawa.org
Web site: www.koenisha.com

Coming Soon
CRUISIN' FOR A BRUISIN'
the fourth novel in the Claire Gulliver Mystery series
by Gayle Wigglesworth

Koenisha Publications authors are available for speaking engagements and book signings. Send for arrangements and schedule or visit our website.

Purchase additional copies of this book from your local bookstore or visit our web site.

Send for a free catalog of titles from
KOENISHA PUBLICATIONS
Founder of the Jacketed SoftCoverᴛᴍ
Books You Can Sink Your Mind Into